THE BODY IN THE BARREL

THE BODY IN THE BARREL

RICHARD G OPPER

KONSTELLATION
PRESS

Copyright © 2022 by Richard G Opper

Published by Konstellation Press, San Diego

www.konstellationpress.com

Cover design: Scarlet Willette

Editor: Lisa Wolff

ISBN: 978-1-7346421-9-3

This novel is dedicated to my mother, Betty Opper, a first grade teacher who passed on her love of reading to me at a very early age, and to Akira Kurosawa, who so artfully illuminated how multiple points of view reveal what is true.

PROLOGUE
OCTOBER 1943

Sticks and Stones

"Sticks," *Palos*, was the nickname the barrio gave my friend Alonzo, because he was so skinny. Alonzo's a funny name for a Chinese kid, but his dad was Filipino. We met at a boxing center for barrio kids in a National City garage. Some guy set up a boxing ring in his garage, what can I tell you? Everybody called me Stones because since I started boxing as a kid, I would take on anybody in that ring. It was a long time ago, but some things don't ever really change.

I grew up in Shelltown, over by the big shipbuilding factory, and I was used to fending for myself. So even though Sticks and I were only fifteen years old, we were scrappy kids. My mom worked in a sandwich joint that fed sailors from the Navy station and factory workers from the shipbuilding company. Never knew Dad. Sticks' mom was Chinese. His dad died before the war. Sticks grew up in Hong Kong – spoke three or four languages before he was eight, when he came to National City with his mom, who married another Filipino guy who came here as a Navy steward. We hung out together. Me, the barrio fighter, and Sticks, the talker.

Sticks was born to be a businessman. He was buying and selling before he was fifteen. In those days, so much Navy equipment was trucking in and out of the bay: jeeps shipping out to the Pacific, planes being built on one side of the bay and flown on the other. He made *inquiries*. He found a sailor, a seller ready to make a deal. Even though Sticks was only fifteen, he had accumulated three thousand dollars. Big money! Put together the hard way over the last six months. In Shelltown, that was enough money to get killed over.

Sticks watched all the truck tires being hauled in and out of the Navy warehouses. Too many to keep track of, he figured. He told me that the sailor said he could drive a truck out, loaded with tires, for three thousand—keep the truck. Sticks thought he had it all figured out. National City is a little bit south of San Diego and only half an hour from the Mexican border. Sticks delivers a truck loaded with tires in Tijuana, and he doubles his money. There's a way into Mexico that bypasses the main gate, and at night you could cross by Smuggler's Gulch with nobody knowing. Not much of a road—but he convinced me that you got to take chances, right? Or you get nowhere.

So he was supposed to show up with the cash after hours. I came with him, but I was supposed to stay back—he had promised the sailor guy he'd come alone. The warehouse was right off Harbor Drive, next to the bay, and it was after seven o'clock. There was a single light on over the door at the front of the warehouse, and I could see a light on in the little office room they had inside. Otherwise, everything looked dark.

No Shore Patrol in sight, no lights on in the gravel parking lot, so Sticks told me to wait outside while he went in to cut his deal. I couldn't believe he was really going to pull it off, so I crept up to the window and peeked in.

Sticks stood in front of a big wooden desk. A fat and grizzled guy in fatigues sat behind the desk, with his hands laced behind his head. He was smiling. The window was open, so I could hear what they said.

"You came alone, right?"

"That's what you said. You got the tires?"

"Oh I got 'em, all right. Where's the money?" and at this he smiled big. To me it looked like he thought he was calling Sticks' bluff. That he didn't think the money would appear. And I could see his eyes widen when Sticks pulled out a packet of cash and dropped it on the table.

"Where's the keys to the truck?" Sticks asked.

"Not so fast, boyo. Let's count up your Uncle Sams first."

Sticks seemed very patient, but I was totally getting freaked out and worried. This guy was making kind of a show of counting the bills and while he grinned about it, it didn't look like he was paying any attention to Sticks. Until he finished counting.

"All here, boyo. Not bad." He stood up, and I saw he had a pistol holstered. Not what you expected from a clerk in a warehouse. "We're done here, kid. Good night, and get your chink ass the hell out."

Sticks stared at him. "You going to keep my money and not give me my truck and tires?"

"You're fast, kid." He drew the pistol. "I'm not going to have to use this, am I?" He pointed the gun at Sticks, then the door. "Scram."

"I'm not leaving here without my money, or my truck."

"Shit-for-brains kid." The clerk got out from behind his desk. I looked around to see if there was anything I could use and spotted a shovel leaning up against the side of the warehouse. I grabbed it and walked quietly over to the door Sticks had entered. The door flung open and Sticks was kicked through it, the clerk coming behind him and telling him to get the hell out. He never saw me, and I doubt he felt the shovel that laid him out. He fell face forward and was silent.

Sticks asked me, "Do you think he's dead?"

I went over and looked at him. I didn't want to touch him, but I didn't see any blood anywhere, and he seemed to be breathing. "No."

Sticks went back into the office and opened the desk drawer he'd seen his money go into. He stuck the bills back in his pocket and looked at me. "I don't think I figured that one out enough."

"No kidding," I said.

"Hey, Gus," he said, and I looked at him straight on. "*Gracias*, Gustavo," he said, "I owe you." That made me feel good. You could tell he really meant it when he used my Christian name.

1

MONDAY, OCTOBER 15, 1973

Gary

I shifted the Smith & Wesson Model 10 to a more comfortable place on my hip, which was feeling tender this morning. The bay had a smell of rotting plants, and together with the smell of the diesel it triggered thoughts about the Mekong—which was not so long ago, even if it was half a world away. It was the reason my hip ached, but that life was over. I was back home in San Diego, and glad for it. Whatever I'd thought I was going to accomplish in the Navy's swift boats turned out to be a bad dream. A nightmare. So the fact that I ended up in the Harbor Police is a whole lot better—but still a whole lot of not much. I was out of the shit storm and into a more peaceful life, but for crying out loud, at twenty-eight here I was with nothing really going on, already going nowhere. But who cared? Other than my dad, I guess, and that only went so far.

Dawn was breaking and the sky was lighting up but still gray, streaked with glowing rose and high silver cloud fingers slipping in from the Pacific. I uncleated the bowline on our patrol boat, the *Pt. Loma II*, which Mark and I rotated onto this morning. We've partnered on the bay patrol before. We're both uniformed boat jockeys, although the term is used derisively by some. Our jurisdiction is the bay, and it ends at Ballast Point and the passage to the Pacific, so what went on out at sea was not our business. Fine with me. From where the *Pt. Loma II* was moored on Shelter Island, you could look out straight through the bay's mouth to the ocean, and the farthest horizon point sea level allowed.

"Casting off," I said, giving Mark the signal to throttle up as I hopped on deck with the line in my hand. We motored out into the bay, engine loud in the still morning. October in San Diego is like summer in lots of places. The Santa Anas blow a warm wind in from the Anza-Borrego Desert, a wind that blows from land out to sea. Most of the year it's the other way around. The *Pt. Loma II* surged forward as we left the protected wake area, and the moment brought on a smile, infrequent these days, as I took in the beauty of the sky: gray giving way to a range of colors, city streetlights still a bright jeweled necklace alongside Harbor Drive, windows in the buildings of the city winking on. There was a light bay chop, a warm breeze, and no one was shooting at me. Felt great. It was peaceful and calming, both of which I appreciated from long disassociation. Then we got a squawk on the VHF radio. This meant the call was from the public, presumably the boating public, and not HQ. We always monitor channel 16.

"This is the *Lady Lynn* hailing Harbor Police. *Lady Lynn* at the tuna docks calling for Harbor Police. Do you copy?"

Mark called out to me as I was standing on the bridge and enjoying the view. "It's the *Lady Lynn*, Gary—you know these guys, right? You told me—the Coelhos? You want to take this?" I went in and took the mike off the hook of the radio.

"Harbor Police, *Lady Lynn*. We copy."

"We need you to come to the tuna docks as fast as you can

make it—we're tied up on the outside quay of the G Street mole. We need you to get here ASAP."

"Is this an emergency call? Have you got a fire or something?" I didn't want to say "bomb threat"—we are trained not to go on public channels with those emergencies. "Lights and sirens?"

"No sir," the radioman from the *Lady Lynn* reported. "It's not an emergency, and I don't really know what it is, but I am sure you are going to want to be here..."

"We're en route." I hung up the mike and turned to Mark. "You heard 'em. Let's boogey."

There are few things as much fun as punching up the cruiser to make smart time down the bay, so I didn't have to ask twice. At this hour, the bay was empty of pleasure boat traffic, and there was no Navy activity or shipping scheduled, so we made straight for our goal at twenty knots. We knew those docks. The commercial tuna docks bring a lot of dollars into this community, and always have, since before World War II. The *Lady Lynn* was one of three purse seiners the Coelhos owned, and I think they also owned some long line ships stationed out of American Samoa. I'd known the family for years. Unlike the TV ads, they were not sorry, Charlie; fishing has been very good for them.

We backed off as soon as we got close to the hull and held station off the side of the vessel. They had the post extended and something was winched out of the water, held suspended above the waterline by a cable looped around it. Day was breaking, it was getting lighter by the minute, and we could clearly see now that it was a barrel. Mark piloted, backing us off a few feet from the starboard side of the hull, while I went out on deck to look up at a crewman I didn't know, who waved at me to wait a minute. I stood for a minute, and Matt Coelho came to the rail.

He took one look at me and smiled. "Hey, Gary, is that you?" he called down.

"Yeah," I said, in a normal voice. It was quiet enough that no shouting was needed; the bullhorn could sit in its holder. "What's up?"

I'd known Matt Coelho since we were at St. Augustine's together. Catholic high school for boys. His family has been fishing in San Diego for three generations, and I had every reason to believe every word he told me. When my mom was killed, his family was at the funeral.

"Short story," he said. "That barrel floated in out of nowhere and starts banging on our hull, so my crewman snags it." He looked up and around. "It was Paco, here." I looked up at the deckhand Matt gestured to. He looked right at me, but he seemed fidgety and nervous. "We snag it and start to lift it, so it isn't a marine hazard, you know, and as it comes up we can see it's draining, like the bottom is full of holes or something. We lift it a little higher, and we can see, yeah, it's full of holes. The barrel has something in it and it was probably designed to sink, but it turned over and floated, and now it's here. My guys call me and I figure it's got to be drugs, right? I don't want to touch it. I don't want anyone to touch it. I told them to call you and I got down here myself."

"So, Matt, if it's drugs you should call the DEA and wake one of them up." Then I jokingly swore at him in Spanish for dragging me into this – truth was, I didn't mind; this was more interesting than just patrolling. My Mexican mom had loved the American sayings – "No time like the present" was one of her favorites.

"I didn't know who was out on patrol this morning, but I knew someone was. You're it, buddy. I don't need a cranky DEA guy at six thirty in the morning." And we knew it was six thirty because at that moment not only was the sky light, but flights out of Lindbergh Field, by the side of the bay, started roaring off.

Now I had to raise my voice. "OK, pull it up and put it on deck." I signaled Mark to a clear patch of dock he could ease into and we tied off and walked over to the *Lady Lynn*, up the gangway to the deck, where the barrel had been laid down on its side. It looked like all the water in it had drained off, so I nodded to Matt and he nodded to a crewman, who walked up with a pry bar and pulled off the perforated barrel end with three sharp moves. The lid clanged on the steel deck like a big coin spinning after a toss. The crewman stepped back, and I walked over to the barrel and knelt down to peer in. It just took a glance.

"Mark," I said, "call PD, we got a body in here. Looks like a woman in a dress." Mark pulled his Motorola off of his belt and called it in. "And give Chief Gus a heads-up, too, why don't you. This is going to stir things up around here..."

We waited on deck; the gentle rocking motion of the tuna boat was a soothing counterpoint to how shocking it felt to find a body in a barrel. I looked up to the bridge of the boat, where I could see my old friend, Captain Matt, who had gone back up the ladder and was behind the glass of the windscreen. I waved him back down.

"You said a crew member named Paco pulled the barrel up?" I asked him. "Where is he? I'm sure PD is going to have some questions. And come to think of it, I have a couple..."

Matt gave me a funny look. Like there was something he wanted to say but couldn't. "Paco seems to have slipped away. I called for him, but he isn't here anymore. Could be an immigration thing, you know? The *migras* might be all over it if he's questioned. He's only half Portuguese," Matt said, looking almost embarrassed about it. "And half Mexican. We brought him on because Tony vouched for him."

"Don't give me crap about being half Mexican, Matt, that would have been his good half!" This loosened the light tension, and we both smiled; we'd been through this routine with each other before from school days.

"Tony is half Portuguese and half Chinese," he said, "so there." But before we got to continue, two black-and-whites and a Ford Vic drive up through the parking lot and out onto the mole. Lights, no sirens. I went down to meet them.

The dawn was quickly becoming day, big jets were lined up and swooping out of Lindbergh Field, and I waved a couple of uniforms and a detective over to where the barrel lay on its side on the tuna boat deck. Naturally, Mark and I held back from emptying the barrel, because anything we did would likely become a note in some report about how the crime scene was disturbed. Not like they were going to get any prints off of this evidence! Still, we left it as we found it, proper protocol if there is no emergency requiring some immediate response.

The detective, in a rumpled brown suit, squatted down without touching the deck and looked into the barrel. All you could see was what looked like a skinny woman with her knees drawn up, her rump and her feet pointed toward us. The detective nodded at the uniforms and asked them to slide the body out by tilting the barrel up and not touching anything. Once lying on the deck, I could see it was an attractive young woman, kind of Asian looking, wearing nothing but a very thin red dress, which clung to her body, revealing every detail of her. She wore a bra but no panties. The detective rolled the body over and the hands, clasped in front of her as if in prayer, fell down and revealed that the ends of all of her fingers had been chopped or sliced off. Long since bled out, the fingers were protruding stumps of bone from which pale white waterlogged skin had receded.

I saw the detective reach into his jacket pocket and pull out a plastic bag and a glove, and after sliding his hand into the glove he reached out and plucked something from the bra under the dead girl's dress. It looked like a card of some sort. He held it in front of him as he stood back up. I could see that the card was on some purple glossy paper, but not what it said. "What does it say?" I asked the detective.

"It's the business card for the owner of a local bar. Says her name is Mona Oakheart. Bar is called 'Tell No Tales,'" he said. "Heard of it?" he asked me, looking up.

"Nope," I answered, "it's a new one on me."

Mona

I sat in a chair in the shadows, scratching an itch under my bra strap by rubbing against the chair back. It felt like a chigger bite, like I got when I was a kid rolling around in the grass back home. That chigger bite was the most feeling I've had all day, 'cause other than that, I felt mostly numb. Like usual. But now I was feeling anxious, even watching something unfold I had seen many times before. There was a woman on the bed, lying on her side under a silk sheet, sleeping even though the room was partially lit. As I watched, a door opened and a man entered. He didn't even glance at me; he looked only at the sleeping figure, and was pulled toward her as though by wires. The shape of her nipple threw an unnaturally long shadow across the sheet. He pulled off his sweatpants, revealing he was up and ready. He came to the edge of the bed and slowly reached out and put his hand on her hip. She moved gently, as though floating on a wave, and stretched, one leg sliding off the other. His breathing quickened. His hand drifted down her thigh. He stepped away from his pants, naked, and leaned over to slide next to the woman. She murmured lightly, and his eyes widened as her body slid under the soft silk sheet. He lifted it and started to slip in with her...

"*Cut!*" I got up and walked onto the set. I'm kind of a tall gal, five foot eleven, with long blond hair that I flip around when I get agitated. "You're supposed to slide the sheet off of her. I don't need the two of you hidden under the sheet. *Capisce?*" I shaded my eyes and turned to look at the director, Susan Rancherd. "House lights," I called out, probably sounded like '*house latts,*' as you can still hear the Arkansas in this girl, and the bright studio lighting went off as the floods hanging from the warehouse ceiling went on. The studio was a big warehouse space that had been insulated for sound and then painted flat black everywhere except the floor. Studio lights hung on a grid made of two-by-fours hanging from jury-rigged plumbing supplies with extension cords running everywhere, held by duct tape. I grimaced. I may be from Arkansas and she may be from Cali-Bezerkly, but I am payin' the piper. "Hey, I am counting on you to get the most out of these two and this shoot. I don't want to jump in and tell you what to do, but jeez, Suze, we talked about this whole scene!"

Suze was pissed. She has a tell; she sort of chills down and gets frosty. I hear a whiny voice in my head: *Just because I own the company and built it with my own blood, sweat, and tears doesn't mean I can stop a shoot on a whim.* My inward grin was grim. Oh yes, I sure as hell could. And Suze knew it.

"You're right, of course," she said with her lips in a thin smile. "We blocked this out, but our man's brains are all located in the usual spot..." She turned to the crew. "Let's set it up to go from the top, OK?" She took my hands in hers, pulled me off of the set, and came up close. "Do me a favor, love? Go take a walk or something. Let me just put this together, as we all agreed? You seem kind of wound up today."

"Do I seem jumpy?" I said. "Maybe a walk would be a good idea. Did that agent, Patricia, ever show up? She was supposed to come in this morning with some hot new wannabees. She's late. By a lot."

"Haven't seen her. And I don't plan to leave this set until we get through scene three. I promise."

I knew this would be best. "Roll it, Suze." I turned and left the studio.

The studio is a middle unit in an inconspicuous cinderblock building, fronted with rolling steel garage doors, sitting in Kearny Mesa, a somewhat gritty, semi-industrialized suburb of San Diego. Next door, they do cheap bumper repairs. Plumbing supplies are sold at the other end. Insulating for sound cost me a bundle. There are a couple of great Korean restaurants up the street, but otherwise it's not a nice part of town to walk around in. Those out on the sidewalk were few and far between, either hustling or lurking.

Coming out of that dark studio, I wanted a breath of fresh air and clean light, which quickly became a determination to see the ocean. It must have been the warmth of the sun talking to me – I'm in San Diego and I want to look at the water. My complexion is pale, as I'm not only a born blonde, I haven't been outside in forever. My powder-blue Mercedes roadster was parked outside in the lot, next to an old Buick Skylark, but even my cute little car couldn't make me happy these days. I took a deep breath to calm my nerves. Maybe the agent simply wasn't coming. Fine. I decided to drive down to La Jolla Cove and look at the beach.

I started the car and released the brake, but before I could back out, Annette, one of the gal go-fers, came running out the door and over to me. I waited.

"We just got a call," she said, breathlessly. "It's the cops. They want to know if you can go downtown. They got questions as part of an investigation." She looked at me, expecting a reaction. "I think they mean right now."

I didn't bother to ask why—I knew she wouldn't know. I waved her off and backed out. I knew the route. I sighed and headed off to the PD's headquarters. I have lived here in San Diego since long before the Beatles played in the park, lately trying to give Hugh Hefner a run for his money. That's sarcasm, by the way. But I do OK. My little downtown bar, Tell No Tales, throws off enough income to underwrite my little company's filmmaking, which is where most of my money comes from these days. Triple X. I own the production company. The movies sell all over. You can rent a hotel room in Europe and see my movies right in the room. Not only Europe, either. Hell, it's the seventies; anything goes. The Supreme Court just ruled that abortion was legal. About time, I thought. The downtown

HQ was a short drive from my studio. I've had to go to the cops for everything from the terrifying to the routine. I know the drill as well as I know the route to police headquarters. Back in the fifties, you had to be willing to be up-close and personal with them to stay out of trouble. Now I think the opposite is true.

I parked in the police building's parking lot and locked the car. This wasn't a great part of town, either. At least I was in my civvies – blue cotton work shirt and bell-bottomed jeans. If I had been dressed in my club owner slit-skirt outfit, especially the one with the spangles, they would have treated me like a whore. That's what they think I am, anyway. But I know I look good. I don't wear a wedding ring because I'm not married— but maybe I should.

The desk sergeant watched me enter with an appreciative gaze. I told him who I was and why I was there. He looked me up and down, then motioned for me to wait in one of the plastic molded chairs on the linoleum floor. I wondered if I should have brought a book.

It only took a few minutes before the side door opened and a head with a buzz-cut hairdo leaned out.

"Mrs. Oakheart? Mona Oakheart?" he asked.

"It's Ms.," I answered, already walking toward him. He turned and held the door for me and I went into the corridor. Everyone inside was in uniform, except for buzz-cut. He had me follow him to a small office with a metal desk and two metal chairs.

"Detective James Exeter." He stuck his hand out for me to shake. "But everyone calls me Jim. Did they tell you why we called?"

"No, my assistant just ran out and said to come down here..."

He motioned me into a chair. "This morning, a fisherman down by the G Street mole called in to tell Harbor Police about a barrel bobbing on the bay. The Harbor jockeys sent a boat and had the barrel pulled in." He looked up. "It was found to contain a body. Like, deceased. Fully dressed, with no identification except for this." He leaned over and showed me a plastic bag that held a business card. It was the distinctly purple card from my downtown club, Tell No Tales. "Any idea why this person should have your business card on them?"

"I have no idea. Maybe if I knew who this person was..."

"We haven't yet identified the body. Have you ever been called to identify a body before?"

"Once."

He looked at me and then said, "Let's roll and I'll explain."

We took Jim's car to the morgue, an unmarked Ford with those shiny moonlike wheel hubs and antenna that said "Police Car" all over them. Just in case anyone was wondering. Jim was talking, but I didn't hear him. I stared out the window, lost in my own memories. The task of identifying a dead body was tangled up in my own screwed-up history. And it all started when I first came to San Diego. Was it twenty years ago? Fresh off the Greyhound from Arkansas, where a skinny boy on his way to be a Marine offered to help me escape to San Diego. Daddy had come back from the Korean War, and he and I had both changed. He had become deranged and I grew tits. His stares scared the shit out of me. Ma was playing like she didn't see anything and I was having none of it. My first job in San Diego delivering liquor led to supplying it for high-profile events, which led to the best and the worst thing that ever happened to me...

"You've been somewhere else while I've been explaining the situation, haven't you?" His voice cut through my reverie. Unperturbed, Jim went on. "OK, what's Tell No Tales all about?" he asked me as we turned off Pacific Coast Highway.

"You've never been there?"

He shook his head and grinned.

I smiled. "It's a first-rate club. Took me years to build it. We get a good customer, lots of Navy and also ship workers. We get people off of the Pacific Coast Highway. Our girls are all smart and good-looking. Miniskirts, halter tops. Nothing pushes the limits. We usually have a little music going on. You should drop by and check us out."

"Kind of a rough neighborhood down there on Fifth Avenue."

"I know. I'm right next door to Wyatt Earp's old place. They've got a plaque on the wall so you don't miss it. Every few months, someone forgets it's the seventies and we have a shoot-out on the street."

Jim turned and gave me a look. "That's something I know a little bit about," he said.

Then we were pulling into the underground parking for the county building, where the morgue was stuffed in between some other nameless administrative necessities. I followed Jim through a door with a pebbled glass window advising us we were indeed at the morgue, and we went into a place that smelled heavily of disinfectant, and not much else.

A bedraggled assistant in a beehive hairdo sat behind a counter. She looked up and you could tell she knew Jim. With a minimum of words, she turned to lead us to the big room with all the locker doors. Except they weren't lockers.

"They won't get to the autopsy for a while yet, so she's in the freezer."

"She?" I asked, with a tremor in my voice.

In answer, Jim nodded to the gal, who pulled out a table from the locker. The body under the sheet was clearly a woman. Exeter pulled the sheet back to her neck. I'd had only one meeting with her, but I immediately recognized the woman on that shelf. Her dark hair was plastered to her scalp, and her skin was waxy and very pale beige in the stark fluorescent lighting. There was still a trace of mascara around her eyes. Thank God her eyes were closed.

I put my hand to my throat. "Oh my God," I said. "I know

this woman. She told me her name is Patricia Peteaut. She was supposed to meet with me earlier today."

"For what?" Jim asked me, nodding his head sideways to have her rolled back into the freezer.

"She's a—*was* a—theatrical agent. She was supposed to be bringing a couple of potential actresses. For movies I make. Oh my God—what happened to her fingers?!" I looked down at the arms, lying outside of the sheet, and was shocked to see that the tip of each finger had been cut off. I could only imagine...

"Let's go back downtown so I can take a statement, OK?" Exeter took my elbow and steered me out toward the lobby. I nodded and allowed him to take me back to the car. The drive back to the PD was tense, and my answers to Jim's questions got shorter, images from the morgue rising in front of me. Especially her hands.

Soon we were back in Jim's office, making the official statement. It started out easy: name, address, and so on; but it was relentless and soon felt like an inquisition. I had no illusions about my own role as a person of interest in all this. Jim no longer felt like a "Jim." More like a "Detective Exeter." We spent a lot of time on who I work with in my business—the films and the club—and what I do. Every time he asked a question, he laboriously wrote out my answer. It was almost an hour before we turned to Patricia, and he asked what I knew about her.

I told him, "She called me Friday, saying that she was supplyin' talent to other SoCal moviemakers and thought she could bring me models and actresses I would want to use. Naturally I said 'sure,' and we met at my club on Saturday to look at some head shots. They looked fine, so she was supposed to come back today with a couple of hopefuls. I was waiting for her down at the studio this morning."

"Where did she get her, um, actresses?" The way Jim said the word you could tell he was trying to be nice, as he obviously didn't think of them as actresses at all. Just trying to flatter as much information out of me as he could. No surprises there.

"It's not like I know; I never met any of them—but I know that most of the talent comes from LA, especially the Valley," I said. "Then there's Tijuana and Guam. And Manila. It's a big opportunity for some. Everybody is over eighteen and no one does what they don't want to. I care about the people who work for me. At least while they're in my house and on my team."

"Somebody went to some trouble to make it tough for us to identify the body. No fingers—no prints, you know. Why would they do that, and then leave us a card so we could get you to ID her for us?"

"I have no idea. I have no idea."

"Where did Ms. Peteaut come from? What was her background?" He made a little show out of the "Ms."

"All I know about her is what I learned on Friday and during our meeting on Saturday. I never heard of her before that. She said she worked with some production companies out of Burbank and San Diego and she was tired of the drive. She said she wanted to relocate because she didn't like being on the freeway, so she was shifting all her efforts to San Diego. I don't know who else she worked with, really. She was an agent." (*Didn't that say everything?*). I looked at my watch and realized I hadn't had any lunch. "Can I go home now? I need a break."

Jim looked over his notes. "Sure, I have enough for now. I'll take you back out to the reception area with the desk sergeant. Wait for me there; I'll get your statement typed up and you'll have to sign it."

I went back out to the reception room and sat in a molded plastic chair. The place was deserted; it must have been a quiet day for crime in San Diego. After about half an hour, the outside door opened and a guy in a uniform different from the others in the building came in. His wasn't blue—he wore green pants and a tan shirt. He carried a pistol on his hip. I looked outside and saw he had parked a truck that was identified as Harbor Police. Dark hair, some tan to the tint of his skin. He turned to me and gave me an appraising look, smiled, and then turned to the hall door where buzz-cut Jim was getting my statement ready. Not that I cared these days, but he looked good from my brief peek at him. He had a funny walk —looked like he was favoring a leg—but he made it work. Nice butt.

It was another hour before I saw Jim again, with a few pages of typed statement taken from our conversation. At this point, whatever there was of my good humor had fizzed out. In his office, I read the statement quickly. It seemed like what I had told him, so I signed it and got up, turning to leave.

"By the way, Ms. Oakheart, you know that I will likely need to talk to you again as we learn more about this. This is murder, with overtones that will be – well, you can bet the press will be all over it. I'm just getting started. You aren't planning any trips in the next couple of weeks, are you?"

Even though I was inside and fans were blowing, I was aware that it was October, and the Santa Anas were blowing hot, dry air into town from the mountains. That puts everyone on edge. In this close-windowed reception room, I still felt sticky. I didn't have any travel plans until November.

"No, *Jim*, I'm not going anywhere."

I got a grim smile from Jim. "Here," he said, handing me a card. "Keep this. Call me if you think of anything else." He turned back to return to his office while I headed out to my car. Through the lobby, stuffy with two standing fans, to a hot, dry parking lot. The air felt scratchy.

As I opened my little car's door, I heard the glass doors to the police building swish open behind me. I looked up and saw the good-looking young cop from the Harbor Police walk out. He veered slightly and came over to me. His truck was parked next to my roadster.

"Hey," he said. "Hold on. You knew the vic, right? I was on duty. I was there when they pulled the barrel out of the bay and opened it up. You heard about the card they found, right? Exeter said you own the club."

I took in his earnest face with a sideways glance. "You mean my good friend Jim?" I asked.

He smiled, then came over and reached out a hand. "Gary Reines. You're Mona Oakheart, right? Jim said you own Tell No Tales."

I took his hand in mine. "Reines, huh. I knew a Reines once and you look more like a Garcia." I smiled at him. "Just talkin'. Look, Gary, I'm beat and this has been one hell of a day. Drop by the club sometime, but not today. I'm going to get something to eat."

For a minute I thought Gary was going to ask me some questions, but he got the drift, smiled, and told me he would drop by some day. He stood by his truck while I dropped into the seat of the Mercedes. The leather was hot to the touch after being exposed to the sun—even in October. I needed a drink. The club was only about a dozen blocks away, so I wouldn't need a pay phone to call the studio and tell them what was up. I glanced up at young Gary, then started up the Benz, rolled it backwards and allowed myself the pleasure of dropping it into first, popping the clutch and zipping neatly around, out of the parking lot and toward Fifth Avenue downtown.

Gary

I watched the Mercedes practically peel out as Oakheart gunned it. Bold, considering this was the police building parking lot. *García, huh?* I smiled. I was lingering over the memory of her legs in tight jeans ducking into her little car, when I heard a SLAM of metal right next to me. It was unexpected, so it was shocking, and I got a buzz in my head. In a split-second I was back in the jungle. It was hot, and sweat was springing out all over my body. My throat went dry as I spun around, snake brain ready for fight or flight. I heard the beginning of noise in my ears and saw red in my vision, but I reoriented even as I spun around, feet on pavement, not rice paddies, realizing I was in the parking lot. Jim Exeter had just walked up behind me and slapped the hood of the truck loudly while I was watching the gal. *Asshole.* I straightened and tried to get control of my breathing.

"Hey, Romeo, cool down; just trying to get your attention," said Exeter. "You seem kind of jumpy. You got some kind of war shit going on here?"

"I'm good." The detective was several pay grades my superior, but I was not going to kiss his ass. Rank didn't mean anything to me and he knew it. It probably pissed him off.

"I came out to give you the chain-of-custody evidence receipt. So you guys have what you need for your files. OK?" He handed me a manila envelope that wasn't too thick. "Are we good here?" It was a put-down, because he was making the point that my only role was to turn the body over to him. That's the way it works. We're just Harbor Police. We work for the Waterfront Agency.

"We're good. I'm out of here." I took the envelope and walked around to the driver's side of the truck and climbed in. Exeter went back inside and I left, headed for the Harbor Police Headquarters out by the airport, which also sits right next to the bay and is part of our patrol jurisdiction.

Harbor Police suited me fine. My last job, in the Mekong Delta, was on Patrol Craft Fast, which everyone called swift boats. I was a swifty. It involved drawing unfriendly fire for a living. I was out there for almost a year before I took some frag in my left leg in an RPG attack. That cut my tour short. They gave me an evac to Naval Regional on Guam for surgery, then sent me to Hawaii for rehab. A few months later, I was back in San Diego where it all started.

San Diego was home to me. Born and bred. My dad knew people—especially around the bay where he built his hotels. He's been building on the waterfront for longer than the Waterfront Agency has been around. His best buddy was Phil Nestor, the head of the Waterfront Agency, and they used to have another compadre, Erick Hansen, who was with the cops but became the Harbor Police chief. The three had been like the Three Musketeers since World War II, long before I showed up. I've known them all forever and I played games with Phil's kids when they were little. The Harbor Police is a division of the Waterfront Agency, and they had a policy of giving preference to returning vets. My leg had healed enough to support the required running and climbing, and the Police Academy was something I could do. The guys at the academy were very supportive. It was about the friendliest thing I experienced on my return to the States. Being a vet at college seemed to be bad timing back then, maybe even worse now. Harbor Police seemed like a good place to be while I weighed my options, so I became a water cop. My buddies on the Patrol hate it when I call us that. Or boat jockey.

I sat in my truck, in gridlock on Harbor Drive, close to headquarters. I was going nowhere. Traffic was stopped in both directions. Over the tops of the snarled traffic I saw the orange tail of a small jet plane, emblazoned with globe and anchors, as the top of an orange fuselage glided across the street and passed in front of the stopped cars. It came from the Coast Guard hangar at the edge of the bay, across Harbor Drive from the airport, and had to cross five lanes of traffic to get to the airstrip at Lindbergh Field. The Coasties had their own special traffic control to shut things down when they needed that access. That added about fifteen more minutes to the drive, while I listened to the police scanner drone on in the background. *Only in San Diego*, I thought. By the time I pulled into our offices—the old Lockheed Martin building from back in the day, stocky and blocky in cast concrete, now Harbor Police HQ—it was about time for me to punch out.

Most of us in the Harbor group shared desks in a large open room, where the dispatch sat strategically located right by the front door. As I entered and headed to the back door for the locker room, dispatch called, "Gary, come 'ere..." and waved at me.

I walked over and gave him a "what's up?" look.

"I just got a call from Exeter over at the PD. He says he wants to know if you got a problem, like with," he paused, "battle fatigue? Isn't that what they call it? He says you were over there this afternoon and he thought you were going to take a swing at him."

"You're kidding me. He called to report I looked like I'm looney, or what?"

"It's not a report. He said he's just following up. What happened over there?"

"Absolutely nothing. Nothing happened. Jeez."

"Be careful how many people you piss off at the PD. You can't get far here if you aren't cutting it over there."

"I'll be sure to remember. That's it?" He nodded, and I dropped the envelope with the chain-of-custody report in the in-box for filing. Then I turned and left for the lockers. I glanced over my shoulder and noticed that Chief Gus was in his office, standing by the window that looked out over the dispatch room. Looking at me.

Gus

I watched Reines' kid walk to the lockers, and wondered again at the unlikely things that come up in life. I went back to my battered wooden desk and sat down. My frame is bigger than Chief Hansen's was; my legs didn't fit so comfortably under the old wood desk. Traces of Chief Hansen were still on the walls. Awards. Photographs. He had pretty much brought the Harbor Police into being. He was a stand-up guy, but he knew something about everybody and he knew how to throw his weight around. He and Phil Nestor, the Waterfront director and my boss, went as far back as the war. Old buddies. And Reines' dad rounded out the trio. The real estate tycoon, Frank Reines.

I don't think I knew what it meant to step into Chief Hansen's place in that trio, and I don't honestly think I could've. Chief Hansen had the goods on what was going on all over, not just around the San Diego Bay, but in Waikiki Bay or Subic Bay. Once, they sent him all the way to Subic—that's in the Philippines—on some strange investigation involving a kidnap case (don't ask me who *they* were).

We all knew he was gone, but we never really knew why. He did some things and knew some things that were not generally shared. I remember distinctly when he did share one big goddamned problem with me, him sitting where I am now, hardly four months before he died at this desk, literally. It's when I started to understand the trio. He let me in on a big Top Secret mess involving Director Phil Nestor, a buddy, but boss of the boss. Nestor later told me that he knew Hansen had clued me in, and that he knew Hansen extracted some promises from me before I got offered the job of deputy, and now, because he trusted I would abide by my word, the new chief. That was OK by me—nothing comes for free.

I looked at the door to my office, and now it was *my* name painted on it: Gustavo Mendoza, Chief, Harbor Police. Once a wayward child of the Shelltown barrio, my mom isn't slinging sandwiches for sailors anymore. I've taken care of her. I picked up the phone and dialed a number I knew well. I thought carefully about what I should say given how much Nestor knew.

"Director's office." The voice on the other end sounded no nonsense and I knew that to be her personality.

"Dorothy, it's me. I've got news for him."

"Just a moment," she said in my ear. There was a clicking sound, a pause, and another click.

"Yes?" Nestor was right to the point.

I would keep it the same way. Direct, no explanations. "It's Exeter," I told him. "Exeter apparently picked up the barrel floater case for the PD."

"Keep me informed," he said, then he hung up.

Mona

Tell No Tales. To me, it was a metaphor for my whole life. Stuff that worked, and stuff that stunk. The club (I didn't like to call it a bar) worked liked a little machine—when it did. When no one was stealing from me, when I wasn't being shaken down by the bad guys or the good guys, when everyone showed up for work (mostly), I made money. That was the point, after all. It paid the rent and then some. But it also stank. I have always hated the smell of cigarettes. The club was always a little rank with the smell of old nicotine, and now was no different.

Tell No Tales was a couple of blocks down Fifth from Broadway. Right past the sex toy store with the papered-over windows. A pizza place down the block had been trying to make it for years. I had no idea how they paid the rent—no one was ever in there. There was a little newsstand between us. The bar had a frontage of about thirty feet, the ground floor of half the building. There were some cheap rentals on the top two floors. Inside the club, I had some tables on the floor between the bar and the window, and a few booths along the sides. To the right, a little hall—left to the toilet, right to the supply cabinet and my "office." I kept the booze under lock and key (of course), but I'd pulled off the doors to the closet next to the supply closet, and that was my office. I was in it now. The phone was on what passed for my desk. A square black plastic box with buttons. No dials anymore; it's the newest thing. I stared at it, thinking about Suze and about Patricia Peteaut. I rethought our conversation.

I'd told Suze that I had ID'd a corpse, and that it was Peteaut. Silence on the other end. Then:

"What happened? Do you know?"

"Not a clue."

Another long pause. "Why'd they call you?"

"She had nothing on her, no ID, except my club's card was stuck inside her bra."

"Well." Pause. "I guess we have to find a new source for fresh faces."

"I wouldn't worry about that. But...shit..."

"Are you in the club?"

"I am."

"Have a drink," she suggested. "We've wrapped up here for now. Let's talk tomorrow when you come in. Noon?"

"Sure. I'll come up to the studio around noon."

Suze hung up without saying anything more. She was a hard girl.

I LOOKED up from the phone and stared at the photos I had taped up against the wall in the small alcove behind my desk. Photos of me and my sweet Angela. Angie. Pictures from her birthdays. I was in one of them, laughing and happy. I reached up and touched the birthday shot. It was as though from another life. I had a small mirror tacked up against the corner of the alcove so I could check myself before going out front. It's been a long time since I worried about tears—but the years have left their mark on me. My face looked lined. My blond hair made me look wan and tired. I considered what might happen next, but drew a blank.

My inability to forecast the future led me to again reconsider my past and the events that led me here. Ten, fifteen years pass faster than you think. My first job was at a warehouse for Old's Market, purveyors of wine, beer, and spirits. But there was better money in running the routes and selling the product than there was in warehouse bookwork. In those days, the California driver's license was black and white, and anybody with a darkroom could make fakes easy as pie. With the help of friends, I quickly aged up to twenty-one and drove the van to make deliveries and push whatever we were told to push. As the TV ad said, we sold no wine before its time.

You meet people when you run liquor deliveries all over the county. Like Stu. He had converted an old car lot into a movie studio out at the edge of town, and he had a liquor license for the building in the front (no one knows how he pulled that off). The first time he saw me, I swear to God he leered like I was going to be his new best friend.

"Well who's delivering the elixir these days? I don't think we've seen you before. You want to see what we're doing here?" He sounded like he was from New York, and asked questions too fast to expect an answer.

"Sure," I said, giving him my clipboard to sign for the delivery. "I'm sure it's really interesting, but not today. You sure you have enough vodka?"

"Look," he said, eyeballing me, "bring an extra case of vodka next week and plan to spend a little time here—I'll show you the studio."

Back in those days, I was curious, and a studio sounded glamorous. I turned to get into the van and swung my butt around just the right amount, looking at him over my shoulder. "Next week?"

"I can't wait."

The next week, Stu took me to the back of his lot, where the studio was set up. I was kind of shocked, I admit it. Not only about having naked people hanging out on the set, but how nobody seemed to mind or care about it. They were all so la-de-da. It was fun to see them film a scene, even if it was pretty raw stuff. Stu was cranking them out; he could distribute everything he made.

Before long, Stu asked me to come back at the end of my delivery shift and help. "Not in front of the camera, Mona," he said, "although I think you'd look great there! I need more production help to keep my balls out of hock and get this series done. Extra cash and a learning environment. You see what we're doing here. Can you help me?"

Hell, yes. Better than the high school I missed out on.

Between helping Stu and building my routes up with the growing hotel trade, I was making fair cash. So I wasn't desperate, I wasn't needy, and I wasn't naïve, and I've got no one but myself to blame for getting pregnant, but it still took me by surprise.

Angie's future daddy was being honored at a big gala at the downtown hotel where the ceiling on the top floor rolls back for parties. I was in the back, behind the star-ceilinged ballroom, bent over and checking my inventory one last time. I had the sense of someone looking at me. Over my shoulder, there he was: an older guy wearing a tux, smiling, obviously a little embarrassed at being caught staring at my ass.

"Can I help you?" I asked, not being too frosty but careful, as always.

He took a moment, looked around, and then smiled at me. "I think you already have. From the look of things, I have you to thank for tonight's libations."

That didn't sound unfriendly to me, so I asked him, "And you would be...?"

"I'm Phil, the lucky guy getting this gala tonight. It's not for me, of course, it's for the new Waterfront Agency."

Phil was a good lookin' man. An older guy, but trim, smooth, in charge, attractive. "I'm sorry," I said, brushing a strand of hair out of my eye, "I don't know anything about who the party is for..."

"Why should you? You're obviously interested in making sure your end goes smoothly, and who cares why?" He laughed. "And I don't blame you one bit. In fact, I respect that a lot. You're getting the job done. Maybe you'd like to consider working for the new agency?" He smiled again, and I started getting the gist.

"Are you offering me a job? Are you going to run the place?"

"Would you like a job?" He looked at me interestedly, but I shook my head no as he told me, "Yes, I'm the first boss. Phil Nestor. I'm going to be the director." He didn't seem to be bragging, but I could tell he was proud. He had a smile on his face that couldn't be all 'cause of his drinking. He looked like a nice guy. "It's the beginning of a new reality for the bay, a new way to do business, and a new government. For this city and every other city along the bay. Wait and see."

"So is your new government going to want to buy any beer, wine, or liquor?" I asked him, always ready to expand the route.

He laughed again, and dug into a pocket to give me a card. "I've got to go back," he said, "but please call me and we'll have lunch and talk about concession agreements for the agency. OK?"

So it's on me, I guess, because I did call him back, and we did have lunch, and over a little time we got into more than one kind of business. He got away at least once a week and we had a lovely relationship in a motel by the pier in San Clemente, a little town an hour's drive up the coast from San Diego. No one would even know the place if Nixon hadn't made it his West Coast White House—but Phil dressed like a tourist and the motel we went to was off the beaten path. No one noticed us.

I knew he was married, and he was more than ten years older than me. I knew he already had two little girls. I was starting to make good money producing sex movies, and I knew how babies were made. I wasn't trying to bust his chops; I just enjoyed the freedom of our relationship. A freedom that came, for both of us, partly because of its secret nature. Known by none. At least that's what I thought back then. So me getting pregnant was not part of a plan, or a plot, but just how life goes.

I wasn't sure how I felt about it at first. People were going to see me at work, and it wasn't like it could be a big secret, you know. But for Phil, shit, it was a bombshell. First, there was the whole Catholic thing. He was married for life, no divorces, and I never wanted to marry him anyway. He told me he could never leave his wife, that he loved her. I didn't really know what to say to that, but my expectations had set the bar pretty low, and I wasn't asking for much.

Then there was the whole public man thing—he was the respected leader of a big new agency that somehow represented the state and a bunch of cities. It was like he was in politics and had to always be perfect. I didn't get it, really. But I know that the idea of owning up to his kid was tearing him apart, and I didn't need or want that.

We met at the motel to have a last roll in our own little hay. Afterward, we walked to the café next door. The surf was rolling in below the pier, relentless and indifferent. I really wasn't sure how I felt.

"I really do love you, Mona. You are a special friend, the kind of friend I've never had before. But this can turn out to be very bad for other people I love, too. I messed up. I know it. I was only thinking of myself when I should have been thinking about everybody else. Including you." He paused while the waitress poured us a couple of glasses of Chablis. "I have a friend I've talked to, and he can help me. He can help us. Although only God can help me, now. I can't acknowledge our relationship. I can't acknowledge our child." The surf filled the pause. It gave me something to listen to during the empty space. "Mona, I am sure you are going to be a great mother to this child, even if I can't be there as dad. First, you've got to have a house to live in that won't get taken away from you, and second, you need a nice business of your own so you can make a good living and show this child all the good things life has in store. That's something I owe you."

"You offering?" I blurted out. Man, I didn't know what to say to that. I'd come to this weekend fully intending to tell him that he could walk away, I understood completely, and not to worry, I'd make do. It's how I've lived my life. The sex was sweet. Comforting, and a little exciting for being secret. But it wasn't my life. I had ambitions. I may not be Catholic, but I never thought of not having this baby. No sir, 'cause now I had something to look forward to, something with a purpose, and being a mom was looking and feeling like it. I would handle things just fine and, you know, I didn't regret a thing. That's what I'd come to say.

I watched as Phil sipped some wine and then looked straight up at me. "I am. There's just one thing," he said, looking downward. "I wouldn't even ask, but my friend who is bankrolling all of this told me I had to. Part of the deal."

"Say what? The deal? I'm a little overwhelmed..."

He put a hand on mine and squeezed it. "We'll set you up in a nice house and furniture, no mortgage, no problem. My buddy is a real estate genius. And you know that one of your oldest customers, Tail O' the Cock, is for sale. Has been for six months. I'm told the market is soft and that he is willing to take a haircut, and the net there is a few grand a month. At least. All yours—but you have to promise me – us, really – that you'll never acknowledge or attribute my fatherhood to anyone. Ever."

"That's it?"

"That's it."

I didn't know what to say. I hadn't thought about his role with my baby. I knew he wasn't going to stick around. Did I really care if he wanted to keep this a secret? I could tell by his face, the way his eyes flicked around, that this was making him nervous. "That's it?" I repeated. "We both stay in San Diego and live our own lives and keep you a secret? Even from your baby?"

He grimaced. "I think so, Mona. I have to drop out of the picture and try to keep things going like they were. Whatever wrong I have done to you and others, I hope to make up for it over time, and setting you up to take care of your family on your own is the first step."

This sounded a little like someone who was making a saint-hood play, but I didn't think I should object. "What do we do next?" I asked him.

"Let's shake on it."

I shook hands in my distant memory, and then I shook my head to clear it and bring me back to the present. Tell No Tales.

I looked around my tiny space, the pictures of my daughter, and I stood up to go back to the bar. It was evening, and time for some business.

Gary

I left our headquarters and headed for home. Dad's house. Everybody knows my dad, Francis Reines, Frank, the real estate genius. Here I was—a vet and on the force, and I was still living at home. What the hell, I grew up there and it felt very comfortable. I parked in front, then walked across the gardened path to the casita my folks built for guests. Now mine—and I needed a shower. Evening was falling and it was still pleasantly warm, so I toweled off, grabbed a Coors from the fridge, and went outside to sit on my balcony and stretch my bad leg.

The big house was dark, so I guessed that my dad wasn't home. Even when Dad's around I don't see much of him, unless I go looking. I don't really know where he spends all his time since Mom was killed. He wasn't around that much when Mom was alive. He and his partners built hotels, and were apparently good at it, since they made a ton of money. Big places for companies like Hilton that had palm trees in the front and the bay in the back. Kept him out late.

The big house was built in the colonial revival style in Kensington, in a neighborhood of big Spanish houses that all looked older than they really were. Stucco was made to look like adobe, with Spanish-styled red clay tiles on top. My dad bought the house after he made his first big hotel score, twenty years ago. Growing up, this house, this was my world. Surrounded by trees, it rambled over to the edge of a ravine. It was large, private, and quiet.

When I was little, the ravine was my kingdom. When my mom wasn't hauling me off to some class or activity I would be out back in my private jungle, armed with my folding Buck knife.

"Gary? Gary, are you ready for lunch? *Ven a comer!*" I can see my mom as she looked then—her Mexican heritage showing in her tan face and long dark hair. Standing on the back patio and shouting for me to come in. I was always out in the back and she was always calling me in for some purpose.

She was my whole world, growing up. My sun and moon. I went to Balboa Park for every sport they had, from archery to judo. She took me. I did a lot of sailing in Mission Bay and I always loved being around boats. Anything I could do to stay outside. I was a busy kid, and Mom was always supportive of whatever crazy new thing I wanted to do, as long as I was not goofing off in the ravine. Which, of course, was where I usually was, because it was what I loved to do. She really loved me, her only child.

She was there for me every single day, right up until my senior year of high school, when she was T-boned by someone who drank his lunch, then drank some early dinner and went out for a drive.

I never saw that much of Dad before the accident—he was always busy with deals and meetings and only home for the occasional holiday—but I could tell the accident knocked both of us off our feet. Losing Mom just threw me. I wanted to kill the drunk driver, and if he hadn't already been in jail I might have tried. I felt it would be a good thing to find somebody bad and kill them. Dad kind of gave up on going to work so much and spent more time at home. I didn't realize at the time that my dad felt as crushed and as lost as I did. Their marriage had been an unlikely union between an upstart gringo and old-school Mexican class. The family in Mexico City never quite accepted my dad, but their marriage worked great right up until that terrible day.

After her funeral, he hired gardeners to take out my jungle ravine and turn it into a kind of memorial garden for my mom. And he started spending more time with me. He was often out and around doing something or other—but I was never sure what, and we didn't talk about it much. I concentrated on getting through my senior year.

It was hard on my dad, home alone, when I told him I was enlisting right after high school. He was hoping I'd go to USD or Santa Clara, one of the Jesuit universities. I had no time for that. I wanted to go to Vietnam and do right by the country and my family. I wanted to go kill somebody bad. I had an unclear picture of what that was. You could tell Dad was unhappy about my decision. It was stiff and awkward between us when I first enlisted, and even though boot camp was at Naval Training Center, San Diego, we didn't see much of each other. Later, we only wrote a minimal amount while I was in country.

When I came home a wounded warrior, though, there was no denying his pleasure at my return. We didn't talk much about my future, but he opened up to me, and we connected. My focus at first was just to get myself suitably mobile and into some job. He told me to take over the guesthouse that sat at the edge of the ravine – now a tropical flower garden—and take my time. He was glad I was around and I was glad to be around.

My dad's buddies were only too happy to help, both Phil Nestor and Erick Hansen, the Harbor Police chief, who'd run the Harbor cop shop for Phil since the beginning of the Water-front Agency. The pain in my leg was hard for the running requirements at the Police Academy, but everything else was pretty doable. Then, just before I became an officer, Erick Hansen had a heart attack. It was really a shame Chief Hansen died before he could retire and enjoy life; he certainly did me some good turns, and it sent another shock wave through my dad. I could see his grief. I guess that now I understood the bond that men make when they've been through war together. It's partly like they've lived through the hardest times, and they just can't believe it when mortality calls later when everything seems cake. Gus Mendoza took over for Chief Hansen, and there I was, still messing around in boats, still in a uniform, member of a new force, the Harbor Police.

I sat on the casita's porch and watched the evening stars come out, visible in our suburban setting because our streetlights were dimmed to the color of a Halloween pumpkin. This was to help the observatory on Mount Palomar. At least, that's what they told us when we were kids in school. I got another Coors and sipped it out of the can. As I finished the beer, my thoughts turned to Mona. Let's face it, like Hendrix sang, she was a foxy lady. I was surprised that I thought I could still feel her hand in mine. It's the thought I fell asleep with that night. I wondered when I was going to see her again.

2

TUESDAY

Mona

I'd had a fitful sleep, and was lost in a deep hole of dreams when I was jolted out of one by the telephone, which sat on a nightstand by my bed, right next to my pink plastic radio alarm clock, which said it was eight o'clock in the morning. I had set the alarm for eight fifteen. "Yes?" I said, warily and a little sleepily into the phone, holding the handset a few inches away from my ear.

"Detective Exeter, Miss Oakheart. I have some more questions for you. I'd like you to come back down here this morning, if that's OK with you." It didn't sound like he really cared very much what was OK with me.

"Look, *Jim*, why don't you just ask me now on the phone. I've got a day of work ahead of me and no one but me to do it."

"I don't want to inconvenience you, but we are talking about a murder. And I'm getting nowhere trying to find out who this person is and where she came from. I've only got you to ID her as Patricia Peteaut." He pronounced the name as though he were spitting it.

"I don't know how *I'm* going to help you in that regard, Detective." I tried to put a purr into it. "Like I told you, I only know this woman because *she* called *me*, out of the blue, and told me she had talent to show me. She knew the names of the other studios and she asked for a meeting. I don't ask for proof of who an agent is – as long as the talent works out, the agent gets a cut. If the talent doesn't work, they don't make anything. I have no idea where she came from, or who she really was."

"How many times did you meet her in person? Or talk on the phone?"

"We went over all of this yesterday, didn't we? I only talked to her on the phone once, then I met with her, *only once*, and she gave me a sample of head shots and a promo letter. She was supposed to bring me actors yesterday, but you know why she was a no-show."

"You've still got the photos, letters, and stuff?"

"I do."

"You probably handled them a lot, right?"

"I did."

"Bring them down anyway. I want to see them."

"I'll tell you what. I have to go to the studio this morning. I'll put the photos and letter into an envelope for you and you can send a patrolman by to pick it up there. Kearny Mesa. You know where it is. OK? I've got a really full schedule that starts in about an hour. Give me a break, Jim."

"That'll work for now. We'll talk more later." And then he hung up. I looked at the handset, said, "Nice talking to you," and hung up. Just then my alarm clock went off with a startling buzz. Eight fifteen. I sighed. Dang it. This was already starting out to be one of those days.

Gary

By eight thirty I was out on the bay again. I had another early shift on the *Pt. Loma II*, so I got up before dawn and drove down to the Shelter Island Station. The island was really a man-made peninsula jutting into the bay, with a long stretch of hotels (several built by my dad) on the bayside street and the Harbor Patrol dispatch HQ at its far end, where the street had a cul-de-sac. It was also our fueling station. The sweet smell of fuel lay on top of the tang of salt water as I walked up to the cruiser, tied to the dock. It had been a still and cool morning. The boat was rocking gently against the pier and creaking lightly against its lines. Dripping fuel left an iridescent swirl of colors on the undulating water. The dawn sky had been pearl-gray, tinged with the pink of reflected sunrise. I took another deep breath of the ocean and it felt pretty good. It felt fine just to head out onto the open bay in a boat.

I bent down to untie the spring line from the dock cleat, then heard rapping on the dispatch window. I looked up and the sergeant motioned for me to come in. When I did, he told me that there was a message from the PD: after my shift, I should connect with Exeter downtown. 10-4. I'd be out on the water until noon, so I'd catch up with him right after my shift. The sarge said he'd relay the message.

Mark Hight was my shift partner again, and with him piloting we slowly turned to the south, tapping forward just a little on the throttle, heading toward downtown. The Navy was all over the bay to the north and to the west of us, so not a whole lot of patrolling was needed over there. The waterfront is really several different pieces, and the Navy takes care of its own jurisdiction. Others, not so much. We slowly cruised by the cut where the sailor recruits at the Naval Training Center were already out training, rowing their lifeboats, and headed toward the Coast Guard Station. As usual, not much was going on at that hour except for the tuna men fishing, and one of the big purse seiners was headed to sea with its huge craned winch cabled to a net skiff, bigger than many cabin cruisers, on the back of the ship, holding down an enormous net.

This was the season when these ships were coming and

going. A normal day. It was a crazy unusual day yesterday when we had to snag that barrel out of the water. Word of it had spread quickly, and no one on the force recollected that happening before—although drownings, burnings, robbery, and general mayhem were well-established at the waterfront. Especially at night. But not too many bodies in barrels.

At noon, we tied up for the next shift to take out the cruiser, and I headed to the PD building. They waved me down the hall and let Exeter know I was coming. He was in his windowless office with its harsh fluorescent lighting. He was smoking, and the place stank of the cigarettes piled in his ashtray. I sat down in one of the two chairs facing him. I had mixed feelings. The guy seemed to be an asshole, but maybe he didn't know that slamming the truck yesterday would really set me off. I didn't know what he was doing, calling my dispatch about it. I wouldn't be a good detective; I often seem to have a hard time understanding why people do things. But I was definitely interested in this case—it was by far the most interesting thing I had come in contact with since joining the Harbor Police. I was in a wait-and-see mode.

"Glad to see you, Reines." Exeter sat there, looking at a file he was holding up in front of him.

"What do you know so far?" I asked. "Was she drowned, or dead before she was stuffed in the barrel?" That was frankly a thought that had been bothering me last night.

He met my eyes. "Well, we don't know shit so far. Autopsy is backed up over a week. All I got is what came out of the barrel. And I want to hear from you about the card. Give me the lowdown again."

I realized he was asking about the business card on the body. Our purple link to Tell No Tales. He pulled out the plastic baggie with the card inside and tossed it onto his desk. I looked at it.

"You said the barrel was bobbing at the surface?"

"Well, actually it was Matt Coelho who told me—his family

owns a couple of the big purse seiners. I was just getting into the shift and it was early, when we get a call on channel 16 to come to the aid of one of the seiners. That was weird—those vessels are set up to be out to sea for months. I couldn't figure what kind of aid they needed while moored at the G Street mole, but they told us to come in a hurry. They thought it might be some kind of drug-smuggling thing. We came alongside and they showed me the barrel. It had been bobbing in the water and had apparently clanked up against their steel hull, and when the watch saw it he used a cable winch to snag it and lift it out of the water."

Exeter just looked at me. I plowed on. "Matt swears he pulled it out of the water only to realize that the lid of the barrel, which had been the submerged half, was perforated. Once they lifted it out of the water, it started draining. At that point he had the winchman stop and just hold it above the water while they called for us. He said he had a bad feeling. He was worried it might be some drug dealer's stuff." I looked at Exeter. "I have no way of knowing whether he actually opened the barrel or not— you'll find out when you question his crew —but I do happen to know their plan was to sail out of here in a few days. Matt's worried this is going to hang him up. They have to go catch fish. I think they are headed to Guam."

"They can wait until I've talked to everybody—and I'm not there yet. I'll make sure they don't go anywhere until we've cleared their interviews. So—what next?" Exeter asked.

"My partner Mark and I came on board as they brought the barrel up and lowered it to the deck. The water had drained out. I watched while the deckhand pried the lid off and then I saw there was a body in a dress, and I told Mark to call you. Well, not you, but PD Homicide. They showed up in ten minutes, pulled out the body, and it had nothing—no purse, no jewelry, no ID, just a thin dress, bra but no panties. It was your guys who saw there was something under her dress. It was a thin dress, you know; you could see the card through the bra because the fabric was soaked. Apparently that was the only thing she had with her—that card slipped under her bra. She looked like a young woman, possibly Asian. It didn't look like any decomposition had begun; she had to have been killed recently, we figured, but you're the detective. Your team looked her over and found nothing. No ID, no nothing, no fingers. Only the card. Tell No Tales. Once the PD's crime scene people showed up to take pictures, we left the scene and went back to the cruiser to finish our morning patrol."

"So, you know this guy—the captain, Matt Coelho?" Exeter asked.

I nodded. "He and I went to the same high school—St. Augustine—but he was a year ahead of me. I know him, though, and his family has been fishing around here for years. Our families know each other. You want to talk to him?"

"I'll catch up with him, don't worry about it. What about the broad? You know her?"

"You mean Oakheart?" He just dead-eyed me. "Never saw her before yesterday." I decided to keep my views about her to myself.

"You ever been to her bar?" he asked.

"Not yet," I answered.

"You know her story?" He looked at me inquisitively.

"No. What story?"

"It's a cold case, now. Six years ago it was all over the news. You must have been out of town."

I said nothing.

"She was the victim of a kidnapping. Little three-year-old girl. They never found her. Sad shit."

"What about the father?" I blurted out the question without really thinking of why it mattered, and Exeter took a moment before answering.

"Something was going on back then. We never found out what. She told the world that she didn't know who the father was. Didn't make her look too good, you know." He nodded.

We just sat there silently for at least a minute, and I felt like he was pulling some sort of power play by making me sit in front of him. "Are we done here?"

"If you see her, remind her I expect her to stick around." He stared at his desk.

"Sure. We done?" I stood up. "And, Exeter, by the way, if you have a beef with me, feel free to call me directly instead of calling my duty officer to ask if I have a head problem, OK?"

Exeter looked right at me and grinned. He said, "I'll remember that, Mr. Boat Jockey. I only got your best interests in mind."

This seemed to be going downhill in a hurry, so I let myself out of his office and ambled down the hall as if nothing mattered. I'd show him how I don't get shook up. When I got back to the parking lot, I checked the bed of the Harbor Police pickup to make sure it still had the boat gear I was carrying back to our storage locker. Just because it was parked in the Police Department's parking lot didn't assure its safety—it was a shaky neighborhood to start with. The gears hardly ground as I backed up and headed to our bayside offices.

There were no Coast Guard airplanes crossing Harbor Drive, so it only took fifteen minutes. I may not have my own desk, but I had my own message slot, and a carbon copy note on thin, crinkly pink paper informed me that a "Mrs." Oakheart had called and asked me to return her call. The only other news was a mimeographed sheet of assignments for the upcoming week.

I went over to one of the open desks in the day room and sat down in the stiff metal swivel chair. I picked up the handset and dialed "9" for an outside line. After a second I got a dial tone, and then I dialed the number on my telephone note. It was picked up on the second ring.

"Tell No Tales."

"I'm returning Mona Oakheart's call. Is she in?"

"Who's calling?"

"Gary Reines."

The hand clapped over the receiver barely muffled her voice as she called out, "Mo-na? Hey, Mona? You got a call from a guy says he's Gary Reines." I could hear some more muffled talk. "Hold on, she's coming."

Mona

I came out from the closet that served as my office and took the phone from Candy, who was tending both bar and phone. "Gary?" I asked.

"I got a message you called." He didn't sound cold and institutional. He sounded cautious.

"Listen, I feel I was a little short with you yesterday, and it is not my policy to piss off the cops. I was feeling a little stressed. Come on by the club and let me buy you a drink."

There was a pause, but not a long one. "I have a few more hours on the clock here today," he said, "but if no more dead bodies float up I'll come by around seven, if that's OK."

"That's not funny. And that's partly why I want to see you. Seven. OK." I hung up. I sat down at the tiny desk in my closet office and stared at the picture of Angie. Yeah, again. And once again I was right back there, lost in my memories of those hopeful days when setting up a house for Angie and me seemed like the promise of a bright future in a brave new world. The house they arranged for me, my new world, was in National City.

I remember getting the letter in the mail. It was the first certified letter I'd ever got! It said that the house was in escrow and I would be the fee simple title holder. Escrow? Fee simple? I had no idea what either of those things meant, but the letter had an address, and I was out to my old Karmann Ghia in a flash to check it over.

National City is a working-class town just south of downtown San Diego, one of the first railroad stops ever built on the

West Coast, and now an industrial place where ships are built and the Navy hunkers at bay. There's an industrial feel to the waterfront, but once I turned inland the street ran uphill to a neighborhood full of cute little bungalows. I found the address in my Thomas Guide and pulled over to park.

The house was on a tree-lined street where there were green lawns and picket fences. It was white, with red trim on the shuttered windows. I was eight months pregnant, but still working at the new bar—I mean club, as the old Tail O' the Cock had become the new Tell No Tales, owned by me. I had hired a few girls and we were trying to make the place look a little more inviting. Getting the paint off the windows helped.

It seemed like a blur going from my downtown apartment to the new house, all while trying to make sure my new business, the club, was functional. It was exhausting enough without carrying Angela. I remember when I was still moving in, the furniture truck had just unloaded a dining room set from Sears and I was standing in the front door, leaning against the door jamb and feeling a little out of breath. This extra weight was getting to me. My feet hurt, I had to pee all the time, and I'm sure I looked like hell.

"You OK?" The voice startled me. I hadn't seen her walk up the side path to my porch. It was my next-door neighbor, Mrs. Aquino, whose husband worked at the shipyard. She'd been really sweet when I moved in just a month earlier, bringing me some Filipino food as a welcome to the neighborhood. Once I got to know some of my neighbors I realized that it was a predominately Filipino block, all of them solid, churchgoing folk. Unlike me.

"How you think you can do everything, you know?" Mrs. Aquino had a lilting accent, having been raised on the island of Luzon. "You should have help. I know the right one."

"I could use some help. Who do you know?"

"Look there," she said, pointing at the largest house on the street. "Esmerelda and her big family live there, yes?" I really didn't know. "She has cousin from Manila who comes with her husband and they move in. Now he gets job with shipyard and they are looking for a place. She wants to work, too. She can come by and clean up your house and take care of you and the baby and you'd have good help. Somebody has to be here with baby while you go to work, yes? Her name is Lola. Lola Lazaraga. I bring her over."

My thoughts drifted back from those sweet days to the present, but unwillingly. I didn't want to leave the memories of those first years on my own with Angie. That was the best. The best years of my life. Me and Angie. All the while I was building the business, making a nicer little place out of Tell No Tales, making a sweet little house for Angie, who loved Lola's crispy lumpia more than anything, except maybe me. Hardly more than three years, that's what we had, and then it all went to shit, and somehow I'm still here. If just going through the motions can be considered a life.

Gary

I hung up the phone after Oakheart hung up on me. OK, maybe multiple barreled bodies was a feeble shot at humor on my part. I wasn't sure why she sounded so put off, but knowing what I now did about the terror of her past, I wanted to go slow. I sat at the desk I shared with four others and swiveled the chair. I thought about the situation, and it made me wonder if she was calling me to pump me about the vic. On the other hand, maybe bringing her some information could be a good thing—as long as it wasn't anything confidential, why not? Maybe she'd remember something helpful. I wondered whether I should even tell her that I knew about her little girl. Hell, she may be a beautiful lady, but I am supposed to be a cop. This was a murder investigation. And there was a detective who was supposed to figure all this out.

I called Exeter's office and they put me through. "What do you want?" he said.

"Oakheart invited me over for a drink, so I plan on visiting her place tonight."

"Really. And you're calling me because...?"

"I suppose it is just possible I might learn something. The vic had to be carrying her card for a reason, right?"

"Here at the PD we call it a clue," he said. Everybody's a comic. "Look, Oakheart's story is that they were supposed to have a meeting and she didn't show up. If there's more, I'd want to know."

"You want me to poke around for anything you can use? Is there anything I should know?"

"I don't know what you think you should know," he said, "but we know fuck nothing about where this floater came from or why she ended up in the bay. I got nothing to tell you, kid. I can't even get an autopsy scheduled until the end of the week. Some highway bus mess comes first. Get her to show you some of her movies—that would be a good time! Let me know what you hear." A quick click and that was that. I was holding the dead phone, and if it wasn't for the spiral cord connecting it to the instrument, I might have tried throwing the handset out the window. Here I was trying to help this guy and all I got was crapola.

I suppose I slammed it down, because the next thing I knew Chandra, the head of the secretarial pool and administrative assistant for the chief, was scolding me. She must have been nearby.

"Don't you go breaking office equipment, Officer Reines! It will take two weeks to get a replacement and I don't have time for that." Chandra has got heft in her voice as well as her body. No one messes with her and she is very good at scolding. "You hear me?"

I immediately felt foolish. "Sorry." I looked across the room to the chief's office, which was dark. "Where'd the chief go?" I asked Chandra. "I think I'd better talk to him before Exeter at the PD does. I don't know what he's going to hear, but I want to tell him what happened."

"Well, you'll have to wait until he gets back from lunch. I don't expect him any time soon, either. He's out with the director, and I thought your daddy was having lunch with them, too. And the councilman, Simon Holier, too, I do believe."

I grimaced. Councilman Holier was going to clean out downtown San Diego with a stiff broom. Sex is a sin, and we're going to chase it out of town. That's always been a favored approach with the church, so not new to me. Paraphernalia shops, movie rentals, lap dances, girlie bars – he wanted them all closed, which was not endearing him to the sailors but has been a great cause for the "Navy Mayor," as the Admiral of the Fleet stationed in San Diego is called. The Navy Mayor swings some weight in this town, with all of its bases and airfields, and city councilmen listen closely when the Navy brass speak up. Holier was trying to earn brownie points with the Navy, so he put pressure on the locals. Then there was the civilian side. My dad was appointed to the board for the Tourism and Visitor's Bureau for the city, and they were always under pressure to come up with money to pay for everything. I didn't know about the lunch, but I was not surprised. And I'd have bet the Waterfront Agency was paying for it.

Gus

We were having lunch at Lubach's, right on the edge of the bay. Classy. Starched tablecloths, fancy food, sexy waitresses in tight black skirts, the whole nine yards. The bay glinted through the big glass windows as the sunshine bounced off the ripples on its surface. Not bad for a poor boy from Shelltown who made it in the Harbor Police. I kept my mouth shut. I was still feeling my way with this crowd. Not too many boys from the barrio in this place, except those busing tables. What with the clatter of dishes and chatter of gabbing power brokers, you had to speak up a little to be heard, so I kept mum. Old man Reines had a glass of white wine in front of him, and a big salad of crisp lettuce tossed with crabmeat and shrimp. He was, as usual, looking every inch the successful clean-shaven tycoon in his Brooks Brothers suit. My boss wore less fancy suits, but looked even more fit and trim than his old friend Frank. Nestor had catch of the day and Holier had a steak. Naturally, I had catch of the day. Frank Reines and the director were listening as Councilman Holier was pitching them on his new anti-smut campaign.

"I'm not looking for support," Holier was telling them. Holier was a small, round man with light balding hair, and it was a little amusing seeing him try to work up a powerful edge to his speech. "I'm looking for commitment!" It was clear that he was including me in this. What does he think, I speak for myself in this sort of thing? I held back and looked at the director for my cue.

Nestor patted his lips with his napkin. Meetings like this were how he made a living. He told Holier, "You know what, we're all behind you in cleaning up this city, but it really isn't our jurisdiction. There's not much I can do at the waterfront that's going to put any kind of spanner into their works. You're talking about a hundred mom and pops. Or maybe just pops." He grinned at his own joke. "You got the bars, the girlie shows, the diners, the tattoo parlors, the locker clubs, the adult book-stores, and at least four or five peep-show palaces. They're all in the city, Simon, they are not anywhere on the waterfront where I can do anything about it—if I even could do anything." Director Nestor paused to drink some of his iced tea—no booze during a working lunch. "And what's more, half of your problem comes from the sailors of the United States Navy. Good luck with that!" Nestor obviously knew who was really behind this push—someone wearing a uniform with gold braid on the shoulder.

Holier turned to me and gave me a hard stare. "I enforce the laws," I told him, "I don't make them." That worked for me a lot.

He turned and looked at Reines. "What, exactly, do you want *me* to do?" was Reines's response to his stare.

Holier leaned back in his chair. "I've got tools at the city. I'm in a conversation about redevelopment. I need some money to back a media campaign about why this is all a good thing for San Diego! Tourism and Visitor's Bureau—they've got the money. At least more of it than anyone else has." Holier turned to the director. "And there's funding you can come up with to help pay for redevelopment if it's on Waterfront lands. Some will be." He turned to me. "And all this smut we live around results in crime. People get hurt. I am going to want to see some successful apprehensions of smut sellers and buyers. And I'm going to want press about it. Got me?" His small, round head swung around to take us all in.

"My men are out there doing their job every day," I told him.

"They are going to have to do more than that," Holier answered.

Gary

My lunch was a tuna salad sandwich from a vending machine in the break room and a cup of coffee to motivate me through the reports. I stayed in the break room during lunch and filled out my reports for the past two days. A lot of guys bitched about the paperwork, but I didn't care. It was better than taking fire. I wasn't paying attention to the time, but when I finished the reports and glanced up, the chief was back in his office and the light was on. Must have been about three o'clock. Even though my day had started early, I still had a few hours to go on my shift.

My intercom buzzed. It was the duty sergeant, who told me

that I had a visitor up front; would I please come out? I didn't have anything scheduled, and visitors were an infrequent occurrence, so I went right out to the front of our office. The gal at the front desk motioned at someone waiting on one of the wooden benches. Through the reception-area window I saw a guy who looked like he was in his fifties, balding red hair going gray, dressed in an orange-and-yellow plaid suit. The secretary and I exchanged glances. We rolled our eyes. I opened the door and walked out to him.

He stood up and stuck out his hand. "Huell," he said, "Huell Hund, *San Diego Tribune*." He gave me a card. "Got a minute?"

"Sure," I said, and led him to one of our interview rooms you can access from the front.

He sat in a straight-backed chair across the bare table from me and pulled out a notebook, although he didn't open it. He put it on the tabletop. "You're the guy who found the body in the barrel, is what I've learned," he said.

"Wasn't much to it. I just looked inside once we pulled it out of the bay."

"Well, I'm covering the case because strange things are showing up, you know?"

"Like what?" I asked him.

"Like you hear she got the tips of her fingers all clipped off?"

"I was there," I reminded him, "but I didn't know that fact had been put out by the PD."

"Maybe it hasn't, yet. I got sources. Thanks for confirming for me. And you know what else I know?"

"I sure don't."

"The broad had a business card on her. Only a matter of time before I find out about the card. Want to tell me what you know? This story gets juicier by the minute, but maybe when *I* tell it somebody ends up looking good, you know what I mean? Why don't you fill me in on some good details and set yourself up to be the good guy in this one."

"You are talking to the wrong guy. It's not my case. I just called the PD when I saw her in the barrel. I've got nothing for you, and believe me, I am not looking to be your good guy. I think we're done here, Huell."

"OK, OK. But something is going on here—I can smell it. People in City Hall are thinking this is part of some bigger deal, and I will find out about it. You know that."

"Great," I said. "Write a great story and I'll read it. But now I really have to get back to work." I wasn't actually rude to the guy, but I didn't spend any time trying to kiss up to him, either. Showed him out, went back to work.

Two hours more on my shift, and I had a change of clothes in my locker. I was just a few minutes away from Wyatt Earp's old stomping grounds, and a lady who might buy me a beer. So near, and yet so far. I thought about the reporter's interest in finding out more about the connection between her and the floater, but I figured it was something I should keep my nose out of. Not my case. I stared at the stack of forms I was supposed to complete. I sighed. For some reason, I couldn't keep my mind on the paperwork. I had a little film loop going through my head that distracted me. It was my picture of Mona, sliding into her little sports car and screaming out of the cops' parking lot.

Mona

Already four in the afternoon and only two drinkers nursing well pours. I figured Reines wouldn't make it over until six or seven. I jokingly call my office "closet-trophobic." It's window-less and still. October, and with the Santa Anas still blowing, it got hot. It was too hot now. Like an Arkansas summer. I didn't have any air-con, and my single fan out on the bar seemed dead. It was a moment in between the moviemaking, inventory checking, money counting, and...whatever. I sat and stared at the pictures thumbtacked to the wall and slid into a reverie...

"...Careful, careful, little girl, let me get you in the chair." It was not a well-attended first birthday party. Only two other grown-ups: Mel from the bar because she was also a mom, and Lola, who had baked the birthday cake, plus Mel's little redheaded Karen. Mel stood by me during the pregnancy and all the awkwardness that it caused. She backed me up for the first year of Angie's life, when it was obvious that whoever Daddy was, he wasn't coming around much. I wasn't talking. That was my part of the deal.

I got Angie in her high chair and put a big slice of her first birthday cake in front of her. I turned to give a slice to Mel, but Mel erupted into laughter and pointed at Angie, who had just done a major face plant into the cake. She lifted her face out and it was coated in frosting. I grabbed the Polaroid and took a picture.

The only other picture of Angie in my office was from exactly one year later. She was sitting in my lap, curled up on a wooden bench on the upper deck of the bay ferry. I had taken her to Coronado for special birthday-party ice cream and we were headed back to the city. She was starting to use words—and she called me Mama. It was chilly. I had a blanket wrapped around her and she was in my arms. This time, we had gone with a small troop of girls, and one of their mothers took a picture of us. The diesel chugged and the big ferry rocked a little, and in less than half an hour we were back at the Embarcadero. That was almost a year before it happened. And now, a few years later, it seems like another life. I find it hard to believe it ever happened and that I ever got to love someone so completely and so purely as I loved Angie.

It was probably the second year we were in the little house that I first heard about Freddie. Our household life had settled into a regular routine. Lola Lazaraga would show up early, because I was running the club and pouring my profits into building a studio for the filmmaking side of things, and it took all day and into the night before I could get home. I got Angie dressed and started her on some breakfast. Then Lola would let herself in and take over for me, smiling and happy, and I would hug and kiss my baby girl and head out to see if I could conquer the world. Every once in a while Lola's husband, Pete, would come over and help her with something, as his schedule was constantly being changed at MASTCO, the shipbuilding docks where he worked.

One day, I got home earlier than I expected. Pete was in the living room, on the couch, hugging Lola, who looked as though she had been crying. He looked up at me with very sad eyes.

"Is everything OK?" I asked, feeling a little dumb. It was obvious that not everything was.

"We just got very sad news from Manila..." Pete said, looking at Lola. "We have a nephew who died."

"I didn't know you had family back in the Philippines," I said, looking at Lola with concern, and glancing around to see if Angie was going to bounce into the room.

"Angie is napping," said Lola, looking up at me. "I cry very quiet."

"Oh, Lola, I'm so sorry to hear about your nephew. Were you close?"

Lola seemed to curl up into Pete a little more, and I heard a muffled cry that sounded like a wounded kitten. She held a necklace in her hands; it looked like a Virgin Mary medallion.

Pete looked up at me. "It's very complicated," he said. "Lola raised her nephew Freddie as her own son, since he was baby. He was her sister's boy, but she died of lung cancer. The boy was in trouble all the time. Always. He grew up with many problems and no friends. We lived in Manila and there wasn't money for things, but Freddie always came home with new things. Clothes that were new but didn't fit right. He take them from people. Always trouble. Lola take Freddie to church so Father Rodrigo could teach him, but he didn't like that. He was angry. He killed Father Rodrigo's pet dog, and the good Father told the police, and they came and took Freddie for jail. Even

though he was hardly fifteen. He had nothing but this medallion," and Pete nodded at the necklace Lola held, "which his
mother, Lola's sister, had on her when she died. He go to jail,
and we leave Manila. It was too hard for us—too many bad
memories. Now I get telegram that he is dead in jail, and
already—what do you say?—cremated. It's a sad, sad story.
They sent us his medallion." As he spoke, Lola gripped the
medallion and wept.

"Mommy?"

I looked toward the little hallway leading to the bedroom.
Angie had climbed out of her bed and was rubbing her eyes,
aware that something was not right.

"Hey, baby," I said. I went straight over to her and picked
her up. The whole idea of a nephew's dying left me sad and
anxious, and I hugged her close to me. "Don't worry, baby, Lola
is sad but she will get better soon. Lola," I said, looking at her,
"why don't you and Pete call it a night, and let me know
tomorrow morning how you feel..."

"Don't worry, Miss Mona, I see you in the morning." She
came over to tousle Angie's hair and give her a quick kiss, then
left with Pete.

The story was never repeated, and Lola kept coming every
morning with her smile, and life at the Oakhearts resumed its
quiet routine. Then it was April. And my world stopped.

I sat in the hot, still closet for—I don't know—it could have
been ten minutes, it could have been an hour. Then the bubble
popped. Marla, a new helper at the bar, stuck her head in to ask
for the key so she could get more Jim Beam from the closet, and
reminded me she was done for the day. As I reached for the
keys, the phone rang. It was Suze up at the studio, and she
wanted to know if the 16 mm Bolex for B rolls was going to
show up for tomorrow's schedule, and just like that, I was back
at work. I went into motion and stayed that way for a couple of
hours, even tending bar for some old swabbies who filtered
down from the small, single-room apartments upstairs,

wandering in for shots with a beer back, and then I realized that the streetlights had gone on outside our window, the sky was darker, and Gary Reines walked in.

Gary

First impression—not very impressive. Looked like just another downtown dumpy bar to me. A couple of ferns and framed movie posters. Otherwise it was Formica, aluminum, and booze. Tell No Tales didn't really look like it had any tales to tell. What did I know? The bar itself looked like it came out of one of those old railcar diners, pleated aluminum front with a zinc top. Behind it, Mona leaned over and poured an old sailor some whisky. As she leaned over, her low-cut blouse emphasized her cleavage. She looked up at me sharply and I shifted my gaze, but shit – busted! Again! She gave me a very slight grin and nodded me over to an empty barstool. I did my best at a nonchalant amble across the small barroom and slid into a seat.

Mona came over and stood right in front of me. She stared me directly in the eyes. I could swear she was arching her back to emphasize her breasts and seeing if I was going to stare at them again. I didn't. I looked right back into her eyes.

"What happened to your leg?" she asked.

"What about my leg? I didn't say anything about my leg."

"I'm observant. I like to watch a man's legs." The way she said "legs" was very direct. "I owe you a drink—so you can take your time and tell me the story."

"Let me have a Coors," I suggested. The place wasn't jumping, but she was doing some business, and it involved keeping track of the guys who were nursing beers. She had a helper, but they both seemed busy. Still, I looked up from my beer and there she was, standing behind the bar, but right in front of me and looking me in the eye. The second time it happened, I smiled at her.

"You want my story...?"

"I'm standing here, aren't I? I may even spring for a second beer, if it's good..."

"I'll trade you stories. Mine is just a simple nothing. I'm from here, went to school here. I enlisted—Navy town, right? Of course, I go Navy. Swift boats. Ever hear of the Mekong Delta? My job was to get shot at and shoot back. I guess I was good at it. Everybody in the jungle was shooting at me. They didn't always miss." I slapped my hip.

"You were Navy before you went to Harbor Police?"

"That I was. A fairly recent transition. Now I'm hanging out at my dad's house. Where I grew up. Hometown boy treads water while the world turns. How about you? What's your story?"

She gave me a look. I couldn't easily interpret it. Then she waved at someone who'd just come through the door, and called out, "It's yours. Are you ready?" Apparently the nighttime shift. What timing.

Mona turned back and looked at me, asking, "You want to get a taco?" She tossed the keys to the gal who'd just walked in, threw a bar towel into the sink, and walked out toward the front door—anticipating, I guess, that I'd be right behind her. Which I was. I guess it was dinner time.

I FOLLOWED Mona out the door into what felt like a dicey evening on Fifth Avenue. I had my department-issue Smith & Wesson Model 10 locked up in my car, but as I looked around, I thought that it might be better if I was carrying the next time I visited. The spirit of Wyatt Earp blasting an end to a rowdy patron seemed to linger on the night air. Mona didn't seem fazed.

"The best tacos, I mean the *best*," she said, "are in OB. I live there. Follow me?"

"Sure. Just don't drive over the speed limit in your hot little Benz."

She smiled and we got our cars—both were in the only lot for three blocks that had a parking attendant—and headed to Ocean Beach, on the other side of Point Loma, that hilly finger of land that gestures out into the Pacific. OB is a classic West Coast beach town, a strange suburb of San Diego that dates back to the eighteenth century. Now it comes complete with beer bars, head shops, and Harley-Davidsons. A hangout for hippies, runaways, some plain old deadbeats, and, apparently, Mona. We headed toward Newport Avenue, right in the middle of the OB scene, but instead of turning down toward the new fishing pier the city opened a few years ago, she drove up another couple of blocks and then turned into a small side road leading to the cliffs. We were in a warren of little alleyways and clusters of apartment houses and cottages. It wasn't too easy to see where I was; I just followed her lights. We took a couple of turns before all of a sudden we were at the edge of the cliff, right by a small grouping of three little cottages around a common courtyard.

"Leave your car here," she called. "At least you can park. We'll walk down to the taco shop. Parking's a bitch down there." She pulled onto a skinny driveway, two strips of cement leading behind the cottages, leaving me to shoehorn my Chevy Camaro (it was from my dad—the same car I had in high school) into a gap on the alley that passed for a street. The lights winked on in the cottage at the rear, and then Mona emerged from the front door.

"Follow me." And we headed out on a dark pathway down a steep hill toward the fishing pier and the lights on Newport Avenue.

Mona

Young Reines followed me quietly. It wasn't fair for me to think of him as "Young Reines," I guess. He probably wasn't ten years younger than me. Maybe. He doesn't really look like he's related to the Frank Reines I met, but if he is, he didn't seem nearly as serious as the old man. He still hadn't asked me why I called and asked him to come by. We'd see how this goes.

"How long have you lived here?" he asked me.

"San Diego or OB?"

"Your story." He smiled at me, and it was a pretty open smile.

"I came to town as a teenager." I gave him a slightly coy smile. "I'm going to be vague about when. I was working for a liquor distributor and I met a lot of people. I learned about hotels and bars, and a client taught me something about the movie biz. When you're a girl people are happy to talk to you, and I learned a lot. Once I got the club, I had what I needed to make my own movies, and they can make good money. Now I've got the club and the production company, and they are both doing OK. I love OB, and a few years ago I needed to make a change, so I bought those cottages. I've been living here for about three years, and it's the best—" I held my speech while a motorcycle blatted loudly by. "Except for the Harleys."

"Why did you have to make a change…?"

"Aren't you the good listener."

"Not an answer. I notice you don't wear a wedding ring."

"I'm not married. Are you?"

He looked a little embarrassed. "I don't even have a girl-friend. I've been busy, lately, getting situated and all." He paused and looked at me as we walked up the block to the taco shop. "You don't want to talk about it?"

"Come on," I told him. "We're here." I knew Miguel, by the comal grilling meat—Christ, sometimes I think I lived on his cooking. "*Dos tacos*, Miguel, *al pastor, con Dos Equis, por favor.*

For each of us." Miguel smiled at me. Gary gave him fifteen bucks, saying, "*Por la cuenta*," and we went to one of the tiny tables off by the side of the taqueria.

Gary looked at me. "We have to talk about something," he said. "So what did you want to talk to me about?"

OK then, here we were. I wasn't going to lie, but I had to be very careful about the truth. The truth was complicated. "Am I a suspect?" I asked him.

"I don't know, to be honest, but I think you ought to figure the police are going to consider every angle, and everybody, and you are certainly one of the persons of interest that have popped up in this thing."

"The police? How about you?"

"I have a different job. Investigating murders is done by detectives. I am not likely to be given any role at all, and I may never know anything more than gossip about what your friend Jim is really thinking."

Miguel came over and gave us each a paper plate of two hot tacos, *al pastor*, and frosty cold bottles of Dos Equis.

"Now if your friend Jim wants a tour of the crime scene, he'll need me. Unless he's a better swimmer than he looks."

"But *Jim*," I said, using the appropriate sound of discernment, "probably doesn't think of himself as one of my circle of friends."

"I think that's fair," Gary said, and then, plunging in, "but he knows something about you." Gary looked at me intently, as if he was waiting to see what I would say.

"What's that mean?" As if I couldn't guess.

"He told me about the kidnapping."

I sat quietly for a minute, nibbling on my taco. It's not something I talk about. What's to say? What's the goddamned point?

"Maybe anything I say is going to come out wrong. But I can't think of a worse thing to happen," he said, after a minute of my silence that felt like an hour. "I think the PD thinks there might be a connection. And I can tell you that things are likely going to heat up. Today I got a visit from a reporter, and that hasn't happened before."

Nothing I could say about that.

"I just want you to know that I know. I lost my mom when I was a kid. Losing someone you love is a bitch. Frankly, one of the things I got drilled into me in Nam was that losing almost *anybody* can be a bitch. Even some guy you've only known for a month. But it's the one reliable constant in life—it ends."

"You trying to make me feel better?"

"I guess I'm just trying to be a friend," he answered. "Maybe I'm not very good at being a cop; my feelings get in the way."

Later, after walking back up the hill to the cottages, I'll be damned if the boy didn't take my hand and draw me into him, leaning in and giving me a pretty spirited kiss. I felt blood flowing in places that had long been still. He smiled at me, but pulled away and headed to his car. "See ya later," he said, and waved. I had to wonder about that.

3

WEDNESDAY

Frank

I t was early in the morning and I stood out on the second-floor porch off my bedroom of our Kensington home, looking across the garden to the casita to see if I could tell if Gary was in. October, and there wasn't a trace of chill in the air. Not like Minneapolis, where I grew up. The Santa Anas blew warm, and there was a hint of smoke, maybe smog, you could smell. It was still early and the traffic sounds were light, buffered by a few rows of houses and canyons before they reached this garden spot. Lord, how Maria would have loved it. Our time together was so precious. Then my thoughts drifted back and I remembered my meeting with Phil last night.

We both sat in Phil's plush director's office. Nice carpet, big dark wood desk. On the top floor of the Bunker, as they call the Waterfront Agency's building, the only floor with windows. I knew he wanted to go home and have dinner. Nestor has done well for himself—given that you can't make a mint working in government. I smiled to myself, thinking what a contrast it was to my own office. I had moved millions in hotel construction, but I had worked out of a cinderblock two-story building in the middle of an industrial development in the Midway district. I'd used a simple metal desk, and did a lot of my own correspondence on my own IBM Selectric.

"Francis," he asked me, "where'd you go to? You didn't get a thing I said, did you...?" When he called me Francis, something only my mother used to call me, I could hear the annoyance that crept into his voice.

"I'm listening. You want to play along with the uproar about city smut until it passes. You want me to get money out of the Tourism Bureau to placate Holier until it does."

I was sitting in a plush chair and holding a scotch and rocks in cut glass. It was Chivas. I sighed. It all seemed like such a waste to me. There were some great things we could be doing for our town. A really classy convention center, for example. Maybe a marine aquarium on the bay... I noticed my glass seemed to have been magically refilled.

"Frank," he said, back to the name I've used since leaving the Navy a couple of decades ago, "we've been friends a long time. I've supported you and you've supported me." I just looked at him, as that didn't call for a response. We'd been through more than just business deals together. Some harrowing times. War. "Stick with me on this; it won't get out of hand."

"I'll go talk to the Board about coming up with some budget for the good councilman's program. No guarantees."

"It will keep the politicians busy and out of trouble," he said, and smiled at me. I can only hope he's right.

I looked across the garden at the casita. Last night Gary had gotten home a little late for him. I heard his Camaro pull into the driveway around midnight, a familiar sound, but it was a workday and he usually had to be out before the light of dawn. This morning, the Camaro was still sitting in the driveway. I leaned against the rough-hewn wooden rails and looked through the large purple slippers of flowering birds-of-paradise and the fringed sago palms to see if I could spot him moving around in there.

Imagine, who would have thought that body would have ended up in the bay, and that Gary would end up pulling it out of the water! It's a crazy world.

Gary

It was hot. Early in the morning, but still hot enough to throw off the sheets and lie naked under the ceiling fan. I'd swapped out my morning shift and I didn't have to show up until ten. As I lay there, I thought about Mona. I knew my dad thought I should get a girlfriend, but what with leaving for the Navy, coming home to heal up, and a new job, I just hadn't had any time to focus on meeting women. And nobody I'd run into made me stop and look again. Mona did. She seemed solid and capable, and different from other women I've met. She's obviously been through a lot. A survivor. She had grit. I bet Dad would like her.

Mmmmm. Maybe not. His best friend is a deacon in the church, and Dad's been pretty observant since Mom died. I didn't know how he would react to a producer of X-rated movies. I was sure the church would frown.

I decided that I wanted to see more of this woman. Get to know her a little better, maybe get her side of the story—assuming there was a story somewhere. Maybe there wasn't, and we'd just get better acquainted. My plan, of course, was made a little dicier because of her current situation as a person of interest in Exeter's investigation. For me to start dropping in on a POI would probably send everybody I worked with through the roof. But maybe I could use my Harbor cop status as an excuse to knock on her door. I mean, how the hell did the vic have her business card? Maybe I could learn something. I knew I'd better let Exeter know what I was doing—not that he

would give a crap about it, but it'd give me cover for being
friendly with Mona.

I rolled out of bed, did some stretching exercises for my leg,
and hit the road after a shower and toast. I almost thought I saw
my dad watching me as I got into the Camaro—but it was a
passing glimpse, gone quickly.

Gus

Eight o'clock in the morning. I sat down at my desk at Harbor
Police HQ to start my day and survey what I'd find there, and
Chandra came in and brought me a cup of coffee. An indul-
gence permitted only to me. And Hansen before me.

"Here you go, Chief," she said.

"Thanks. Anything going on?"

"No—but it's early; there's plenty of time for things to get
messed up." She and I both grinned at the tired joke, and she
left me to thumb through the first papers to reach me that day. I
get reports about ship traffic as well as other facts. It looked like
one of Coelho's purse seiners had left for the Western Pacific
last night. They'd be using Guam as a transshipment point for
the frozen tuna they'd send home, and not likely be seen in
port for a couple of months. Keeps Bumblebee Tuna, their
buyer, fat and happy. I noticed that his other purse seiner, the
one his son, Matt, captained, was rescheduled to stay in port for
a couple of days. Police orders. Exeter wasn't going to let it
depart until he was done with interviews about the floater from
that source. I paused. Should I still call it a floater? Even if it
was in a barrel?

I knew from the beginning that I had an obligation to deal
with this thing. I knew what I'd promised Chief Hansen, who
had done everything to try to help his friend and my boss,
Nestor. His best friend from the war. To whom he owed everything. And Hansen had gone above and beyond and pulled off
some detective work in the Philippines that was amazing—

even if it wasn't enough. So here we were. I promised what I promised, and when it came down to me, I had tried to do my part. Maybe this time it would really be over.

Suze

I was supposed to be at the studio bright and early, but I was a little late. I pulled up to the studio in my glamorous ten-year-old Volkswagen, conscious of the fact that my MFA in film-making from San Francisco State had not yet taken me to greater heights. My car – maybe a little banged up and rusted out—looked right at home in front of the industrial building that housed the studio. It wasn't exactly a red carpet in front of Grauman's. I looked at all the traffic driving by on the street, smoke pouring out of tailpipes, and thought about the scenes we had to finish that day. It was an ambitious schedule, and I was working with some new talent that I had never met. Suboptimal. When the deal with that Patricia lady blew up (how weird was *that*?) and no new faces were going to come from her, I covered with Stu, Mona's old buddy, and we came up with some actors from TJ and one who was in town from Manila.

I looked at my watch. Resisted the urge to light another Marlboro. God, I hoped Mona wouldn't be such a bitch today. The past few days she'd been nothing but trouble. I looked at the studio.

"Showtime," I muttered to myself, and got out of the car.

"Hey, excuse me, hey, are you Mona Oakheart?" The voice came from behind me, and I turned to see a guy standing in the shade of the building across the narrow parking lot. Wow, what a suit! It was, like, green plaid threaded with purple.

"Who's asking?" I answered.

He walked over and handed me a card. Huell Hund, *San Diego Tribune*. "Took me an hour with the county recorder, but we finally figured out that you apparently own this building as well as the bar downtown. Can we talk?"

"About what?" I said, not moving toward the door of the studio.

"What do you think? I'm tracking down a murder and your card shows up, right? What's going on with that?"

"What do you think is going on with that?" I figured I might draw him out and learn something good for Mona. "And by the way, where did you get that suit?"

"TJ," he said. "Can we go inside?"

I figured I'd played out the string. "No," I said. "I'm going to work and I have nothing to tell you. And, by the way, I'm not Mona Oakheart and I'm pretty sure she isn't going to want to talk to you either. She isn't here yet, I don't think. Do you want to leave a message?"

He looked a little confused, and maybe pissed. "Don't jerk me off, lady. If you're not Oakheart, who are you?" I didn't answer. "My boss buys ink by the barrelful and when the *Tribune* gets angry, there are often a lot of angry citizens that go along. Talking to me would make sure Oakheart's story got heard. Tell her that. Looks like she's tied into a murder and it is stirring up a hornet's nest at City Hall. City Hall talks to me. It sells papers. Have her call me."

He glared at me, then wheeled around and headed back out to the street. I didn't know what Mona got herself into with this dead agent, but it sure looked like it wasn't good! I turned and went into the studio.

Exeter

First thing in the morning, and I was on the phone with the coroner's office. "Ma'am." I kept trying to interrupt her nonstop story on the telephone. "Ma'am, Marge, please, I get it—you guys are overwhelmed with the bus accident. I know it, but you can't just put us in line one after the other. I've got a murder here and I am coming up with absolutely zero. I NEED that autopsy. I can't wait until early next week. You go tell Doc

Sleizer he's got to bump me up in line. Or I'm calling the mayor and the supes." I waited for another outburst to finish. "I will call, you know I will. We are all taking heat on this and I need some results. I need them today!" Another outburst. "Yes, ma'am. Thank you."

The patrolman, as instructed, had gone to the studio to pick up the envelope of photographs the so-called agent had left with Mona Oakheart. It was evidence, and he bagged and tagged it on receipt. He brought it straight downtown to crime scene forensics to have the papers dusted for prints and photographed. Over a dozen glossy eight-by-tens—perfect for prints. That was the problem. Too perfect. The goddamn photos were covered in prints. It would take a long time to sort this out. I had been waiting on forensics since yesterday for the papers and the photos. Finally, I got a buzz on the intercom that I could pick the stuff up for inspection before it went to the evidence locker.

I used light cotton gloves to handle the letter. It was on cheap paper, with a letterhead that looked like it was printed with a rubber stamp. It read "Sweet Pea Talent Agency" in a swirling, colorful script that looked like something off of a Beatles record.

> Dear Miss Oakheart,
>
> Please find enclosed some examples of talent we can provide. We specialize in adult entertainment, and can arrange for professionals in the fields of dancers, strippers, and actors representing a wide range of types and styles.
>
> As we discussed, I will meet you at your bar before you open so we can talk. I am looking forward to it.

It was signed, simply, "Patty." The return address, cheap printing in swirly letters, was in Baguio City, in northern Luzon, in the Philippines. Well, shit, what was that about? The phone number was a Los Angeles exchange—area code 213. I picked up my phone and called the number. I let it ring for a minute or two, but no one ever answered. I made some notes to follow up with Ma Bell. I looked at the glossy eight-by-tens. Some black-and-white, mostly color photos of young people and some faces that didn't look so young anymore. Nothing that looked kinky young. They all looked to be over eighteen. Blond girls, black dudes, Asian...I'm not sure what. A party pack. I sighed. Then I called over to the studio, where Mona Oakheart said she'd be working that morning. A woman answered.

"This is Lieutenant Exeter. Can I speak with Miss Oakheart, please?"

The woman said she was the administrative assistant at the studio. "She told me you would probably call. Can I have her call you back? She's in the middle of production and there's probably a dozen people here who are being paid by the hour. She told me to tell you that."

"Look, just tell her I need her to come back downtown so we can have her fingerprinted."

"Fingerprinted? She didn't do anything!"

"Calm down, this is standard stuff. We need to identify her prints on all the photos she sent me this morning so we can tell them apart from the others, like prints that might have come from the victim. Process of elimination. I need her to show up sometime today because we're working on the ID right now. OK?"

"I'll tell her."

"I'll be waiting."

I turned to thumb through the material in the envelope again, when the phone rang. It was Marge. My threat of going to the superintendents had done the trick. The autopsy was now scheduled for first thing tomorrow morning, and I was welcome to be there. I thanked her, but told her not to wait on my account. Just get me answers.

Gary

I still had the Rolex my dad gave me when I graduated from St. Augustine's. That and my old Camaro— artifacts of another life. The watch said nine fifteen. Not a lot of time before I had to be down at the dock, but I hustled over to Exeter's office and knocked on the door.

"Yeah?" He looked up as I pushed it open.

"I wanted you to know that I went to see Mona last night. We didn't talk much about your case. She did say that agents are basically unreliable and sometimes they're grifters, but I didn't learn much else." He just kept staring at me. "I'm probably going to see her again, unless you tell me you're thinking she may be involved somehow..." Sounded pretty thin to me, but I figured I might as well lay it out there.

"Listen, Reines—I never think anything about anybody. I just collect evidence. I think it's dicey to get cozy with a wit on a murder case, and you probably ought to clear it with your chief. But I don't really give a rat's ass one way or the other. You two have a good time?" He leered at me.

"You are a piece of work, Exeter. I'm just trying to keep you informed. Maybe it could help."

"Tell me something I don't know."

Despite the fact that Exeter played like a rough guy, I had the feeling that he wasn't really an asshole. He'd just chosen to live in an asshole's world. I played it straight. "What can you tell me about the kidnapping? Why do you think that it's connected?"

He answered in kind. "I don't know shit. But I do know that coincidences aren't usually just coincidences. There's some kind of Filipino connection—and Mona Oakheart has got some history with this department."

"What—did you arrest her for something? Trouble with her bar?"

"Nothin' like that. But we do think she lied about her age

when she first came to town." He grinned. "She got a license to drive for Old's Market and deliver booze to hotels. Somehow, she got away with it."

"Really?" I stared at him. "So that's your big scoop on her? She lied about her age—what—ten years ago?"

"Closer to twenty. I wasn't here, but the guys who were remember her. Then she is the mom in a kidnapping. I told you. Six or seven years ago—maybe you were off to the Navy. It was all over the papers. Young mom, owner of a local bar, has her three-year-old daughter kidnapped. The people around here remember—we don't get that many kidnappings, and this one had a murder tied to it. I went back and started looking at the files, naturally." He looked at me. "Did you talk to her about it?"

"I told her I knew it happened, but she didn't say anything about it. What went down?"

"After the grab, no ransom note was ever delivered, but we brought in the FBI anyway. Chief of police back then wanted cover. Nothing ever happened. No notes. No communication. They never found the kid or the kidnappers—coulda been one of them, coulda been two, nobody saw them. Only their van, tearing out of the driveway. The scene was a mess—kid was grabbed right out of the home along with the housekeeper, whose husband was shot dead. Never heard from the house-keeper again, either. Two weeks later we get a call from the *policía* in TJ because they found an Econoline that matched our BOLO—abandoned at the airport. We showed photos to the neighbors, who thought it was likely the same van that the kidnappers used, but trying to trace it backwards got us nowhere. *Nada*. It was purchased for cash in LA a week or two prior. The feebs got prints off of everything in the van—and somehow it took them to the Philippines, but nothing ever came of it."

"She never talked about the father?"

"Well, that's a funny thing. She would never tell us who the father was. She said she didn't know. It wasn't something anyone ever figured out. Four, five years go by—nothing has changed. She never told you any of this?"

"It wasn't what we talked about."

"She's a looker. As far as I know, she's a loner. She's been on the radar screen of the department since she got here, but we never made her for taking her own kid."

"You think there may be a connection with the floater?"

He shrugged. "I don't believe much in coincidence, and right now I'm just collecting evidence." He looked at me. "The murdered guy in the kidnapping was Filipino. The house-keeper, his wife, was Filipina, and I'm trying to run down indi-cations that there was some kind of follow-up investigation on the kidnapper that went down to the Philippines. Somebody apparently went to Manila and got prints. Oakheart gave me the letter from the floater, the talent agent Patricia, who has an office in Ba-gui-o City." He drew out the name into three distinct syllables. "It's in the Philippines. Just so you know. Let me know if you learn anything."

I nodded and left for my shift.

Mama Rose

I looked at the trembling man in front of me. My disgust, like always, would have been very hard to read. I was taught young how to keep feelings inside. My people have been living here for a long time. "You think you are a sailor?" I asked him. "Because when sailors make bad mistakes, they don't come home." He held a cap in his hands, turning it around.

"I've hired you to do jobs for us before. This one was supposed to be quiet. You remember our talk? *You* told *me* we'd never know what happened. You *told* me that it was in good hands, as good as done. 'Don't worry about it, Mama.'" I glared at him. "You think I can have police all over my place who want to know what's going on? Who's going to take care of this now, *you?!*"

"Mama," he said, "it must have been some freak tide. It must have been some freaky current. It wasn't my fault—"

"I don't want to hear about it. You gave me a promise. You said you know your business. 'Freaky tide' sounds like a lame excuse. The tide hasn't changed. My great-grandfather fished in this bay. You know what a sampan is? They used simple wooden boats more than a hundred years ago. They fished for squid. He knew the tides. You fish here now with a motorboat —I think you know the tides, or you *should*. What were you thinking!!?"

I can see him staring intently at my weather-beaten face. It would have looked much the same as the faces of my Chinese ancestors when they first came to San Diego Bay in early times. "It's very bad that this body floats back, yes, very bad—but even more bad, she has a business card in her bra! No fingers, no prints – but we don't need fingerprints; we gave them a card! What were you thinking! This job, it was clear, yes? No come-back on this. No ties to our contractor. This is exactly what we didn't want. Now I have to pay for it. Now I have to fix it up. The body comes back, and you provide a road map. Idiot! Worse than idiot!"

"Mama," he said, panic in his eyes, "you told me to dump the body with no ID and no way to check prints. We took the purse. I clipped off all her fingertips so there could be no finger-prints, right? That was what I was told to do. I'm supposed to feel her up under her bra? A skinny dead girl? A cheap dress? She didn't have any pockets! You could see everything, Mama, there was no way to see this—"

"The people who call me Mama, they are my friends. You don't get to call me Mama. Get out of here, Paco. You work it out with Tony. I don't want to see you again."

"But, Mama—"

"We're done!" It came out as sharp as a pistol shot. "You're lucky I'm not telling Tony to put *you* in a barrel. He knows how to do it right. They don't come back."

Paco slunk out and I went through my back door, back into the shop out on the boardwalk by the bay where I sell this and that to the tourists. Like T-shirts that say "My parents took me to San Diego and all I got was this lousy T-shirt!" I turned the sign around in the door so that it said "OPEN." It was hardly five minutes later that a couple of out-of-towners—underdressed, straw hats, shirts with words—came in and started thumbing through my goods. I took out my abacus and sighed, thinking about the phone call I had to make.

Suze

Making movies for Mona has its ups and downs. I got up from the desk where I was hanging and left the little office. I went through what we all laughingly call our green room and took stock of the stock. Four girls, two guys, white and brown, trim. Fine. I kept walking through to the studio. There was a workbench at the back where Eddie, our cameraman, was taking the new Bolex out of its box and attaching some lenses.

"This is so cool, Suze—I didn't really think she was going to get it for us."

"It's just a camera, numb nuts. Weren't you supposed to arrange for an assistant today? We're shooting, right?"

Eddie grinned at my sarcasm. "Keep cool, Suze. I got a guy who is supposed to be here by nine. He's hot for this job—hasn't shot sex before and he is really pumped. He'll show. Where's Mona?"

"I haven't seen her yet. Be careful, you know—she's on a short fuse these days."

"I noticed. It's the dead lady thing, right?"

"I suppose so. She's had more than her fair share of bad breaks."

And with that thought hanging in the air, Mona walked into the studio and said good morning.

"Isn't anybody going to turn some lights on in here?" she said. "It's as dark as a cave. Time to go to work." She smiled, so we'd know she was just being the friendly boss.

"Sure. You want to walk through the blocking before we get started?"

"Before I do, I want to meet the talent and get a little better sense of them. Join me when you can, OK?" Then she turned to walk into the green room. I made a last-minute review of the lighting and the shot, then turned to follow her. I caught up with her as she reached the soundstage door—muffled with egg cartons stapled to the inside.

"Mona," I told her, "a reporter was here earlier, looking for you."

She just looked at me. "What did he want?"

"He thought I might be you, so he started out telling me that he knows about stuff—like, he knows they found your card on that agent's body. I didn't think that fact was out."

"Suze," she said, "I'm not sure what's out and what not. What else did he tell you?"

"He wants you to call him. He made it sound like he *could* tell your side of the story, or else he could make you look bad."

"I don't have a side, Suze. Feels like I'm just a bug caught on some flypaper. I've got nothing to tell him." The way she looked at me, I saw more of the little girl from Arkansas than the hard-boiled porn producer.

"Yeah, I figured." I looked at her. "What do you want me to do if he shows up again?"

"Take the Fifth. We don't need press." She looked at me and sighed. "Showtime."

Mama Rose

I took a deep breath and called the grandfathers on the telephone, and the secretary put me right through.

"Yes?" the voice answering said. Very abrupt. OK, I was talking to a grandfather, so I had to show respect, but I was not happy.

"Look," I said. "I know this is a mess. I'll fix it somehow. You've got to share with me. Who do we work for? What's the connection to this bar?"

Nothing.

"So what do you want me to do?"

"It's very easy," he said, "to know what I want. I want this didn't happen. Now—what else can we do but make it right? To save ourselves! I can't tell you who our contractor is, but he is a man of great influence, and he speaks for another man of even greater influence. Our instruction was so specific, and I don't need to remind you, do I? This was supposed to be quiet, like it never happened. No come-back. No come-back!" He paused and took a breath. Then he started in again. "A business card!" He was as upset as I'd ever heard him. And I've heard him pretty upset. "If our contractor is threatened, he throws us to the wolves. This contract is with someone who could take us down, and now it's news, and the cops have a lead to someone. This is big trouble. The biggest." There was a pause. "We were discharging an *obligation*."

"Our obligation can still be discharged. I will fix things. Why can't you tell me more?" I couldn't understand why he was being evasive with me and it made me wonder, who was this contractor? Who hired us? Why?

"Indeed," he said, "we are going to have to fix things. Come for the meeting this afternoon. Regular time." Then he hung up.

Sweet Jesus, I thought this was originally supposed to be a favor for a friend. This was supposed to be easy money! Aren't those always the ones that go sideways? Why the devil did Tony leave this one for Paco to do?

At lunchtime, one of my nephews came to keep the shop open and I took a walk on the waterfront, not very far from what is left of San Diego's old Chinatown. Our family is very big, and it is spread out all over the state, and Mexico, too. This is because when the whites imported all the cheap coolie labor from China to build the railroad, they didn't like it when we started building a community, and they tried to kick us out. The Chinese Exclusion Act of the last century pushed many of my people into Mexico, and many are still there. I shuddered. But this is how the Tong was formed. So we could protect ourselves.

The walk along the Embarcadero was not far; only a little bit of it had sidewalk. I knew it so well I could do it with my eyes closed, but today I felt tired. Even the honking and creaking of the boats pulling at their ropes failed to make me feel good. Maybe I just bore the weight of the mistake we'd made. The grandfathers were the head of the San Diego Tong, which was originally set up to help protect us from the whites and the Mexicans and everybody who wanted our rice bowl, but it evolved into a well-oiled machine that scoops up money for lots of things, protection being only one of them. Many in my family have had a connection with the Tong, even though its leadership shifts over time. I am not the first in my family to be in the chain of command, and our generals are the "grandfathers," who have, indeed, fathered and grandfathered many over their long lives. I had to go back up the chain to these men who started this thing, who I have known most of my life, and who knew my father, but who seldom listen to my counsel when they are worried about blame. This mistake will bring blame. I turned around and headed back to the shop so I could prepare for my meeting later. The grandfathers. We have been here a long time, and I hope I can continue to be the fisherman, and not the fish.

Mark

Back on the bay, piloting the launch, it felt great—it was the best part about this job, as far as I was concerned. We were cruising on a late shift for us, so it would be another hour before we could tie up and grab some lunch. Which wouldn't be down here! The waterfront can be a tough place. Weapons everywhere. Everybody carries knives, the Navy has lots of sailors with guns, and it's obvious that the Mafia has their fingers in...something. You got the Italian Mafia, the Chinese Tong, the Mexicans tied in with both of them. Hell, I don't know what. I looked across the bridge of our cruiser, at my partner sitting in the nav chair, scanning the bay. Gary had been through a lot. The war thing, that was tough stuff. He was a solid guy. Life always felt best to me when I was out on the cruiser, and I was always glad when I pulled him as my partner on these bay tours, because sometimes shit happened, and you want a steady guy. He was very steady, OK? Like for the past half hour he hadn't even said anything. He was just looking out the port at the bay going by.

"What are you looking at, buddy?" I asked him, after the last burst of static from the VHF marine radio split the silence.

"The usual. Dope runners and petty criminals." He looked at me and grinned. "Not a lot going on in Coronado today. I guess I got kind of lost in my thoughts."

I prompted him. "About...?"

"I met this gal."

"No shit!" I had to laugh. Gary was so serious. I corrected our course to port slightly. The diesel was chugging away like a conga drum. *Pucketa pucketa.*

"She's smart, trim, and foxy. A little older than me, I think."

"And...?"

"She owns a bar and makes sex movies."

"You're shitting me!"

"She's not like, *in* the movies, she just makes them. It's a business. I met her because she is a wit on the unknown floater thing we picked up the other day."

The helm of the cruiser was like a big truck steering wheel, and this made me tap out a drumroll on it. "Man, everybody in the department is talking about it. We're famous. How are you going to get by hanging out with a wit? That's crazy." I looked at Gary, who was staring straight ahead. "What if the chief hears about it?"

"Well, it's not like she was charged with anything. The floater was apparently going to bring her new girls for her movies. They were going to meet up, so she had Mona's card on her. That's all. The cops know I'm talking to her. I just came from downtown," and at this, Gary's voice kind of trailed off. Something was bugging him, I could tell. A family on a Kettenberg sloop sailed alongside, heeled over, and prepared to tack —the children bundled up in orange kapok life jackets sitting on the high side with their legs over the rails. They waved at us, and I waved back. I turned back to Gary as they wheeled about.

"You already have a thing for this gal?" I asked him. "Trouble on the hoof!"

"I don't have a *thing*," he said, "but I am interested. I guess I'll have to wait for this investigation to be completed before I can get to know her better."

"She's good looking, she makes X-rated movies, and you want to get to know her better? What's to know? You don't even like being a cop, anyway." I gave him a big grin to show I was joking.

"No matter how hard you fight it, Mark, someday you are going to grow up. You can't be Peter Pan forever."

"Why not? It worked for him." I laughed again. We cruised by the moorings off Glorietta Bay on the Coronado side, and headed under the high sweep of the still-new baby-blue bridge.

"So I learned something this morning and I'm trying to think it through," Gary said.

I waited patiently, looking at him. He was chewing on his lip, which I'd never seen him do before.

"You ever hear of Mona Oakheart? That's her name," Gary asked me.

"Unless she works in the department or is a professional basketball player—which being a woman, can't happen—how would I know her?"

"Her name came up in the news while I was overseas. She had a kid a few years back, and apparently it got kidnapped. Never found. Little girl."

"Oh man—that's horrible. That's the worst. Worse than being killed, I think. What did she tell you about it?"

"I haven't talked about it with her. I just learned about it this morning. And you're warning me I'll get my ass canned if I go talk to her."

I didn't know what to say. *Pucketa pucketa pucketa.*

"So what are you going to do?" I asked him.

"I'm pretty sure I'm going to see her again..."

Mona

It was already afternoon by the time I walked into the green room and said hello to the kids. I guess I shouldn't think of them as kids, and the woman from Taipei looked a lot older in her eyes than her body. There were three other women: a Latina, a blonde, and one that looked vaguely Eurasian. The two guys looked like bikers from LA; they were wearing leathers and boots.

Our movies are shorts—they like to call 'em *vignettes*. People meet in lifelike situations, and then readily agree to ever-greater intimacy until they are driven to a private room (or public space) where their imaginations run wild. We can do a lot of different takes on this basic formula, but right now I have a contract with a major distributor going into hotels all over the world, and they want half a dozen "three-vignette" films. Each vignette generally runs about half an hour, so my films run ninety minutes. I get paid well to make them. Our production schedule is based on shooting one vignette per day, at least, but we could take a lot of different riffs on each vignette. Today was special; we'd already shot our first and were planning our second. I looked at the talent, and they looked back with various levels of enthusiasm.

"What we're thinking about here is that these two guys go into a diner and order burgers, and you girls are waitresses who are attracted to them. We'll throw in some extras for other customers, who leave quickly when it's obvious that you waitresses are thinking of jumping all over these two good-looking guys. The diner is closed, we draw the blinds, and then we get wilder. I was thinking of some two-on-one, you and you?" I pointed. I started asking them direct questions and got acceptable replies. Ideas formed. "OK—makeup and costume will come to you in here in about five or ten. Be on set in twenty minutes, OK?" I'd be lucky if they were there in half an hour.

I went back out to Suze, who was pushing our set dresser around, and telling Eddie what they wanted in terms of lighting effect. We talked about the blocking, and I had no doubt that Suze was all over it and could direct the scene exactly like we wanted it. I used to say "it ain't rocket science," but now I say "it isn't rocket science, you know." And it ain't. As I saw everybody filtering in, taking on their roles—Eddie's new assistant, Annette, with Suze in charge—I figured that I could, no, I *should*, slip away and the show would go on. I had to accept that with everything going on the way it had for the past few days, I was stressed. I thought work would help, but I just seemed to be getting in the way.

As I stood to the side of our dimly lit soundstage, I couldn't help but think back to the most horrible period of my life, still raw and painful even if it was almost six and a half years ago. Angie's birthday was December 13. She would have turned ten in a couple of months. *Would* be ten? Is? It was all just too viciously evil. I no longer had much faith in the power of fairness. It was the unknown, the uncertainty, that was so hard to bear. The possibilities ran from horrible to much worse. It was my hell, which would never end.

Without even realizing it, I had walked out through the studio and was right beside our front door. I looked through the pebbled glass pane in the door. You could tell if it was daylight, or if someone was standing right in front, but everything else looked more like an abstraction of blotchy color. Just an impression of what outside must look like. I thought, what if Angie was ten and asked me what I did for a living? What would I tell her? I wasn't sure, and speculation was meaningless. I literally shook my head to clear it, and thought about what to do next. I decided to go down to headquarters and let them take my prints, like they'd asked. It wasn't like it would be the first time. I'd had to do this back when I got my first license to drive the booze routes for Old's Market, and then again when I opened the bar and got a liquor license, and then later when... the shit storm happened. But I guess they needed them again. I learned a long time ago that it is dumb to argue with City Hall.

I thought about calling him again. Phil. That would make it twice in more than eleven years. Asking him what he thought was going to happen now. Funny how I couldn't even name him in my mind anymore. It was just *him*. We'd kept secrets for so long that I no longer even attributed them to a person. It was just *him*. I really didn't even think of him anymore. But given what had happened since the one time I did call him, I figured I'd keep my thoughts to myself.

I pushed open the door, and the pebbled colors in its window became the drab industrial parking lot in Kearny Mesa. I smiled at my little Benz and figured that I would think of some way to weather the storm. Started the car, entered traffic, and headed south.

Frank

I was using my home office to try to move some things along, and noticed through my windows that the afternoon light was growing amber and evening was on its way. All this work for a local politician that Phil wanted to bamboozle. I put the handset into the phone cradle very slowly and deliberately, thinking about how much time I had already invested in trying to satisfy the current political priority. Smut. I wouldn't be putting all this energy into it for Simon pudding-brained Holier, that's for sure, despite his direct request. But if Phil Nestor was going to make such a big deal about it... Well, we go back and I owed him. Some of my best hotel jobs happened because a particular thumb weighed in on the scale.

I looked on my list at the next name I was going to call. My list was of the commissioners at the Visitor's Bureau. My fellow commissioners. My friends. I needed to gin up enough support that the request to spend some unbudgeted money on Holier's quacky anti-smut campaign would be approved without too much squawking. I heard those words in my own mind and smiled. We had a commission meeting set up monthly, and it was only a week away.

My next call was to Father Jeff, one of the commissioners. He was championing a church-led program for the homeless and destitute living downtown. I've steered money his way often enough, but before I dialed his number, the phone rang.

It was Phil Nestor. "Francis," he said, and I immediately feared the worst with his use of my given name, "as if things weren't complicated enough, I think we have a twist that I hadn't foreseen." I stayed quiet, knowing he wasn't talking about the money for the anti-smut campaign. "It was certainly a shock when it turned out that Gary pulled that body out of the bay, but now I'm told that Gary is, um, spending time with Mona."

"Spending time?"

"Well, I don't think he's actually been *spending time*, but he's definitely been seeing her."

"I haven't heard anything about this. You sure about it? I can't see a cop getting involved with a crime, uh, witness. I don't see Gary walking into that one, and he is a cop, you know." I was feeling a gentle tug pulling me two ways as I digested this news. On the one hand, this looked like possible trouble for Gary, but on the other hand, it would be nice if someone could help pull him out of his shell.

"Believe me, I'm crystal clear on that one. Don't forget who the chief reports to."

There was a pause in the conversation, and I chewed on the new facts. Such as they were.

"Let's not get ahead of ourselves," I said, "because there really isn't anything to do about anything, is there? And when there isn't, it's usually best to do nothing. You know as good as anyone that the past is never dead, right? We'll deal with it."

"We'll deal with it," he said, in seeming agreement, and hung up.

For my own part, my mind was swirling with what it would mean if Gary and Mona connected. As unlikely as I would have thought it, I realized I'd better start thinking of just what I could say to Gary when he started asking me about Mona. Poor Mona. What a heartbreak.

Mona

I went for a drive up the coast before turning around and heading back to the city. A rebellious act of freedom? Was I worried there might be a limit to them? It was almost the end of the day; things were winding down by the time I pulled into the lot in front of the downtown headquarters for the San Diego Police. To Protect and Serve. It's written on the car doors. It's just that no one can really protect you from anything. I was in a glum mood as I walked into the familiar linoleum-floored entryway. I stood in a short line to get to the desk sergeant. He looked like Dwight Eisenhower. I remembered Eisenhower's campaign slogan: "I Like Ike."

"Yes?" he asked.

"I'm here to see Lieutenant. Exeter. I'm Mona Oakheart."

The sergeant consulted a notebook in front of him, and then turned behind him to what looked like a key shelf in a big hotel, but these shelves held messages on flimsy paper. Ike pulled one out, read it, and told me just to go down the hall to the clerk's office so they could take a fresh set of prints.

"Does the lieutenant want to talk to me?" I asked, almost fearful the answer would be yes.

"Apparently not," answered Ike. His name badge said Harold Greene. I followed where he pointed and walked down the hall to get my fingerprints taken. I sat in the little chair by the big wooden desk, and went through the inky business all over again. They have some stuff to wipe off the ink, but even with those rough brown paper hand towels you can't get it all off. I was staring at some ink still stuck on my skin and remembering the last time my fingers had looked like this.

It was April 1967, spring in San Diego, a bright sunny five o'clock in the afternoon, blue sky and small fleecy clouds. My old Karmann Ghia was parked in a lot that had an attendant, because downtown could be dicey. The waterfront was only a couple of blocks away, but even though I could take care of myself, I knew that you don't go there alone, especially at night. I remembered all the moments of that day so vividly, so exactly. I remembered being glad to get out of Tell No Tales and its smell of stale cigarettes and spilt beer, and taking deep breaths of the fresh breeze coming off the ocean and across the bay. I got into my rat-trap of a car and headed down Harbor Drive to National City. Lola had promised to make pork adobo and lumpia that night, and Angie loved the deep-fried lumpia.

Angie was my love. I would take a shower to get rid of the smell of cigarettes, and Angie would cuddle like a puppy. This was the best time of day—going home. I turned off Harbor Drive and left the industrial grimness of the waterfront, headed back into the hills of National City and my own little California bungalow. And the beautiful spring day became a nightmare. I wished I didn't remember it all so clearly: how my blood ran cold as I saw three black-and-white police cars and an ambulance parked in front of my house—lights flashing—and a small crowd of neighbors gathered around. I drove into a neighbor's driveway and jumped out of the car, running to the house. Neighbors gave me looks of fear I didn't understand, but I took no time to talk—running in my work flats up to my front door, where a uniformed officer held out his arms to stop my entry.

"What happened? I live here! Where's my little girl? What's going on?" The words tumbled out in a rush and I tried to push the officer aside, but he stood his ground.

"Ma'am, you can't go in there now. It's a crime scene. Your name is...?"

"Mona, Mona Oakheart. My little girl is Angela. This is my house! She was home with the housekeeper. Lola. Lola Lazaraga. Where are they?"

"Hold on a minute, ma'am, I'll get the detective out here." He turned around and called into the house behind him. "Lieutenant?! Hey, LT, I got the homeowner out here..."

After a moment, a man in a rumpled suit came around the corner from the rear of the house. "Ma'am, I'm Detective Rivera. Will you please follow me around back?" And in front of the gathering crowd of neighbors, I followed Rivera into the backyard, where a couple of uniformed cops were standing by the door and the alley in the back, to prohibit anyone from coming in. As we rounded the corner, two paramedics came out the back door handling a gurney, its passenger shrouded in a white sheet from head to toe.

"Oh my God! Oh my God! What happened! Where's Angie?"

"We don't know. There was only this one body in the house when we got here. Can you identify him? Are you up to that?"

I gave a tremulous nod, and the detective waved at the paramedics to stop at the bottom of the landing. He motioned me to come over and flipped the sheet down enough to show the face.

"Pete!" I cried, in fear and despair. "Pete Lazaraga. This is my housekeeper's husband. He comes over to help sometimes. Lola and Angie, where are they?!"

"Ma'am, we don't know yet. Neighbors reported hearing gunshots, then a van went screaming out of your driveway and disappeared. They made a 911 call. We got a description, but it wasn't much. White Econoline with rust marks. We have a call out to try and find it. Our working theory is that someone, or some people, made off with your housekeeper and your daughter, and in the process they shot and killed the victim. Do you have any idea who might want to do something like this?"

I heard that question as if through a fog. I was trying to listen, but all I could see was my baby, my Angie, and she's... Angie's everything to me. My chance to have a life, to make something for somebody, to get past the muck that life handed me. I looked at the cop and tried to focus. Hurt my baby? Hurt Angie?

"Of course not. Absolutely not. You're saying my baby was kidnapped?"

"It's really too early to know, but it looks like that's what happened. Our standard operating procedure is to notify the FBI. They've got resources..."

Just then two other vans pulled up, emblazoned with the logos of local TV stations. A photographer jumped out with a heavy 16 mm camera and immediately started filming.

Detective Rivera turned to me. "Ma'am," he said, "you can't go in there right now—we have a crime scene investigation in progress. Why don't you come with me to the station and we'll try to get some background? I'd rather not leave you here at the mercy of these reporters." I bobbed my head in assent, and dumbly followed him into an unmarked car. The searing memory of that day stilled burned. Almost seven years ago, but it was really a lifetime, and here I was, with ink on my fingers again.

"Miss Oakheart?" I didn't have to turn around; I recognized Jim Exeter's voice.

"I thought you just wanted my prints," I said, turning to look at him.

"It turns out that I do have some more questions, and I'd appreciate it if you'd follow me back to my office so we can talk in private."

I did not think of a conversation in Exeter's office as private, but I got right up and cooperatively followed him down the hall and into the small room I'd been in just yesterday. So much for leaving a set of fingerprints and then getting out of there easily.

Exeter motioned me into a chair and sat down himself. "Let's go over it again, OK? Exactly how you met the deceased...?"

I took a deep breath. *Again? OK.* "On Friday, last week, I got a message from our go-fer at the studio, Annette, that an agent had called. Annette thought her name was Patty something, she put it down on the message as question marks, and," I said, anticipating the question I saw forming, "I'm sure I threw that message slip away a long time ago."

I went on. "It was just a number—an LA number, area code 213, and I left a message to call me later that evening at my bar." I looked at Exeter, who was looking at me. Was this enough for him? Did he have a problem? I'd told him all of this already... "She called around six, as I suggested, and made a pitch to show me some head shots and set me up with new talent." I looked at him, and he still said nothing. "I naturally said OK, as we are always looking for new talent. She agreed to come by the bar the next day, Saturday. We would meet before we opened at three p.m." I looked at him challengingly. "I get some regular early customers at Tell No Tales." *It's a business, buddy.* I went on.

"She left an envelope with me, a little material and mostly photographs, all of which I turned over to your cop yesterday morning. She promised to come back on Monday morning with three of the girls I liked the look of, but I never saw her again. That's it. End of story."

"What race would you say Miss Peteaut was?" Exeter asked.

"I don't have a clue," I answered.

"Oh, come on now—you work with girls from all over the world, right? You got all kinds of nationalities in your movies. Don't tell me you're blind to it. You're not going to tell me that gal was German. And she sure wasn't a Viking."

"No, that's fair," I said. "I would guess Miss Peteaut, if she is a *Miss*, because she could be married for all I know, is Eurasian. Like a little of both, you know?"

"Why do you say that?" Exeter asked, looking directly at me. "Why didn't you assume she was a Filipina, seeing as she lists her office address as being somewhere in Baguio City? Have you ever been to Baguio City?"

"No, Mr. Exeter, I have not. And I said she looked Eurasian because that is what I thought. That's all."

"Well, that's fair," he said, "if that's what you thought. I was naturally curious about the connection to the Philippines, given your own history."

Shit. There it was. My history. Coming back to bite and gnaw and tear at me again. No matter what I did and where I went. No matter what happened, people rooted around in the pain of my past and tossed it back at me like it was meat. Bloody meat. I knew where he was going with this.

"My history?"

"Listen, Miss Oakheart, I'm really sorry to bring this up again, really, the reports all sound terrible. But when your daughter was abducted right out of your house, everyone thought the most likely suspect was the Filipina babysitter who disappeared that same day. Not a lot was covered by the newspapers, but our records show you were aware that we were following up on the connection between your housekeeper and the Philippines. This department followed a trail from National City to Mexico, and later the FBI took it to the Philippine Islands, but it died there." I saw a brief look of concern in his eyes. "Our trail," he added. His look when he said that "it" died there, and his feeble attempt to cover, made me feel as cold as ice. "I'm told that the FBI or some other department sent someone to the Philippines to track the kidnapper, but I don't know much about that. Yet. I'm tracking down a report that was filed. Did anyone tell you how the search went? Did you know that they tracked the kidnapper to the Philippines?"

I had heard of the investigation going to the Philippines, but no one ever told me what came of it, and even talking about what I heard and how I heard it would lead me into the black hole of my secrets. We were done here. "I'm sure I have no idea and I don't know anything about it. Do you have any further questions for me, Lieutenant? This discussion has become an extremely painful interview."

"No ma'am," he said. "Not now. But we're still at the very beginning. I'm sure we'll talk again. Why don't you go get some rest? See if you can remember anything else about this talent agent. Anything at all. Call me." With that, he got up out of his chair and opened the office door for me. I was only too happy to leave.

I have no real memory of walking down the hall, out the door, into the warm Santa Ana breeze and into my car. I think I sat, immobile, in my car for a while. A couple of minutes? Twenty minutes? I don't know. I felt hot. I didn't know if it was internal or the sun beating on my uncovered head in my little convertible. I've been on my own for a few years. I know how to put my game face on. But now it was all flooding back. I had put layers of insulation around my feelings after spending so long learning how to live inside of myself and not share anything, but the downside was that now I was slow to pick up on what I really felt...and I realized that I wished I had a friend. I was, at least at that moment, exhausted from always slugging it out on my own. You'd think I would learn, right?

Frank

I was in my home office, where I spent a lot of time these days. On my desk was a paper with my notes about the friends I had called for support for this new city initiative when the phone I had been using all afternoon rang. Friends, money, and politics. You'd think I'd have had enough of it already. As soon as the phone rang, I glanced up from my chair at the clock. Almost six o'clock, and time for me to wrap things up. Who was calling at the last working minute of the day?

"We have a problem." The voice needed no introduction. "I just got a call from Holier."

"What now, Phil?" I asked, dreading his answer.

"He's very excited. He's ready to jump out of his clothes. He thinks he's got his poster girl for the anti-smut campaign. He wants to put her head on a post."

He didn't need to say more. I knew exactly who he must mean. I grew silent.

"Councilman Holier is apparently bosom buddies with the *Tribune*'s reporter, Huell Hund, and Hund has apparently been out sniffing around, digging in the dirt, and believes he has uncovered some story involving the floater in the bay and the sex business. Once he got a thread of a connection he was on full alert, and he is ready to push it to the max. Hund has dug up who Mona is, a local bar owner implicated in the murder of that poor innocent woman—and not only is she connected to the local porno industry, but so was the floater. The sex industry, it seems, is taking over San Diego, infecting our local establishments and leaving dead bodies, as well as living naked ones, in its path."

I'd first met Mona back when Phil got into this mess, so I'd known of her for a few years. I'd done projects downtown, and that's where her business sits. I'd followed her, sort of, from afar after our meeting. From what I'd seen, she was always a stand-up gal (the phrase gave me pause), given her struggles. Just like you would usually think of a stand-up guy, she was one of the few stand-up gals I'd ever met, other than my Maria. But her life—she was a regular female Old Testament Job. Left alone to raise her child, then a kidnapping, and now a pillorying. I felt powerless in the face of this threat to her, and more concerned than ever because of the new connection with Gary. This could lead to pain for both of them.

"What's he plan to do with his new knowledge?"

"He wanted me to know he's working on a deal with the *Tribune* to run a special this Sunday. He plans on a major splash and they're going all out with photographers, the whole thing. He said he'd splash this filth across the Sunday news and show how *we*, and he emphasized that pronoun, were going to clean it up."

"The Sunday news?"

"Yeah. That's his plan."

"She has no idea, does she?"

"Nope. This plan bubbled up with revelations he got today."

"Revelations from the PD?"

"I don't know and he didn't say. But I'd say we have three days to find a way out of this mess before it all gets so much worse. For everybody." There was a pause. "Meanwhile," he said, "I know Gary has been seeing her."

"Not much I can do about that," I said. "And I suppose stranger things have happened."

"I suppose you're right about that."

"I think the funding I was trying to squeeze out of the Visitor's Bureau to help support Holier's campaign might be better spent elsewhere," I said, "or perhaps not at all."

Phil readily agreed with me and retorted, "We're going to

have to come up with a new approach. I can't let Holier crucify her." *Good*, I thought, *I'm glad to have that confirmed.* "Clam up on the funding, for sure," he said.

"Look, it's getting a little uncomfortable not sharing anything with Gary, now that he's in this. I think he has to know about what's going on. "

"You mean with Simon Holier and Mona? Or do you mean with my past with Mona? Or do you mean what the cops have in mind?" His tone was clearly pushing me to get back in line with him.

"For crying out loud, I'm not sure, but I don't like where things are or where they're headed."

"Three days 'til the Sunday paper comes out and Holier smears Mona on the front page. As if we didn't have enough trouble. Let's talk tomorrow." And he hung up.

Mark

It was after six, and I had just come off my shift. I got back to HQ and got a note to go talk to the chief. I wasn't with Gary today; I was paired up with Bill Peters, a rookie, but a straight shooter. He was on his way home. We'd done a land-based eyes-on survey of the public buildings along the harbor, which involves driving around pretty much the whole bay, even though most of the important public buildings are in downtown. All the public buildings around the bay fall under the jurisdiction of the Harbor Police, so we check them out.

"Yeah, Chief?" I said. "You want to see me?" I closed the chief's door behind me and he gestured me to take a seat. Even though he was the chief of the Harbor Police, he didn't have a fancy office with leather chairs. Just a couple of straight-backed wooden chairs, some file cases to the side, and a big desk that looked like it could have belonged to a schoolteacher.

He gave me a look that drilled right into me, and then told me he had heard that Gary was starting to hang with Mona

Oakheart, the person of interest on the floater, and he thought that would be a very bad idea.

"Is that what this is about?" I asked. "I don't know about Gary's love life, and I would guess he is smart enough to know what he should and shouldn't do. Right?" I looked encouragingly at the chief, as if expecting him to smile and nod his head. Didn't happen. "What do you want from me?"

"I like to think that all our officers are smart enough to know right from wrong. But I don't like to leave things to chance. I know that you two have been sharing a shift for the past few months. I know how time goes by while you're out on the water. Partners talk. We are a small shop—I want to know what's going on. I want to hear about it if someone is drifting over the line. This would be a line. Understood?"

When I can't keep staring someone in the eyes—like being in a staring contest—I tend to look at their mouth. Chief's mouth was a very thin straight line.

"Chief, I can't come running in here with stories of Gary's sex life. That's not right."

"I don't want to hear about his damned sex life, Corporal! I just want to hear if he's getting tangled up with a person of interest in a murder investigation. And I expect you to cooperate! Do you understand?"

"I understand what you want."

"Then we're good here?" He glared at me.

"Yessir."

"That is all." I didn't need more to tell me that my visit was over and my orders were delivered. I left his office and went back out to the lockers.

Mona

It was after dinner, and I was still in the studio—our green room had been converted into a dining room. The table was littered with white cardboard boxes of Chinese food with a red dragon on the side. Double Happiness. It had been a long and trying day with new people, but we got what we needed (if not what we wanted), and after paying them all as day laborers, the crew sat down to a meal from up the street. Take-out. I telephoned the club and my night manager assured me that she had it all covered. She told me that she had plenty of people and I should just take it easy. She'd close up. Now the studio was quiet—probably the quietest spot in this part of town. Kearny Mesa and the industrial district go dark long before the wild and woolly life downtown, where Tell No Tales is planted. Everyone was gone and I'd told Suze I'd clean up the mess. We'd all had enough fried rice and pork chow mein and God knows what else, and I was alone to clean up and lock down. Which was what I wanted.

I threw the garbage away and then hauled the can around back to the big steel dumpster. I was keeping myself busy with simple tasks because I didn't want to think about the mess I was probably in. I went back into the studio, picked up a big push broom, and started sweeping. I sure as hell had nothing to do with stuffing someone in a barrel and trying to sink it. What were they thinking? Now I was in the middle of this, all because of my business card. Exeter thought I had a target painted on my back. I had nowhere to turn for help; no one working for me at the club or the studio could help, even if they would. Promises made, I couldn't look to my past for help.

I sighed. It was most likely my past that had come back and resulted in this mess, but nobody was going to jump out and say, "Don't worry, Exeter, she didn't kill anybody!" It never works like that.

Even though it had been almost a decade since I'd rubbed up against a man's flesh, it wasn't like I'd totally forgotten about it. I had just ceased to care. Would I just be using the kid if I had a tender night or two with him? I had to do something to steer this away from me, and I couldn't say why, or what exactly my plan was, but I had a strong sense that if I could get young

Gary to feel like he owed me, I'd get something good out of it. Thinking about setting it up made me feel kind of excited, actually. I decided to give him a call. It was five minutes after eight by my watch.

Gary

After all the excitement we'd had, today felt like a totally uneventful day on the waterfront. I got back to HQ, filed the three reports that related to the day's activities, then took a shower and changed into some civvies I had in the locker room. I came back into the dayroom and dispatch waved at me to come over.

"You got another phone call from *Ms.* Oakheart," he said, emphasizing the "Ms."

He gave me the little pink slip, tearing off the top piece of our office's form, with a check in the little box that said "Return the caller's call" and Mona's name and number filled in. Dispatch looked at me but didn't say anything, then just spun his chair back around. I walked back to my desk and sat down for the call, facing the rear of the dayroom, with my back to the office. Everybody might know we talked, but it was my private business what I wanted to say. Except it wasn't much of a conversation. She got right to the point.

"Your day over yet? Checking out?"

"You caught me on my way out the door."

"Did you eat yet?" Then, not waiting for an answer, she said she'd had Chinese food an hour ago and was hungry again. Would I like to join her for a burger and a beer at the Waterfront Bar & Grill? I told her I was hungry and only ten minutes away. "See you there," she said.

Mona

The Waterfront Bar & Grill is a classic old place that looks out on the thoroughfare of Kettner Boulevard, named after some local congressman. I knew Gary would get there first—he was a lot closer than my studio in Kearny Mesa; and as I drove by looking for parking, I saw he had arrived and snagged a little table off to the side. It looked like he already had a beer in front of him. In this warm weather, the front of the bar was opened up to the road and passersby. The place looked like a dimly lit patio. I slipped the Benz into a street spot and fed the meter with some dimes.

I had taken a minute at the studio to put on my face and change into a blouse —cream-colored silk that let the light shine and slide around my curves and went really well with my hair. Most of the patrons at the bar were men, and it felt like every eye was on me as I turned off the sidewalk and walked toward Gary, who stood to meet me. I gave him a quick hug and sat down. After all, he had kissed me last night; we weren't strangers anymore.

A waitress came over to check on us, and I ordered an Anchor Steam and a Jack back, and smiled at Gary. "It's been a long day," I told him.

"Well, I'm not going to let you drink alone," he said, and told the waitress to bring him a bourbon as well. Then he looked at me directly, right into my eyes, and asked me what was up. *Oh hell*, I thought to myself. *What's he going to do, hate me?*

"Can we talk about the weather first?" I smiled weakly.

"Sure," he said. "It's a warm fall evening. So why did you call me?"

"Look, Gary, you believe me, don't you? I didn't kill anybody."

"Sure," he said, "and I don't know that Exeter thinks you did it, but he sure thinks you know something about it. So what do you know?"

"Sure is a warm fall evening, isn't it?" I said.

He leaned back in his chair and smiled. "Mysterious lady with her secrets." The waitress brought us our drinks.

"Everybody has secrets, Gary," I said. "I have 'em too. But murder is not on my list. You may feel that Exeter just thinks I'm holding out, but to me it feels like he's turning the spotlight on me. I'll be honest with you: I'm scared. I can't fight City Hall. What if I get set up because there aren't any other patsies?" Gary just looked at me. He seemed sympathetic and thoughtful. "Hell, Gary, I need a friend. But being my friend is likely going to put you in what we used to call a shit storm."

"We still call it that," he said.

"I need a defense lawyer, probably, not a cop buddy."

We sat and talked about my fears. He proved to be a good listener. I didn't have to make anything up, after all. Just because I'm paranoid doesn't mean they aren't out to get me. I danced around some of the issues that involved the central secret of my life and how it had led me to motherhood. After a few drinks it got a lot easier, and I suppose I opened up a little, enough to let him know how deep I had been cut. An hour or two later, we left the Benz on the street and I climbed into his Camaro and drove home with him. Mission, I guess, accomplished.

Gary

She seemed beautiful, vulnerable, and lonely. I asked her a little bit about the dead gal, but I felt like I was taking advantage, and my interest soon veered from the case to the woman. I hadn't been with a woman in almost ten years, not since I left high school for the Navy. She slid into my Camaro and I felt like I was back in high school. I was in my old high school ride, the bright orange beast, and I reached over and put my hand on her thigh before keying the engine to life with a growl. I didn't want to have to explain myself to a black-and-white on the way home, what with all the beer and Jack Daniel's, so I drove pretty cautiously. I pulled into my driveway and killed the lights.

"I've got the guesthouse," I said.

"Looks lovely."

I took her hand and pulled her along. "I'll show you the garden tomorrow, but I'm back on morning shift, so we'll have to get going early. At least, I will." She laughed a clear laugh and followed me along the path to the casita.

4

THURSDAY

Mona

I woke up and knew exactly where I was. No confusion. It had been a very long time since I'd woken up in any bed but my own. With anyone next to me. He was on his side, facing away from me, breathing gently, still asleep. The muscles in his back were pronounced enough to throw their own shadows in the early morning light. It had been my experience that outside of people in my world, most everybody else had trouble with knowing I make sex movies. I got a lot of people whose gaze shifted from my eyes when they learned that. *If you make those movies, then you are working with whores. You must be a whore, too.* Screw that and screw explaining myself. This is why I naturally saw few people socially, which frankly was fine with me after I lost Angie.

I didn't get any of that from Gary, and it surprised me. Given he had this privileged rich-boy background, living in the guest-house, I didn't expect him to be so honest and so accepting of me. So open. I'm that poor gal from Arkansas who would do whatever the hell she had to to get ahead. And I did.

Let's face it, I was totally prepared to do whatever needed with this man so I could get some leverage on this mess with the cops. Maybe I *was* being a whore, in a way. Not for money, but not for love, either. Yet here I was. Lying next to him in the warm dawn and thinking about how nice he was. Having a warm body that I could grab on to, that smelled like a man and was gentle and kind, touched me unexpectedly. *Shit.* Now what was I going to do? I knew I should've thought of this the night before when he proposed taking me home. His home. What if his old man came out and saw me? What would I say?

I'd only met his dad twice, a decade ago, when he helped put me in the house in National City and got me the bar that became Tell No Tales. Once to go over what he proposed to do, and once to sign everything when it was done. And that was done in his home, with a notary who came to his house to sign everything. Another first for me. All private and quiet. This house. Next door. At his dining room table. Dad. How had I gotten myself into this? If Gary put together his dad's connection with me, then two and two would start to look like four and my big secret would be blown. Not good. I guess the rhythm of my breathing changed, as Gary rolled over and opened his eyes.

"Hey, beautiful," he said.

I had to smile. "Nice night," I ventured.

He smiled. "I was a little worried you were going to want me to do something I wouldn't know how to do, you having seen it all," he said, clearly teasing me and enjoying it.

"I guess I'm just a simple girl at heart," I said. It came out without me thinking about it.

"I expect to learn more about that," he said, "but not this morning. I've got an early shift on the cruiser." He stroked my arm and then swung his legs off his side of the bed and sat up. "Can I make you some coffee? It's about all I'm good for."

"I'm sure it's only one of your talents." I smiled at him again. What can I say? I felt great. "I'll take a fast shower and get out of your way." I got out of the bed, glanced in his mirror, glad that my butt still looked good, gathered up a few scattered clothes from the floor, and headed into the bathroom off the hall. When I came out, he was wearing gym clothes and the smell of coffee filled the room. He poured two cups and nodded me over to the side of the living room, where sliding glass doors opened onto a little balcony that overlooked what I remembered as the backyard of the huge house.

I took one of the mugs of steaming coffee and followed him to the balcony. I'd been thinking about this all through my shower. I didn't have any idea what to say. Should I ask him if his father was home? What if he saw us? How would I explain any of this? I felt unusually distracted. That was my only excuse, really. I was so nervous about how to explain things, about being spotted, that I just wasn't thinking. I'm sure that's how it happened. I didn't want to be out on that balcony, clearly visible from the main house. Then I looked down and, to my surprise, saw how incredibly beautiful the backyard had become.

It used to be a rolling grassy lawn, as I remembered looking down onto it, with some pathways and patio furniture, bordered by a rough overgrown ravine. Now it had become a lush tropical paradise of flowering plants climbing in twisting vines up palm trees, birds-of-paradise bursting through the scented plumeria, a small orchard of fruit trees on a hillside, glossy lush greenery spilling over itself, with bright splashes of color from banks of wildflowers. "Oh wow," I said, "this has changed..." and then I thought about what I'd just said. *Oh shit.*

Gary

What? I looked wonderingly at Mona. It felt as if a cleaver had struck down between us, separating me from the warm glow of the morning and leaving me staring at her. She didn't shrug it off or act like it was nothing. She looked straight ahead, holding her coffee, staring at the garden, and it was obvious to me she'd said something she regretted. She'd realized that she had inadvertently opened a door to something. More seconds passed.

"Are you going to tell me how you know the garden has changed?" I asked. I had a growing sense of disquiet. One of those gnawing-in-your-gut things. Here I was with the first woman I felt totally relaxed with. First woman in years. We were good together. I thought I could have something going, and now there was this. Whatever the hell *this* was. What was it?

More seconds passed and she still looked at the garden. Then she turned and looked at me. "Yeah, I've seen this backyard before. It's awkward, right?" She put the coffee mug down on the balcony rail. "I'm in a hard spot here. We haven't talked about it, but now we have to. I am not going to lie to you or tell you stories. I'm going to be honest. But there's a problem, because there are some things I can't talk to you about. Important things, but they are part of my past, and I really can't say more about it. I don't know what to tell you." She looked at me. "Gary, I won't lie to you, I've been here before, but I can't tell you why. It was a long time ago. It doesn't matter to me anymore, but I made a promise and it's something I can't talk about because that was my promise. OK?"

"Hell no, not OK." I could feel my blood pressure start to rise. "I can't believe it. When were you going to tell me?" She said nothing. "Or were you just not going to say anything?"

"That was my plan. I wasn't going to talk about it. It doesn't matter anymore to me."

"I don't even know what the hell *it* is, so I sure as hell can't tell you that it doesn't matter to me!" I was getting myself a little worked up, but I could see she was looking beat up. I didn't want to pound on her, but I wanted to know. "I presume you were here to see my father?" I asked her. A thought flashed into my mind—the years back after Mom. Jesus Christ! Could my father be Angie's dad?

"I think we'd better call it a morning," she said. "Would you take me back to my car?"

I didn't know what to think. I guess I'd let myself feel too much, and now I was paying a price. I had the early shift, and I had a spare uniform in the locker room on Harbor Island— better if we just went. I was wearing sweatpants that said NAVY on them, so I grabbed a sweatshirt. Mona looked like she was ready, so I held the door open for her and we walked back out onto the Saltillo tile pathway to the Camaro. Not saying anything to each other, and not saying anything on the twenty-minute drive back to the Waterfront Bar & Grill. I pulled up next to her Benz. She still didn't say anything and neither did I. I didn't know what to say. Mona opened the door of the Camaro and gave me a sad smile, pulled out the keys to her car, and slid in. I felt like shit.

The Waterfront Bar was only minutes from our Harbor Island HQ, a quick drive until I pulled into the parking lot and went in to suit up for the morning. Mark was already there, thumbing through some files, and I looked up just in time to see the chief pull the blinds closed on his office window. It was still early, but I told Mark I'd be back in ten minutes and went to the showers. We were at the dock of the *Pt. Loma II* about half an hour later. The cruiser was already fueled, so we slipped the lines and headed out at a slow "wake speed" glide of less than five knots.

We were hardly moving before Mark turned to me and blurted out that the chief was on him to report on me. He asked me how he got into this goddamned spot. "Everybody's worked up because of this woman you're seeing, man. That's why the chief wants me to give him a report. About your damned sex life. Shit!"

"Don't worry about it," I told him. "I don't think we're going to become a number."

He blinked. "What, you're not seeing her anymore?"

"Not exactly. I spent the night with her, but it got complicated."

"You spent the *night* with her?! What am I supposed to tell the chief?!"

"Don't ask me—I'm just telling you how it is today. I think I pissed her off. And she pissed me off, too. I don't know why it matters to the chief."

"Because she might be involved in a murder, you dumb shit! Why do you think?"

I was quiet, and Mark said nothing as he tapped the throttles forward to pick up speed.

"She says she didn't kill that girl in the barrel."

"Now *that's* new and different. I guess it's case closed." Then he started shaking his head and laughing. "Man, it's lucky for you that your daddy's loaded, because your career in law enforcement looks like it may be challenged. You're amping up Exeter over at the PD, you're tweaking the chief's nose with this girlfriend, and you're treating your partner," he turned and looked at me, "me, like he's a total fucking idiot."

"That's putting it a little harsh, don't you think?" I said. "You're not a *total* idiot," and damn it if we both didn't start laughing. I didn't want to say anything else about Mona, and Mark didn't ask.

The rest of the morning was spent arguing with some long-haired hippies in tie-dye T-shirts who had moored a disaster of a barge at the edge of Glorietta Bay on the Coronado side, under the shadow of the blue Bay Bridge. Their goal was apparently to set up a floating commune. By the time they understood that they had to move or we would move them, it was the end of our shift. We motored back to our dock. As we cleated off the mooring lines, I heard that familiar tapping at the plate-glass window and looked up to see the sarge waving a pink telephone call slip at me. Naturally, Exeter wanted to see me again. Perfect.

I was still in my uniform when I made it to the PD's office

downtown. I went straight to Exeter's office. His door was open, a cigarette was burning itself out in an ashtray, and he was going through open file folders on his desk. He looked up, saw me, and nodded me into the chair in front of his desk in the small cubicle.

"You've been spending time with her, right?" The question threw me off base, because I really had no idea what he knew. He didn't wait for my answer. "And you've got nothing to tell me that's useful, right? There's stuff you ought to know."

"I tried to get her to open up about her connection with the dead gal, but she basically kept saying she didn't know anything about it. Whatever it is, she isn't talking about it."

"Well, that surprises me none at all!" said Exeter. "I know something is connected, and I sure as shit don't expect you to hand it to me."

"What do you mean by that?" I wasn't sure if this was worth getting riled up over.

"Let me tell you some things, Mr. Harbor Man, and *you* tell *me* what *you* can do to help. OK? First of all, there's the Filipino connection. It's all over this. I pulled the case files from the kidnap case. There it tells me that her kid is snatched with her Filipino housekeeper, Mrs. La-za-raga," he said, reading off the file notes. "And Lazaraga's old man, Pedro, is found DOA at the scene. Gunshot wound at extremely close range." He paused. "Apparently, a .38 caliber round." He looked up at me. "Now here's where things get interesting. They follow the perp's trail to the border, mostly following leads on the van, and they get great cooperation from the cops in TJ, who find the abandoned Econoline at Rodriguez International, in airport parking, dirty with prints. FBI team goes down for samples and prints, but that's all they ever get. No bodies or perps were ever recovered."

I felt bad again for Mona. No idea what happened to her little girl. "But the prints pay off," Exeter continued. "FBI traces the lead to visa docs that were used by someone from Manila called P. Aquino. FBI has the resources; their guy goes to Manila and tries to run this down. You following?"

"Sure. You're telling me that based on some prints from the Econoline used in the kidnap, they traced them to the Philippines, where the FBI continued the investigation. What'd they get?" I asked, already figuring I knew the answer.

"Fucking nothing. That's what. Couldn't track this guy down, but they tell me that working in the Philippines is a ball of wax. Now, here's where it gets a little weird. Ordinarily, when the FBI picks up a case, they run with it, and the locals stay out. They're touchy. But the feebs, who had special permission to work in the Philippines, couldn't trace the prints farther than the consulate. Then the story takes a twist—and maybe you can help me figure it out. All of a sudden, a grant of money appears to finance some local investigation in the Philippines."

"Money? From whom? Or where?"

"Pedro Lazaraga worked for MASTCO, based in National City. They apparently put up the bucks to fund a local agency investigation. Sounds weird, right? I never heard of them doing that before. I don't think they ever did it again, either. And it gets a little weirder, too." He looked at me. "You know what local agency was sent over to the Philippines to conduct the investigation?" He paused and his eyes narrowed. "It was you guys. The Harbor cops. Apparently one of you guys had World War II experience in the Navy stationed in the Philippine Islands, 'cause it was a US territory back then, and he spoke the language, and everyone wanted him to see what he could find. Can you believe it?"

I could believe it, all right. I knew whom he must be referring to. Chief Hansen. My mind was busy trying to wrap itself around all of this information. I wasn't sure that I could connect any of the dots to make a picture, but the number of dots was growing pretty damn fast. "So what do you want from me?" I asked him. "You obviously think I can do something for you, or I wouldn't have been called down here."

"Sit tight. There's more to this. The chief of the goddamned Harbor Police is the guy who goes down there, and he does a great job. He spends time in Manila and starts where the feebs ended, the visa docs for 'P. Aquino,' and somehow backtracks that record to the local juvie jail. The prints are on record there for a kid, but there had been a terrible fire a couple of years earlier, and the kid was supposed to have burned to death. Burned so badly he was identified only by some jewelry. The kid's name: Federico Lazaraga. Lazaraga. Get it? Familiar name? Yeah. But the record that Federico Lazaraga died had to be wrong, because it was his prints that were used to get a visa a few years later using the name P. Aquino. It was your chief who figured out that the kidnapper's prints were really Freddie Lazaraga's, and he believed he was related to the lost house-keeper and the dead vic at Mona's place after the kidnapping. Freddie didn't die in the jail fire in Manila, the way everyone thought, and in the next couple of years he somehow came up with the funds to get a visa and fly to the US of A." Exeter looked at me. "Now his report is like a summary, not a detailed investigation, but that's the story—Freddie assumed a new identity, Aquino, to get visa docs to visit the US. Came here with evil intent—we don't know why—and when he got here he did the deed. Killed his uncle. Kidnapped his aunt and the kid."

"You're telling me that Mona's kid and her housekeeper were kidnapped by the housekeeper's relative," I said, "and he shot and killed the husband in the house before he took off with them in the van—that they recovered later in TJ, by the airport?" The way it came out was half a summary of the facts and half a question about whether that was the picture. Exeter nodded, watching me. "OK, I'll bite: where do you see me fitting in here?"

"You can get into some things I can't. You scratch my back and I'll scratch yours. What the hell is the Harbor Police doing sending their chief to the Philippines? You're an insider—what can you find out for me? And I got to tell you, I think the floater has more to do with Mona than she's admitting. The connections to the Philippines are all over the place. You want to bet that it's all a coincidence? Now you know something. Go talk to Mona. She's sure as hell not talking to me. Don't tell me she doesn't know *anything* about a relative coming after her housekeeper. Get her to talk to you about it. Shit—make her talk. You're not going to arrest her—you don't need to give her a goddamned Miranda warning. Just get her to talk and tell me what she's saying."

When I left Mona that morning, I'd felt angry and possibly a little betrayed, but this was a preposterous proposal. I was going to go spy on some woman I was sleeping with? Or at least, slept with once? It didn't sound like a good plan to me. I guess my reaction to his proposal was plain on my face.

Exeter leaned forward. "Let me tell you something else, Reines. You don't want to hook yourself up with this broad. She is trouble, and she's got trouble coming."

"Seems to me she's already had plenty of trouble," I said. "More?"

He nodded. I'll give him credit; he didn't look happy about it. "My department, and our boss, was told to go to bat with Councilman Holier, who is planning some kind of big anti-smut campaign and wants to splash your girlfriend's picture all over the front page to start it off. He wants what we have on her, and he's ready to go to war. When we bring her in for questioning, the press will be all over it. She's going to look like hamburger all over the highway by the time this is done. So be a cop. Get her story but stay away from her, or you might get caught in the cross-fire. And get me something I can use!"

What a mess. I was trying to sort out my feelings for the woman, while Exeter wanted me to pump her for the story about her kid, all the while not telling her that more trouble was on the way. This sucked. "An anti-smut campaign? What's that about?"

"What is any politician about? Getting reelected! Word is that City Hall is working with the press on a campaign to clean up the city. All those tattoo parlors on Broadway, the locker clubs where guys get a little special something. All that shit. He thinks that when we arrest Mona at her bar he is going to start a big local event."

"I didn't know you planned on an arrest."

"My boss believes that playing ball with City Hall is how you keep your job. We sure as hell will drag her back in here for questioning. I'm not predicting who gets arrested after that. But likely somebody." He grinned. It didn't seem funny to me.

I stood to leave. "So how did Hansen's report conclude?" I asked Exeter.

"Huh?"

"Hansen. Our old Harbor Police chief. He had to be the one who went to the islands. What happened?"

"Same as everyone else. In his report he says he now believes it's this Freddie Lazaraga guy who killed Pedro, but after Lazaraga dumps the van at the airport in Mexico the trail ends. He disappeared. He could have gone goddamned anywhere. By the time they went looking for him, the records in the Mexican terminal weren't very good. He was in the wind. No one could follow that one. The FBI tried for months before giving up. Nothing on the vics at all, and when bodies are disappeared in Mexico, they are truly disappeared."

I stood up. "I'll help, but it needs to go both ways—you have to share what you get about Holier's schemes." He smiled at me, and I walked out.

I left the building and walked across the half-empty parking lot to a phone booth on the corner sidewalk. I pushed open the folding glass doors and slipped in. Graffiti was scrawled all over the glass walls of the confining booth, and the black binder of the phone book dangled empty on the end of a chain, most of the pages torn out. You'd think that a phone booth right in front of the central police building wouldn't get so trashed, but maybe callers felt like they were somehow getting back at the cops. I fed it two dimes and dialed a number I didn't have to think about; I've been dialing it my whole life.

"Hello?" he said, a question.

"Dad," I said, "we have to talk. I'm coming right over." I figured he was going to be home, but I wanted to be sure. I needed to know what the hell was going on.

"That's fine, Gary. I'll be on the back patio. Under the gazebo."

It was late in the afternoon and my official shift had been over for an hour, so I radioed in that I was going off duty and headed for home.

I pulled into our driveway, but instead of taking the path to the casita, I took the flagstone stairs that led downhill, into the ravine and through the garden toward the patio on the other side. It had been a warm day, almost hot on the water and definitely hot in the car—the vinyl reeked of chemical decay. But when I got to the garden, it was cooler: shaded, rich with green foliage and the scent of flowers. I had marched down the steps determined to look into my father's eyes and find the truth, but my march slowed on its own accord as I got into the garden. At the low point in the ravine, where I was almost hidden in the plants before ascending to the other side, I slowed to a stop and took a couple of breaths. I thought of Mom. That, after all, was the purpose of the garden. Mom has been dead for almost a dozen years, and I suppose whatever Dad got into afterward was his own business. But still.

I headed up the embankment to the patio behind what I thought of as the big house. A gazebo sat on the edge of the patio, looking out over the verdant ravine. Dad was sitting in the gazebo, watching me as I approached. I went in and sat down on the banquette that ran around the perimeter of the gazebo. I had thought about what I was going to say on the drive over. I would be direct and clear. I had a path in mind, but when I sat down and looked at my dad, who looked really tired and kind of sad, I was at a loss for words. We sat in silence for at least a minute or two. It seemed like a long time.

"It seems obvious," I said finally, "that you know more about what's going on than I do." He, of course, knew exactly what I was talking about.

"Gary," he said, "there are some things that I've promised not to discuss. With anyone. Ever. Even with my son. Can I just ask you to trust me on this, and not try to push on it?"

"Shoot, Dad, I don't even know what the *this* is. All I know is that I am on the outside, but connected to a murder investigation, and everywhere I turn, I bump into a reference to you."

At this, my dad gave a weak smile. "Everywhere? I find that hard to believe. What am I supposed to know? What are you hearing about me that riles you up?"

"First thing I hear is that Mona Oakheart, who has become public enemy number one in the eyes of the homicide detective, knows you—and that she's been to this house!"

"How did you come by that knowledge?"

"Well, this morning she let it slip that she hadn't seen the garden the last time she was here. But the fact that there was a 'last time' was something she refused to talk about."

"She was here?"

"Yeah. With me." He looked at me, part reading me and part questioning me.

"Look," I said, "it's complicated. I've only known her a couple of days, but we were doing OK together. I like her." I looked at him directly and asked, "Do you have an issue with that?"

"No."

"That's good. Then why do you know Mona?"

"It's part of what I can't get into, Gary. It happened a long time ago, but I made promises I have to keep."

"Promises to Mona?"

My dad gave me another weak smile. "Is that it?" he asked.

"You learn that Mona has been here before, and you assume that therefore I know about things happening today?"

"Did you make promises to Mona?"

"Gary, that's all wrapped up with the things I can't talk about."

"OK, then, Dad, help me understand why later in the day I learn from Exeter, who is the detective on this murder case that *I* brought him, that something kinda screwy happened back when Mona's little girl was stolen—I wasn't around, but I am sure you know about it." I paused, but he didn't say anything. "It seems that MASTCO offered to fund a search to the Philippines for the kidnapper, and your old friend, Chief Hansen, was hired to go back to investigate fingerprints there." I stopped and took a breath. "There is no way that Hansen would have gone to the Philippines without you knowing about it. I know how you guys were friends from way back in WWII. I can see that something was going on. Your old friend, chief of the Harbor cops, for cryin' out loud, is investigating a kidnapping? And the victim has been here to this house?" I paused for another breath. This wasn't my usual conversation with my father. "Now the cops are connecting Mona to the body in the barrel because they think the floater had something to do with the kidnapping, too. Right now they don't have more than the connections to the Philippines and her business card on the dead body. Not only do you know more than I do about what's going on, it's possible that I am getting involved with her, and I don't know if she's guilty or innocent—or even if you are!"

"Guilty of what?!" he snapped. "Whatever you think I'm guilty of, you're wrong. I just can't talk about it."

"You can't even talk about Hansen going to the Philippines?" I'd heard the stories of how my dad, who was a Seabee who helped build up Subic Bay at the end of the war, met Erick Hansen, who was a Catholic Dane held by the Japanese as a prisoner of war in the Philippines. The two Catholic boys connected in a war-torn place. With Phil Nestor, they were three. They hit it off and were buddies until they got their discharge not long after. They stayed friends until Hansen died.

"Of course I knew that Erick got asked to travel to the Philippines. And you're right, you weren't around. You were in Vietnam by then."

"And...?"

He sighed as the breeze went through the garden. "He went because, as I am sure you know, Erick was very good with languages, he knew several before he was captured, and he got quite fluent in Tagalog and even knew some Japanese. There were obvious reasons he was asked to take on a task in the Philippines, I would think."

"Dad, you're being purposefully misleading. The point is, Hansen was sent to investigate connections with the jerk who took Mona's little girl. You can't skip what you know about that part."

My dad just looked sad. "I wish I could tell you," he said to me, "because even though it is all in the past, there are still stakes in this for people and my promise still holds. I really can't talk about it."

I took a deep breath. This was harder than I thought. "Was Mona's baby yours?"

"Gary, that's a ridiculous question." He stared back at me. "And I told you, I can't talk about it."

"Mona's baby?! Is that what you can't talk about?"

"Gary! Enough! Leave it alone."

I stood up from the padded bench and looked out over the garden. It didn't feel quite so peaceful and beautiful anymore. I looked down at my dad. He looked older. "This isn't going away, Dad. The PD is all over the connection between whatever happened then and whatever is happening now. Your secrets are probably not safe. I'll see you later."

And I walked back to the casita.

Frank

I watched my son as he receded down the path and up the other side. Even though I had no one to share this information with (oh, Maria, it still and always hurts...), ayy, Gary, what was I going to do? And as I watched his back rise up the other side of the garden made to honor his mother, I thought to myself that I would do as I always had with this mess—nothing. *Que será*, as they say.

I really liked Mona. Of course I'd kept an eye on her and followed up on things. And I'm sure I wasn't the only one. I liked her grit and determination. Even if her bar was in a tough neighborhood, it was still a neighborhood, and she built a rep for running a tidy ship, from all accounts. The movie business was her own business; I didn't know anything about it and I didn't want to. I'd heard about it, of course, and I heard she makes money. Nothing I would tell Deacon Nestor, but it gave me a smile to think of her pushing on in a world that was not set up to help her. Probably the opposite. I couldn't even imagine what it would take for a young woman to make it in that world. You had to hand it to her for that.

Suze

This movie business is one hell of a world. It seems I'm always in a rush. I was late and in a hurry to get back to the studio for our next take, so I drove quickly into our parking lot and didn't look up until the last minute. The creepy reporter was back, this time in a yellow-and-orange plaid suit. Hard to believe. He was leaning against the rail that leads up to the studio door. If he thought he could block me, he was going to learn otherwise. I parked my bug and got out, walked over to him, and stood there, saying nothing.

"You know, it wasn't all that hard to find your boss's name from her liquor license," he said, "so I know about her club, and from there to the county recorder to find that she owns this building. So maybe I know what's going on in there," he said, motioning to the building with his thumb, "or maybe I don't. But I want to know: When are you going to stop being her guard dog and let me talk to her? I'd hate to think she was hiding something."

"I'm not her guard dog. She makes up her own mind about talking to people. I gave her your card. I guess she just didn't have anything to tell you."

"You tell her that I'm not done. If I find out that she has her fingers in places where she isn't supposed to have 'em, it's not going to go too good for her. People are losing fingers on this one, get it?" He grinned at me, but I honestly had no idea at all what he was talking about.

"I'll tell her you came by and you want to ask her questions. That's all I can do. We're busy around here."

"I'll bet," he said, and sauntered off to where his car was parked on the street. I turned back to go into the studio, and once inside I was quickly consumed with getting everyone organized for the first shoot after lunch. I checked the clock on the wall and saw that it was already getting on in the afternoon. Gotta get going...

Mama Rose

My souvenir shop backs right up to the water, with big windows in the front for the goods, and little windows that looked over the bay from my back room. On a shelf in my shop over the door there is a rosewood carving, or maybe it's just stained like rosewood, of a large happy man or god, smiling, who could be Buddha, but he is not Buddha because his belly is a clock. Now it says it's five o'clock, and that means the door can be shut and locked. No more foolish tourists. I flipped the sign over so that it said "Closed/Cerrado" and pulled the dark green shades halfway down in the front windows. I turned, slower now, I know, and walked into the back room. Perched on the edge of the Embarcadero, I could hear the gentle and rhythmic surge of the bay and smell the salty tang of the water. Soothing, as I have thought all my life. I put on my black cardigan sweater even though it was still warm outside. I locked up the shop's modest takings in the metal box and put that in a locked drawer. I stood and nodded to myself. I could put it off no longer. Time to meet with the grandfathers.

It's a five-block walk from the waterfront to the Wong Grocery Warehouse, which has been the center of Chinatown here for more than eighty years. Those residents who survived the anti-immigration laws of the 1890s, at any rate. I have walked this walk for many, many years. Upstairs in the grocery warehouse are offices, so at the end of my walk I had to climb two flights of stairs. It's OK—nah, don't worry, they say it's good for me. I talked to myself as I climbed the stairs, pausing between flights. At the top was a landing with some space, and two young women sat at a table playing mah-jongg and ignored me. Two men were nearby, in easy chairs, reading what looked like race sheets. I ignored them all and walked to the closest door. I knocked, opened it, and slipped into the smoky room that is the office. The windows had long been fogged with cigar smoke and who knows what else, but there were paintings and scrolls on the walls that held your attention much more than the industrial views out one of the windows.

There was a big table in the middle of the room, big enough to seat many people. If invited. Three men occupied three sides of the table, leaving an empty chair at the side closest to the door. These were the grandfathers. For today, at any rate. The makeup of the grandfathers has changed over time, and I'm sure it will change some more, but now it was the people at this table who called the shots. I knew what to do; I've been here before.

"Sit, sister," the oldest of the men, Mr. Archibald Hu, said. Mr. Hu was still wearing a bowler hat he must have gotten in the thirties, cigarette holder in his lips. He was the voice on the phone yesterday. He ran the warehouse—and pretty much everything else. I knew who the dock worker was who sat at one side, as he was my usual contact when work had to be done, but I didn't know the man on the other side. Maybe a new grandfather. Very nice suit. Maybe he was the connection to our contractor, but I didn't know and they were not telling me.

I turned to Mr. Hu. "I put my trust in the wrong man," I said, "but we have used him many times before. I thought he was reliable." This was not easy for me to say.

"Stop, sister," Mr. Hu said, holding up his hand. "Later may be time for blame. Now we only have time to fix this. Do you understand?"

"Yes, of course. What would you have me do?" As always, I tried to be calm and expressionless, but inside I was feeling like my guts were twisting because I could tell I was going to have no options. Blame would come later, all right. Their decision was final and would reflect their will. And even though I'd been around a long time, I did not mean much in the big scheme of things. I knew this better than many others.

"We did explain to you that our contractor for this job had a number-one rule for us—*this must not come back to me!* You remember, yes?"

I was now thinking that I knew just how Paco had felt, facing me. "Of course, yes. You were clear. I was also clear. Things were done to insure there would be no come-back, just like you told me. But Tony—who you all know—gave the job to Paco. We've used Paco before, but this time he made a big mistake. No fingerprints, no ID, no clues – except he missed a business card to a local bar, and they found it. We all know that. That bar's been there for years. What's the connection between the bar and our contract?"

Mr. Hu stared at me levelly. "We have no idea. This contractor is in need of great secrecy, and thought we could deliver that to him. That is why he contacted us through anoth-er." He looked at the man who could be a banker. Was he the contractor's man? "But nothing is clear. We think we know who is contracting us, but they are working behind curtains. I understand this. We have no understanding of why this target was chosen, or why they say remove the fingers, but we can imagine. We don't know who this person is or was. We know the man who contacted us, of course, but we know very little about his contractor. He isn't sharing. He only insisted there be no come-back." The man in the nice suit studied his finger-nails. "This was a very big point—no come-back can happen! Or we unleash problems for everybody. Problems we cannot afford, of course! Life or death, sister. If that business card links Mister Detective Exeter to our contract, we could all go down! It will be worse than when those Taiwanese assholes pushed us out of Macao."

I sat and thought about this. I didn't know anything about the contract or the target; I just work out what the grandfathers say, and for that I get my shop on the Embarcadero and, of course, a little something extra. It would be sweet if I lived to enjoy it. But this bit about the business card was bad. "Why would the business card lead to our contract?"

Mr. Hu looked at me somewhat archly. "I don't know, sister, but it's a connection. From the cops' point of view, they have a clue. It's not a good thing that they have it. It is a link. We know that the police think the bar owner, a lady, has something to do with all of this. And now we hear that Councilman Holier has finally got enough votes to fund his cleanup campaign, he even called us for money too, and the bar lady, I can tell you, is going to be dragged out in the street and made to look very bad in front of the city. If she leads to our contractor, I don't know, but we created this link and that makes it a very dangerous link for us. We have been discussing it all day, and we have come to a conclusion."

Then the dock worker spoke up. "To help our contractor, we need to cut the link."

Eyes casually shifted from one to another around the table, each surmising, from the very slightest of signs, what the others were thinking. Mr. Hu puffed slowly on his cigarette in the long black holder. The man in the suit also held a cigarette in his fingers. He said, "I agree. We need to make sure that whatever link this bar has to our contractor, it is cut. Our contractor can never be connected with this. We have far too much to lose in this case. Cut the link."

Mr. Hu turned and looked at me, his face tilting. "You understand?" he said.

"You really think that if I just get rid of the bar owner, there will be no more link to this mysterious contractor? As easy as that?"

"Dead people can't talk. No talking—so there would be no threat. No come-back. This is what our contractor would like, we are sure."

This did not seem like a good idea to me. This lady had been around a long time; people knew her. I'd seen her. I thought I knew her name—Mona? There was something about her that I couldn't remember, but it was a memory that scratched, something bad. Or sad. The idea that we could fix this problem by killing her seemed crazy to me.

"OK," I said to Mr. Hu. "I'll take care of it. Of course." I bowed my head at him deferentially, then stood up, looked directly in the eyes of the other two men, then turned to walk out the door and back down the stairs into the warm evening air on the street below. Seven o'clock and still light out.

Exeter

"Marge," I said into the phone, "you promised me!"

It was almost seven o'clock. I wanted to get home and eat dinner, but I was stuck in this cramped, stale room and I couldn't even charge it to overtime. I was just wasting hours! I'd left three messages with the coroner this afternoon to follow up, and now they were telling me sorry, they didn't get to it, but the good news is that they'll do it first thing tomorrow morning. What was the point?

"Does this mean you haven't even started the blood work? Can't you give me anything?"

She explained, again, what I already knew, and promised me the office would do the autopsy on Miss Patricia Peteaut tomorrow first thing, and I'd get a complete report just as soon as they had it, signed it, and filed it. Which I also already knew. She said goodbye and hung up. After all, she was working late as well. I sighed and was thinking I would close it up when the phone rang. The whole first floor was "after hours" quiet, so the jangling ring seemed louder than usual. Who was calling at this hour?

I picked up the black plastic handset. "Exeter." Only then did I glance down and see that of the five square, clear plastic buttons at the base of the phone, the one that was lit indicated the call was internal.

"Lieutenant Exeter, this is Nancy from the chief's office. I'm glad I found you in."

"I was just on my way out." Now what did I step in...?

"That's OK, don't let me hold you up. You don't need to come upstairs for a meeting or anything, I'm just supposed to pass on a message for you from the chief. Two, actually. The chief has been getting calls from Gonsalvo Coelho, the old man who owns the tuna boats?" It sounded like she was asking me a question, but I knew she wasn't. "They know you have to do a thorough job, but they only fished that barrel up, and they were on their way out to the fishing grounds when it happened. They say you've already interviewed almost everyone who was on board when it happened—except for someone who isn't with them anymore, or something like that. They have got to put out to sea because he's got a crew on pay status and it's costing him to stay tied up at the dock for days, like you told him to. The chief wants to know, just for information, mind you, if you can wrap it up with them so they can get out and back on their schedule. Unless you find something incriminating on board, of course." Her tone made it plain that such an outcome would be humorous to consider.

"Duly noted, Nancy." I just hated this crap.

"And also, the chief says the city is planning some kind of event at the G Street mole for Saturday night. He wants to make sure you know about it, because apparently it is the Harbor Police, and not us, who are issuing the permit. He plans to send a black-and-white there to observe. Seeing as I caught you in, I don't have to type out a note for you, so that's good for me."

"I'm really glad." But I suppose I may have sounded just slightly sarcastic, as she then hung up. That was the end of the call. No goodbyes. OK, I was done. I got up and stretched, thinking I would start the day tomorrow by completing the interviews on the boat so I could clear them to take off.

Frank

I had spent the afternoon sitting and thinking. My house felt cavernous and empty. I watched the sky darken into night. The phone call I was waiting for broke the stillness and I picked up the handset.

"Yes?"

"Frank," Phil said, as I knew it would be him, "it isn't good."

"They are not going to get any big bucks from the Visitor's Bureau, I can tell you that."

"I'm way past talking about giving them money. Remember when I told you the good Councilman Holier was working with the *Tribune* for some kind of Sunday exposé? Well, it's grown. The forces of our city have orchestrated a show—you're not going to believe it. For some reason they are talking about having Mona arrested tomorrow, with coordinated press coverage of her, handcuffed, and then some kind of prearranged political rally the next day, with Holier crying for blood and the mayor apparently willing to join him. Sunday, of course, they expect full color coverage of both events in the Sunday paper. They already pulled a permit for the event Saturday night. I'm at a loss."

"Look, I need to tell you, she was here last night." There was a pause.

"At your house?"

"At the guesthouse."

"With Gary." It was a statement, not a question. "I guess I would be happy for her in other circumstances. Right now I don't know what to say. They are planning to pillory Mona for making her porno movies, running a bar, and being mysteriously connected to a recent murder. Maybe they think they can tie her to the murder. For all I know, they'll probably blame Angela's kidnapping on her."

Wow, I thought; I hadn't heard him mention Angela's name in many years. "Does Gary know about this?" Nestor asked.

"Gary is suspicious of me. He knows I'm involved in something, but he doesn't know what or why. As far as I know, Mona isn't offering any explanations. Have you talked to anybody?"

"Only Father Murphy. Confession."

"We have to do something for Mona. She can't get hung out to dry," I said.

"I know. I just can't figure out what. Yet." There was another pause. "Sleep on it, Frank. I'll talk to you tomorrow." And we ended the call.

Mark

I was headed off my shift and coming out of the back way at HQ when I saw Gary drive one of the trucks into the back lot. I stood there and watched as he parked. He didn't notice me until he got out and headed over to his old Camaro. His mouth was smiling. "Hey, buddy." He waved at me and slowed down. "What's up with you? Shift over?" I was feeling a little uncomfortable, as earlier I'd had to go up and brief Chief Gus about what I knew about Gary. Which included my latest wisdom— that he wasn't getting along so good with you-know-who and I thought it might be over.

"Yeah," I answered. "I'm headed out of here. How about you?"

"I planned on...," and then he stopped. "I don't know what. This has been a crazy day. Maybe I'll just go get a beer."

It was all the opening I needed. "Let's go," I said, and he grinned and put his hands on his hips. "Meet you at the Waterfront," he called over his shoulder and went to his Camaro.

Parking was easy, even though it was almost seven o'clock. Never that busy on a Thursday, I guess. We got a little table out by the sidewalk, with a hanging chain barricade to indicate where your right to drink beer ended. We ordered a plate of their little burgers and Gary ordered an Anchor Steam.

"When did you start drinking that?" I asked. "I thought you were a Coors man." He just smiled. Not too many people in the tavern, but enough so that we blended in. We both drank some beer, and then Gary reached for a little burger and I unloaded on him.

"The chief called me in today. Told me I was to report to him about you, buddy. He wanted me to blab on you about your old girlfriend. I told you he would. Jeez, I really hate this shit. He makes me feel like I'm a spy."

Gary took a bite, ate half of the little burger and told me, with his mouth still full, "Lucky for me you're shitty at it. What did you tell him?"

"Same as you told me. That you were on the outs and didn't think you'd be seeing her. I didn't mention anything else. Like who you spend your nights with."

"Aren't you a clever guy."

"I'm just trying to walk a fine line. I'm being up front with everybody. It isn't easy!" And we both laughed at that. "You gonna tell me? What's the deal?" I asked. "What is going on with her?"

Gary sobered up and looked at me appraisingly. "I really don't know, Mark. I really don't. I tell you this, it has something to do with Chief Hansen."

"No shit?!" Chief Hansen predated my time on the Harbor Police, but everybody spoke about him like he was some kind of saint. I stared at Gary, who looked as confused as I was. "How did Hansen have anything to do with Mona?"

"I don't know. At least not yet. He was part of the investigation into the kidnapping of Mona's little girl. It's all kind of strange, to be honest. Nobody knows why he got into the middle of this, but apparently he was sent on a mission to the Philippines to do research and filed some report about the kidnapping. The PD thinks that report links Mona to the shit that's going down now. The floater we picked up. And somehow," Gary paused, "my dad is involved. Somehow."

I didn't know what to say to that. Naturally, I was trying to figure out how all this got Gary into trouble, when trouble came walking down the sidewalk toward our table. *Oh. My. God.* It was Mona, looking like a total fox, filling out a blouse with a loose tie around a sailor's collar, tight, tight jeans with bell bottoms, and red sneakers. Every male eye (and every female eye, as well) watched as she walked straight up to our table. She stopped in front and smiled at both of us. Then she looked straight at me and asked if she could have a minute with Gary. I picked up my beer and a little burger and said I'd be hanging at the bar if they needed me for anything.

Holy shit. Now what? The back of the bar was plastered with all these decals and stickers and stuff, but there was a mirror, and I could see them in the reflection when I sat in front of it. Mona came around inside the chain-link barrier and sat in my seat. I saw her start talking, but I couldn't hear what she said.

Mona

"I've been looking for you for a couple of hours. First I drove past your Harbor Police building, no car, and then I went out to Shelter Island and drove past the boat dock, and then I drove all the way back to Kensington to see if your car was parked in front of your place. No dice. I figured the only thing left was that you were back here." I paused. "Because I feel we need to talk. And I saw your Camaro on the road."

"You should be a detective," Gary said.

"Ha." I must have looked as uncomfortable as I felt. "Look, I want to tell you something. Not all the things you want to know, because I made a promise, but something that I want you to know." His stare back at me wasn't unfriendly, but it didn't tell me much. "I wish this morning did not go the way it did. I made a mistake, and the goddamned cat was out of the goddamned bag. Which I very much feel sorry about. I didn't want to argue with you this morning. I really didn't. For some reason I've been wanting to tell you that all day. For a gal who makes sex movies, I hadn't slept with a man in years. Actually, lots of years." I paused. "I liked being with you."

"Kind of a frank admission," he said, looking at me with his warm brown eyes.

"I haven't had very many man friends at all. I'm in a business that turns them off—or it turns them on for all the wrong reasons. You're kind of a new thing for me. I didn't want to piss you off. I'm sorry. I also wanted to tell you that my promise about secrets really doesn't have to mean anything to you. It's all in the past but it still matters for others, even though not me anymore. Can't we just let the past be the past?"

"I haven't had much luck with that in my life. How about you?"

I sighed. "OK. Point taken. I still feel better having found you and told you that I'm sorry. But I'm not sorry for who I am or for the promises I've made. Maybe I'll see you around." I sat there looking at him and he looked back at me with a conflicted expression, but he didn't say anything. I figured it was going to be a fast visit—I'm not sure what I expected. I guess I thought he'd give me a kiss and come home with me. But he didn't do that. He sat there looking confused and unhappy, so I smiled at him, got up, and walked back out to my car. I'd go home for the night, even if it was another night of being all by myself.

Mark

I was looking into the bar mirror and saw her get up from the little table, so I turned from looking at them in the mirror to staring at them directly. Gary just sat, gazing into his beer like it was a crystal ball, and Mona smiled at him and walked out. I figured it was just like I told the chief: things were over and cooled down; all would be good, right? I grabbed my beer and headed back to the table where Gary sat with at least three uneaten burgers. I sat in the chair that was still warm from Mona. I didn't want to think about it, so I picked one up and took a bite.

"Hey, man—everything OK?" I asked Gary.

"I really don't know." He went back to staring into his brew, and didn't say anything else. I took that as a hint. I didn't need to gab, I'd just drink this beer and eat these burgers, and as I reached out for another one I saw Mona go by in her convertible. Then, as I watched, the headlights went on in a black Lincoln Town Car that had been parked in front of her little Benz. I didn't see anyone get in the big black car, but as soon as Mona took off its lights flashed on, it pulled out, and it took off in the same direction as the Benz. It looked like a Chinese guy was driving, but the windows had a heavy tint, so I couldn't see who else was inside. *Odd*, I thought, and reached for the last little burger. It didn't occur to me to say anything about it to Gary.

5

FRIDAY

Mona

It was a fitful night for me. I stared at the ceiling a lot. Trying to divine something from the cracks in the old plaster finish. As it got gradually lighter, I thought about my planned day at the studio. Suze had the production well organized, and I didn't really have to be there, but where was I going to go? This is the life I've made, a way to bring dollars into my bank account, but it feels like I'm living in another world. Some kind of different universe. Maybe that's why Gary didn't want to come home with me. I'm, like, an untouchable. I have often thought to myself about the difference between a kiss and a fuck. I mean, if you're kissing you've got your tongue in somebody else, right? So what's the big dif between a tongue and a cock? It could only be the baby thing. Can't get pregnant with your tongue (although that gives me an idea for a scene). It's the goddamned seventies! We have birth control pills! Nobody has to have a baby! Nobody is going to drop dead from screwing! Why don't they just cut me a break and not act like my movies are so terrible. Like I must be so terrible.

I rolled my head to the side and my pink plastic clock told me it wouldn't ring to wake me up for another half hour. *Great.* I reached out and turned off the alarm. *I'm up.*

I put on a short French robe that I got in a shop downtown and went to make myself some coffee. It was too early to show up at the studio, so I poured myself a cup, then went outside to pick up a copy of the *Ocean Beach Rag*, our neighborhood news sheet. It was almost dawn; soft shadows were shrinking as the misty morning light grew. I looked around the street, but nothing moved. The *Rag* wasn't a paper so much as a neighborhood newsletter, but that was all I wanted. I don't want to read the news; I don't want to know it. Maybe the *Rag* was obsessed with Watergate, but I mostly read about the Junior Lifeguards training by leaping off the OB Pier. The kids all looked so happy and innocent. Within thirty minutes I had finished the coffee and the paper and was feeling like I ought to go to the studio, even if only to open it up. I'd get some coffee and donuts for the crew. Thing is, we may be untouchables to the world, but we have each other. We are our own support group. I was ready to get back into it.

I put on my working clothes, jeans and a cotton work shirt with sneakers, tucked my hair under a cap, and left by the back door, which opened onto the driveway and the carport that protected my little powder-blue Benz. I hopped in and it started up nicely, like always. I backed up and headed out onto Sunset Cliffs Boulevard so I could drive over the hills this peninsula was named for and pick up some first-class fresh-made donuts, then head out to Kearny Mesa and the studio. I felt great backing out of the driveway, but once on Sunset Cliffs I had to brake quickly for a light change and it seemed like the brakes got spongy. I'd just had this car at Hans's shop off Pacific Coast Highway, and everything had been checked. What was up with this? The light changed again and I turned onto Narragansett to drive over the hill. I breezed up just as the sun broke over the tops of the palm trees by the top of the hill, and then I started hurtling down the hill to the next light. I instinctively stepped on the brake as I was picking up speed and the light was changing. *Holy shit!! No brakes!!* I started stomping on them, over and over. Nothing. I was rolling into a four-way intersection at forty miles an hour, and I could see that there were cars driving through. Traffic! My heart was pounding; my hands were sweaty. I tried to pull on the hand brake but my hands were slippery, and then it was too late. I found myself charging straight into the intersection and heard a blast from a horn that seemed right in my ear, and then it was fade to black.

Exeter

I'd just sat down at my desk to start my day and was patting my pockets to find some cigs when the phone rang. I picked up the black plastic handset, then punched the clear plastic button with the light on. "Exeter," I said, and waited to hear what's what. It was a nurse from the hospital in Hillcrest. They'd gotten an emergency admit from a car wreck who had my card in her purse. "Yeah?" I said. The nurse said she wasn't conscious and they weren't sure of her condition. Did I know her? Her ID said her name was Mona Oakheart.

"Huh," I said. I'm great at small talk. "I'm going to swing by."

I called over to Traffic and asked the sergeant to get me the news on what happened. Not a lot to go on—they weren't sure where the accident occurred—but there couldn't be too many emergency rides to the ER from a car crash at this hour. He said he'd call me back ASAP. I leaned back in the old wooden swivel chair and thought about it. No reason I should go down there right away. It didn't sound like she was in critical condition, and she sure wasn't going anywhere fast. I drummed my fingers on the desk and reached for my coffee mug. Tasted like dishwater, but better than nothing. Only took minutes for the phone to ring.

"Exeter?" the sergeant on the phone call asked.

"What happened?" I answered.

"It was over by Narragansett and Catalina. Controlled inter-section, luckily not so busy at seven a.m., when she goes barreling across Catalina through a red light. This is according to the guys in the moving van who hit her. If they didn't have good brakes it would have been a T-bone, and she'd likely be gone. As it was, she got clipped in the rear; she was in a little car, some kind of foreign convertible, and it was light enough to spin around, miss some cars headed eastbound on Catalina, and collide with a parked car—apparently a Chevy Impala. She hit her head and was unconscious. There was some loss of blood, so the black-and-white called a wagon to take her to the ER. I got no report on her condition. Good enough for you?"

"What? Did she, like, fall asleep at the wheel at seven in the morning?"

"I'm sure I don't know, Detective. I'm just telling you what I got from the guys at the scene."

"Anybody look at the car?"

"I got no notes it was anything but negligence. We're towing the vehicle to impound. It's on its way now. You good?"

"Yeah, thanks—I appreciate what you got."

I knew that coincidences happen; I just didn't believe in them. Something was off about this. I mean, was she a delicate flower and the very thought of getting involved in a murder investigation made her want to end it all? I didn't think so. And when people chose suicide by car, they usually did it off a bridge or a cliff. I knew she used to drive for a living before she got into her bar. Had she been strung out on some kind of drugs? I decided that it would make sense to check her out, maybe she'd be up, so I got in the car and headed for the hospi-tal. It wasn't far, and when I finally got up to her room she was awake. The back of the big mechanical bed had been raised and she was brushing her hair, very gingerly. Big bandage on her forehead.

"Stitches?" I asked, nodding at her head.

"Well if it isn't my good friend Jim Exeter!" she answered. "What the hell brings you here?"

"The very same question I had for you." I looked at her. "What happened?"

"What—did you think I was trying to get out of town? Why are you following up on me?"

"Look, the nurses found my card in your stuff, and they gave me a call. They do that routinely when there is no next-of-kin or other connection to call. You OK?"

She thought about it. "Yeah," she said, "I think so."

"You just missed the red light?"

"Hell no! I saw the light," and at that point she slowed down as if remembering something, and then looked up at me. "It was my goddamned brakes! They failed. I was going downhill into that canyon Catalina runs up, and my brakes were gone. I remember. I was stomping on them, but nothing. Hey, I take care of that car—it wasn't cheap, you know—and I go to Hans, he's a pro with the Benz. This shouldn't have happened."

I looked at her. "You going to be all right? You want me to call somebody? I wanted to talk to you today, but I think you better get back on your feet first. I'll call you later—OK?"

She looked a little confused, and I started to feel bad because I knew what they planned for her later. My boss and his bosses had planned on bringing her in and making her Queen for a Day (not!) with the press. That shit always stinks. I headed back to the office. I wanted to look at the little Benz.

Impound. Now that made it convenient. Impound was only a couple of blocks away from our downtown headquarters, so I drove back from the hospital and parked in our lot. It was early enough that it was not yet hot, weather was nice—a little walk seemed like a good idea. I went to check out the car. There was a uniform on post next to the gate, and after I badged him he slid open the chain-link barrier for me. He pointed at where the newly arrived sports car was sitting. I headed over and walked around it, slowly. On the driver's side, the rear quarter looked totally caved in. The wheel and its tire, snapped off, were dropped in the back seat of the convertible. Handy, as it wouldn't have fit in the trunk. The front of the car looked like it had sideswiped something painted red, big streaks and creases down the body. To me, the car looked totaled. I looked inside and the driver's compartment seemed pretty intact. Other than some blood, still tacky, on the leather seats and the carpet, nothing looked broken. Driver's door still opened, so I grabbed on the edge of the windshield and stuck my foot down on the pedals without getting into the bloody seat. I pumped on the brake pedal—and confirmed what Oakheart had told me. No resistance at all.

I got down on my hands and knees and bent low so I could see up into the engine compartment. I spotted what I thought was the master cylinder, but the hood was too twisted to open, and I had to rely on my flashlight. I was no pro mechanic, but I could tell that the clear plastic tube dangling off the master cylinder had been neatly sliced, as the other part of the tube was dangling right by it. I didn't think this problem could be blamed on Hans.

As I walked the couple of blocks back to my office, I wondered about what I thought I'd seen and made a mental note to send forensics over to take some pictures. That brake line had been sliced, and that likely meant someone was trying to take the gal out. It sure as hell wasn't a very effective approach—more like a gambit from a movie from the thirties. Was it a warning? What else could it mean? Why would that be happening? Was she connected to something that was a threat to someone? I didn't know what to think, so I went back up to my desk, where I do my best at not thinking.

I had a phone message in the in-box. Chief wanted to know what he could tell Coelho about getting under way on Saturday. It was all about money, right? What did I care? I wasn't going to learn anything there. They just fished up the barrel. I'd interviewed a handful of the fishermen, and the captain, whose papa owned the ship, but the guy who pulled the barrel up had apparently split to Mexico and hadn't been back. My missing link. These guys were not real reliable, and what the hell was I going to learn by talking to him anyway—what was his name? —*Paco*. I figured I could let the boat go and track Paco down later.

Instead, I looked at what I had spread out from the files. I saw that the older files on the kidnapping from '67 had been dug out of central and shipped over. It was a thick bunch of paper: our own casebook, and the FBI files that they shared with us, and some kind of weird Harbor Police expedition report as well. Looked like we had a lot of paperwork. I checked the log sheet that went with the materials; it told who had viewed them and when. Didn't look like the file had been handled much after 1969, except that the last entry, before the file was sent to me, was smudged and illegible. It could even have been recent, but I wasn't sure. I started opening the big manila envelopes the files came in and made little piles of the reports. A lot of reports to and from TJ—when those guys found the Econoline at the airport it sparked a lot of communication—and different requests to and from the FBI. Even if the perp had disappeared cold at Rodriguez Field in TJ, the prints from the van could be traced, and they led back to the Philippines, because of a visa application at the US Consulate. Most of the FBI report was a record of how the investigation using the prints ended up at the consulate in Manila, but got no further because the name on the application seemed to have first appeared at that point out of thin air.

I started looking through the files to find that weird report, specifically. The report written by...what was his name... *Hansen*...from the Harbor cops. I was really jazzed to find it— and what a story. This guy takes FBI print cards of prints from the scene and from the van, no question that they are the perp —but who the hell is he? Hansen goes back to Manila (where the FBI's carefully constructed trail goes dead) and runs him down. He must have had money to spread around. How the hell he made matches for prints from the US Consulate for a visa application, and tied them to prints that were on record for a supposedly dead kid doing hard time in Manila, man—I'd like to know how he pulled that off.

I turned to the back of the report to see the prints themselves, but the print cards weren't attached. Now what! What happened to them? The report wasn't going to help anyone make a link if we didn't have the goddamned prints! I wanted to match them to the photos from Mona. I spent about ten minutes turning over every piece of paper in the envelopes. I had the report, but not the goods! I didn't have time to try to figure out how the print cards had gotten separated from our copy of the report—I needed answers now. What if the prints on the card matched prints on the photos?

Then it occurred to me that copies of the report and its cards had to exist somewhere. Getting it out of the feebs was not going to happen in my lifetime, but maybe the Harbor cops had a copy.

I decided to call Reines and see if he could be useful, but before I could call him the phone rang. "Exeter." It was Nancy. Following up for upstairs about the *Lady Lynn*. Money. I could smell it burning. "Fine," I said, "I have everything I'm going to get from them—they're clear to go if you want to give them the word." I knew that, of course, the chief would like to be owed a favor from Coelho, so he wanted to be the one to give them the word. Then Coelho's boat could get the hell out of there and start making money. Again. I reached for the phone and left a message for the boat jockey.

Gary

Mark was piloting while I casually surveyed the bay from the bridge of the *Pt. Loma II* as we cruised through a mild chop. Fridays can be busy—even though the real action, the movement of cargo or Navy ships, followed schedules that weren't linked to the days of the week. They came and went anytime. Still, Fridays were busy. Maybe a lot of people were playing hooky from work, out on boats because it was so damn nice out. A light breeze, even if it came mysteriously out of the east, powered a fleet of sailboats, large and small, dodging each other while someone was luffing his sails in a failed tack. Man, did it feel good to be out of the jungle.

The bay breeze, the blue sky, and the scent of brine from saltwater spray was almost shifting me out of the funk I'd felt all day yesterday. And all night, for that matter. I really wanted the shift to happen, but it wasn't a totally successful strategy. I still felt like shit, and Mark wasn't talking about it. As far as he was concerned, the way last night went was a good ending. I can still hear Exeter telling me to dump her, because now the chief would be happy and I wouldn't be in anybody's crosshairs. Didn't feel so good to me. Mona had got under my skin. I had all these conflicting feelings: my dad, her kid, my job, her job... but all of them were a sort of backdrop for a feeling in my gut— was it warmth?—that was gnawing at me. It had meant more than I thought it would to have someone I could hold. It was obvious from how I felt today that I'd missed that. More than I thought. I remembered holding her and feeling very...I don't know...centered? And here everyone was giving me more pressure to walk away. All the reasons that were screaming at me to let it go were still yammering in my head when the shift ended and we tied up the cruiser at our dock. Mark and I hadn't talked much. I was going to drive us back to HQ when dispatch tapped on the big glass window and motioned at me to come over. Another telephone note. The message had come in hardly an hour earlier.

The sarge looked at me when he handed me the slip of paper. "What have you got going with this Exeter guy? It's like you two got an affair or something. He calls you every day!"

"Very funny."

"It's that floater case, right? What are you still doing hooked up with the dick who's working it?"

"Are you kidding, Sarge? They can't do anything without me." I looked at the message.

Call me. MO was in accident but OK. We have to talk ASAP.
Exeter

That stopped me cold. *Accident?* I turned and yelled at Mark to tie up and clean up himself, told him I had to run. It was an early shift, so I had parked my car in the lot in front of the dock, and I jammed into reverse, then took off down Shelter Island Drive to head downtown. Mark had come to the dock with me in the truck, but he would just have to grab a ride back.

It was a fast ride downtown. No Coast Guard jets crossing in their private runway extension. I didn't run any red lights but I did push it a little bit, gunning the Camaro down PCH and screaming into the left lane onto Broadway. I was still in uniform, so I took advantage a little. I pushed open the big glass doors to the downtown headquarters of the Police Department and took the hall to the left to Exeter's office. I'd been there before, and the desk sergeant hardly even looked up at me. I rapped on Exeter's door.

"Yeah, I'm here, what do you want?" The voice came through the thin door.

I opened it.

"You!" he said, looking annoyed. "I told you to call me!"

"Yeah, well, I'm here. What the hell is going on?" Exeter's desk was at least a foot deep in paperwork; his tie was loose and it looked like he'd been in there all day. Smelled like cigarettes.

"That's the question I got for *you*. Sit down." He gestured at the chair in front of his desk.

"What happened to Mona?" I asked, as I sat in the chair.

"She's in a shitload of trouble, that's what. She's tied up in this thing and I got too many loose ends."

"For Christ's sake, Exeter, what the hell happened?!"

He paused and looked at me. "I thought you were done with the fling thing?"

"What does that have to do with anything?"

"I hear it in your voice. You're not done, you're worried about her. You still seeing her?"

I glared at him.

"She lucked out, kid. Her pretty little convertible is kaput, smashed as she goes tearing through the intersection at Narragansett and Catalina, and a split-second earlier she would have been clobbered head-on in a T-bone." The word brought up memories that chilled me deeply. I caught my breath. "She was KO'd, and they took her to Hillcrest in an ambulance. They called me 'cause she had my card in her purse. Good thing. She was recovered and talking when I showed up—remembers her brakes failing. For grins I go take a look at the little car. It's in impound. Now, I am not a forensic laboratory," he said, drawing out and emphasizing the syllables of each word, "but it looked to me like the brake line was sliced. And that is a fact that is going to get looked at."

Wow. I got what Exeter was telling me. I didn't see that coming. Was someone trying to kill her? Why would anyone try to off Mona? She was the victim in all of this. "That doesn't make any sense," I said to Exeter.

"I don't disagree with you; I'm just telling you what I saw. And there's more."

"OK, I'll play. What?"

"I dug up the report we got from your old chief of Harbor Police, Hansen, and it details how he took prints from the crime scene of the old kidnapping of Mona's kid, and from collateral sources—mostly the van—and linked them to a visa app in Manila for someone who is supposed to be dead. Hell of a story. Except for one thing—our official copy of the report is missing the print cards. They're just gone from the file. This isn't supposed to happen. I need the copy of those print cards because I have a feeling they are going to lead me to the floater's perp, even though there's limitations to ID'ing the floater. No fingers, right? You've got to have a copy of this report in your offices—this came from you guys. Go get it for me."

I stared at him.

"What's the problem? Go to your file room and dig up this report—I need those print cards. OK?"

I thought about what Exeter was telling me. Maybe I could get a little help out of him by letting him know I was on board, and hell yeah, I *was* on board. I wanted to know who'd done this. In fact, I had more than one question on my mind. "How'd you leave it with Mona? She still in Hillcrest?"

Exeter rolled his eyes. "Kid, you got to be crazy. City politics is about to turn her into grilled meat. I don't see how she's going to keep her bar, once they run her up for making dirty movies. They'll find a charge in there somewhere. Maybe zoning. She is still in the middle of a murder investigation, and at the heart of a miserable crime in her past, and in the crosshairs of a councilman who's got the press slobbering for the story. This is not going to go good for her—or you."

Tell me something I care about. "You left her at Hillcrest?"

He shook his head. "Yeah, but she's probably gone already. She was looking pretty recovered when I left. Tell her to lay low and be careful."

Maybe he isn't a total asshole, I said to myself. "I'll see if I can't find you that report. I'll call you as soon as I do."

"I sure as shit hope so," he said, and I left to go back to our own HQ by the bay.

Gus

Naturally, I heard about it as soon as Reines's kid came in and went straight into our file room. Chandra called me because it was so unlike Gary. He stayed as far away from paperwork as he could, and none of his patrol duties involved any file research, so she wanted me to know he was in there. I could only imagine what he was looking for. *Jesus.* I didn't have to imagine. I knew. The Hansen report.

I remember the day when Chief Hansen told me about the report, and why it was meaningful. They'd ID'd the killer, even if they didn't catch him. Hansen was sure he'd come back. I owed Hansen. It wasn't that I doubted myself; I knew I had gotten here by my own effort—but I did have help along the way. Father Jesse at St. Augustine had taken pity on my hard-scrabble upbringing and my path that seemed headed toward gang life, and he set me up with Chief Hansen back when he was a captain with the PD, long before he became chief of the newly created Harbor Police and was looking to build a force. It was an angle right out of high school, a path no one in my family had ever had: the Police Academy and then a job, and I quickly took it. Captain Hansen was like some kind of uncle to me. He gave me time and service credit for attending City College so I could get a degree. He was looking out for me, and when it was announced that he was going to head the new force, I was one of the first to go with him. Later, when his budget was going up and he could add to the leadership staff, I was so proud when he called me into his office. This office. This very office.

"Gus," he said, "I am proud of what you've done here with us. You're a good man and a good Catholic. You know why you're here?"

I nodded, but didn't dare say anything.

"Whoever I put in the seat of deputy chief is going to be on a beeline to rule this roost when I let it go, understand me?"

"Yessir."

Hansen looked at me and nodded his head a few times. "The man who will sit in that chair needs to know something that isn't on our books, and needs to promise me that certain things will never be forgotten. Understand?"

"No sir. I surely don't."

"I'm in a hard spot here, Gus. I gave a man a promise I

would keep his secret, but in order for you to give me the promise I need, I have to share his secret with you. If I didn't trust you, it would be problematic. Can I trust you to keep this secret? And before you answer me, know that this is something that can never be shared—except between you and your confessor. Lives are at stake." I remember nodding at him.

"Here at the Harbor Police, we work for the director, you know? He runs the Waterfront Agency, and we are a part of that. You know, I've known Phil Nestor since World War Two," he went on. "You knew I was a prisoner of the Japanese on the Philippine Islands, didn't you? I went over there as an MP before the invasion, and my timing couldn't have been worse. I spent years in a Japanese prison camp on Luzon. Almost didn't make it. When the US showed up, there was Phil and his pal Frank Reines, with the Seabees. They knocked down the walls of our cages, and he was there to give me a hand when I needed one bad. The Seabees were put to work restoring structures and laying the beginnings for the first construction work on Subic Bay Naval Station, even before the war was over. The two of them got me on my feet. We helped each other, I learned to live again, and we all ended up in San Diego after discharge. And here we are. I owe those guys. I owe them everything." He stopped and looked me square in the eyes. "You still with me?"

"Yessir." No hesitation now. I was getting the drift of where this was headed. Debt. I got that.

"No man, Gus, is above making mistakes. We know that, right? Even a very good man can make a mistake. The trick is what you do about it. My friend Phil, our boss, the director, fell for an attractive young woman, and even though he already had a family, he started another. He knew it was wrong, and he did what he could to make things right, and that was all good. No one—I mean, *no one*—other than me and Frank Reines and our confessors knows anything about this. Now you know— and you will never share it, will you?"

"No sir."

The chief looked me straight in the eye. "In the eyes of God, Gus, I'm holding you to that." I swallowed.

"Mother and father agreed to a life apart from each other, as it had to be. Then, a terrible thing happened, and this child was kidnapped, stolen from her mother at the age of three."

All of a sudden I put two and two together. This had happened just a couple of years ago—it was all over the papers, the whole town read about it. Single mother loses child—but the "father unknown" part created waves for a while. Didn't earn her any brownie points, that's for sure. Wow—that meant that the kidnapped kid was the director's daughter. *Shit!* And then I remembered—Chief Hansen had been sent out to the Philippines a few months later, and was on some assignment there for a couple of months. No one knew much about why, but the word in the department was that it had something to do with the kidnapping. The papers said the big shipbuilder, MASTCO, was funding it because they'd lost an employee in the kidnapping. Unusual. Now I was getting the picture. This must have happened because of the relationship between Chief Hansen and the director, and the connection he had with the kidnapping.

"Gus," said the chief, still looking right into my eyes, "now I am getting to the part where you have to make me another promise, if you want to step into these shoes. This is a harder promise. This is a condition of this job. Not just from me. I've already given my word about you—but you have to tell me I did the right thing." He paused for emphasis. "I know who stole that little girl, the Oakheart girl. I got his prints. It's in my report, and I figured out who he is, but I just don't know who he is *now*, or *where* he is. And I sure as hell never found out where *she* is. My gut tells me the guy who did this is not gone forever. This was some kind of family crime, not a money situation; there was never a ransom demand. This killer kidnapper is a total psycho, and although *no one*—except me, the director, Frank Reines, and now, you—knows the connection, we will never forget. This animal will always be hunted. He is always on our radar screens, and by God if he does show up we will take him, and he will answer to justice. And there will be no links to *anyone* in this agency. We will take care of it and protect our own. Understand? Commitment? When he shows up, we will protect our own. No matter what. It's going to happen someday—trust me, he'll be back."

He gave me a moment to absorb all that, then said, "Are we good here?"

I knew what he was asking. Would I fill his shoes when he retired, and keep his promise to his two old friends? Would I not just protect them, but keep the secret about the girl's paternity, if it threatened to come out?

Damn straight I would. Not for a chance at the top job one day, though that mattered to me. But because of what I owed to Hansen, and because he'd taken a big risk telling me all this. I needed to do the right thing. I stood up straight, stretched my arm across his desk, and held out my hand. Chief Hansen took it. "The director will send out a memo about you becoming the associate chief," he said. And that was it. The kidnapper had stayed away. I was thinking of the unfairness of this animal escaping into the unknown after such crimes, when there was a knock at the door, and I was pulled from my reminiscences to the here and now: same office, new occupant, years later. Time travel by means of a knock on the door. "Yes?"

Gary Reines poked his head in. "Chief?" he said. "Chandra said you wanted to see me?"

I nodded for him to sit down. Then I smiled; no time for small talk. "What are you doing in the file room?"

It seemed to throw him off guard for a moment. "I'm looking for a report," he answered. I kept staring at him.

"Exeter told me about the report Chief Hansen did on Mona's kidnapping perp. His copy doesn't have the print cards attached, so he asked me to get him our copy so he could see them. Chief, I know it sounds crazy, but it looks like Chief

Hansen was somehow tied into this kidnapping thing. It's like everybody is tied into it," he said, looking lost.

"Yeah, yeah," I said. "I know about the report. Why didn't Exeter put in a request or come down here himself? What have you got to do with it? Is it a crime occurring out on the bay?"

He shifted uncomfortably in the chair. "I'm just trying to get some answers, Chief. It matters to me. Maybe a lot. Exeter probably asked me to help because he thought I would. Paperwork can take a long time to get from one place to another."

"Don't I know it," I told him. The conversation paused, and Gary kept looking at me. There was really nothing I would rather do than tell him what was going on—but that wasn't my call. I had promises to keep. I would rather keep this kid out of it, if I could.

"Let me tell you about the report," I offered. "Chief Hansen did an amazing job of running down a set of prints in the Philippines, and the report went to the FBI. We were supposed to have a copy, and so was the PD's office downtown. Chief Hansen told me himself, while he was still sitting in this chair, that he couldn't find that report. We tried to locate it, but our copy is gone. Now you're telling me that the PD's copy is missing the print cards? Sounds hinky to me, Officer, don't you think? What do you think is going on?" I was counting on the fact that the files containing the report, now locked in my lower desk drawer, would not emit any noise or sign to reveal my misdirection.

The kid could make a great officer. He shook himself and looked back at me. "I don't know what's going on, but there's no way I'm not finding out."

"Why?" I asked him. "Is it because you aren't staying clear of Mona, like Mark told me you were?"

"Mark is reporting to you about me?"

"He reports to me about anything I ask him to. And I expect you to do the same, Officer. What force do you think you are a part of? A force unto yourself? You know better than to stick your nose into some matter that doesn't involve you, right?"

"How does it not involve me? Everywhere I turn, somebody I know is in the middle of it. And I'm not even sure what *it* is, but I am sure it has something to do with Mona's kidnapping case. I'm also sure you know more about it than I do. What the hell is going on, and what does my dad have to do with it? And who else is involved?!"

I paused a beat. This situation was heavy. I wanted to protect Gary, and I had to protect others. "Look, Gary. I don't know what you think I know, but I do know that you could make it pretty impossible for yourself in the San Diego law enforcement community if you don't stick to your job and let other people stick to theirs."

"Did you know someone tried to kill Mona this morning?" he demanded.

"What?" That caught me by surprise and held my attention.

"Exeter thinks someone sliced her brake line last night. She was in a car wreck this morning and survived by a thin margin." As Gary was talking I could see his face darken, full of blood. I could see where this was going.

"Exeter told you this?"

"Yeah. And he thinks that Chief Hansen's report on the kidnapper from the Philippines has got answers for him in the print cards—which are somehow missing from the PD's copy."

"Who does he think sliced her brake line?" I was hoping redirection would serve me.

Reines shook his head. "I'm going to try to find out, Chief. One way or the other."

My heart went out to young Reines. I knew his dad was a stand-up guy, one of the Three Musketeers, a close friend of my patron, the director. I knew young Reines had been through a lot. And so, obviously, had Mona. Maybe the two of them were connecting. That's not supposed to be a bad thing. Plus, she was the mother of Phil Nestor's lost child. That had to mean something. It meant something to me. I wanted to help him. I wasn't sure how to do it, because I had promises to keep. Important promises. But this was a new twist. If someone was trying to get to Mona, it was going to backfire on them big-time. Nestor was not going to want her put at risk, and neither did I.

There were two things I could do. One of them was a risk for both Gary and me—if things backfired. But it would be telling to see what Gary Reines might learn if he could catch up with this Paco guy. It would have to be off the books. Out of our jurisdiction. Probably leading to Mexico. Possibly a career-limiting move for Gary if something went south down south. I knew enough to know that's where this would lead him. I doubted he cared about his career that much—he had his dad to back him while he was still finding his feet after his time in Vietnam. But I did care—for both of us.

"Look, Gary," I said, jolting him a little with the use of his first name, "I may not have what Exeter wants, but I can think of a lead for you. On your own time; I am not paying for any of this." *Shit*, I couldn't believe I was doing this.

He leaned forward. "I'm off duty, Chief—I already put in my shift."

"Did you know the Coelhos are putting to sea tomorrow? *Lady Lynn* is on her way back to Guam. They were cleared to go by the PD, OK'd by Exeter."

Gary looked confused. "So?"

I took a deep breath and told him something he wasn't supposed to know. "We've been working with the DEA on a drug connection, and Matt Coelho, the tuna boat captain, has been helping us. The B-52 bombers in the Arc Light program come from Andersen Air Force Base on Guam and land at North Island Naval Air Station, Coronado. DEA intel thought product was probably coming out of bombers and into some distribution system. It seems to start from the bay. There's a Joint Strike Force with the feds and some of the locals. Strictly need-to-know basis. I'm one of those who needs to know. I learned from your partner Mark that Captain Matt's your buddy. He's been talking to the strike force. He thought he had a deckhand that knew more than he was saying. Guess who?"

Gary squinted at me. "Uh..."

"It's Paco, who fished the barrel out of the bay for you. They thought he was good for a connection, and then he pulls the barrel up, and now he's a no-show. The task force thought the floater was tied into this drug thing, but then this whole kidnap connection came up because of Mona and the business card. Since then, we think Paco has fled south, and that puts him out of our reach. Unless we do a lot of paperwork." At his confused look, I elaborated: "I'm suggesting you talk to Matt before he sails. Maybe you'll get farther with it."

"What does Paco and this drug thing have to do with Mona getting attacked? With the kidnapping? With anything? Chief, I respect you and I am not trying to be difficult, but you obviously know more than you're telling me. Why can't you just tell me what the hell is going on?! It seems to me that practically everyone knows something more than they're willing to say. Even my own father."

Sometimes, I find sitting behind this desk easy. Chandra brings me coffee, I go out for lunch. But sometimes I find that being the chief is a hell of a burden, and God knows what was going to come of this. I recalled a friend's advice to me one time that you don't get anywhere without taking risks.

"I'm telling you what I can tell you. Look, this gal Mona was fine until the body in the barrel showed up with her card. That's the connection, and I think Paco knows more about it than what we've heard so far. Maybe—unofficial, of course— you can learn what it is. Good luck, Officer. Go talk to Matt. He's only here overnight."

I made a hand gesture shooing him out of the office, and he got up and left. As I watched him close the door behind him, I thought, "Been there, done that." Trying to figure out what was going on when you only had half the story. Chief Hansen was the only one who knew all the connections, but I was sure he'd shared them with the director. Frank Reines probably knew, but nobody was telling me. I didn't know. I only knew what the chief told me, and what I'd promised him. And I had kept my promise. So far.

I looked down at the scarred face of that drawer in my old oak desk, inherited from Chief Hansen. It had a lock. I had a few things in it. One of them was our department's copy of the Hansen report from his investigation of the kidnapper's prints in the Philippines, and the other was the set of print cards that had been attached to the San Diego Police Department's copy of the report. Which I had purloined, in an effort to hide the tracks. Getting my hands on those print cards had been dicey, and if anyone looked hard enough it might come back to me, but I'd risked it.

I reached for the phone to call Sticks. Sending Gary after Paco was the first thing I could do to help him. This was the second thing I could do. If someone was bringing heat down on Mona, they'd better be stopped now, and Alonzo Lee, my old amigo Sticks, was my connection to making that happen.

Exeter

I got a little pink telephone message note from the front desk. Gary Reines left a confusing message about locating Paco, but I was sure Paco was in the wind. I didn't think Gary would find him. I stretched my legs out to the side of my linoleum-topped metal desk. Even I could tell the office stank of cigarettes. It had been a long day. The afternoon was a little long in the tooth, and Fridays always left you with wanting it all to be over. But it wasn't over quite yet. Our building isn't air-conditioned, and this hot October wind was blowing through every window that could be opened, pushed along by rotating circular fans on tall stands in all the hallways. Hot blowing hot.

Ever since I had scoped out Mona's car I'd been trying to

figure out how she became a target on this one, to the point where someone wanted her dead—assuming that's what the sliced brake line meant. Was I missing something? I pulled out my field notebook and reviewed what I had, flipping the pages on the wire-bound pad. I had underlined the word "kidnapping," as it is a relatively uncommon crime and lightning doesn't strike twice, but maybe it was something else? I flipped the page. Porno movies and porno actors. Was this all tied up in her dirty movie business? Was somebody moving drugs, somehow? In film cans? I shuffled through the papers on my desk and found the letter from Baguio City. I get how she had a meeting with the porno casting agent, and how the agent ended up with her card, but the next thing that happens is that the agent turns up dead in the bay. And now someone was trying to take Mona out, because...? How the hell did all this tie into the kidnapping she suffered almost seven years ago? Or did it?

These thoughts had been rattling around for hours, and frankly, I was dog tired of it and ready to call it a Friday, when, naturally, the phone rang.

"Exeter."

"Hold on please, Detective, the coroner would like to speak with you."

I recognized Marge's voice immediately. Hey, about time! But I wondered why I was getting the special call. Last I heard, they would run their tests and send me a report when they were done.

"Detective Exeter?" said the voice on the line. I recognized it as the man himself.

"Dr. Sleizer," I said, "it's not often I hear from you directly. What's up?"

"I'm calling about the body found floating in the bay. Detective, it's late and I don't think we are going to get a report written and out to you this evening, but there's something I'm sure you should know right away. Something quite unusual."

"I'm all ears."

"That young woman was a man. Who had altered himself, or herself—I'm not sure what you say in this situation. We've heard of these operations being performed in Thailand, but I had never seen evidence of it prior to today. The autopsy was irrefutable. There were surgical alterations to the genitals, the breasts, and the throat. That woman was born a man. And another thing—not all our tox screens are back yet, but initial tests showed a very high level of heroin in her blood. I mean, his blood. Lungs are not very saturated. We will likely say dead before drowned. You'll hear more next week, but I wanted you to have a heads-up. Most unusual."

"Thanks for the news." I was still digesting it as we hung up. The floater was a *guy*? Well, that clinched one thing for me— Mona was definitely not telling me all that she knew. How could she not have known that? A gal who makes sex movies couldn't tell she was talking to a guy? Maybe, but I'm not buying it. And here I was starting to feel sorry for her. It was time Ms. Mona and I had another visit. But maybe tomorrow. Right now it was hot, and I was tired, and I had new things to think about. I pictured myself with a nice cold Budweiser by the side of my apartment house pool. *Later*, I thought.

Gus

Reines left my office, and I sat behind my desk and thought about next moves. I got Sticks on it, but things were still pretty dicey. Once I'd made a match of the prints on the photographs that "Patricia" had left with Mona with the prints in Hansen's report, I knew we had a positive ID, and that others would be able to make it as well. "Patricia" was Freddie, the dead house-keeper's nephew, or stepson, or whatever—as unlikely as that seemed to me at the time. So far, the director and I were the only ones who knew. Nestor was the one who'd told Mona to take a walk and leave the photos that the "agent" brought with her on the table so I could drop by, dust them, and compare them to the kidnapper's prints. I made a positive ID, and I'm not even a fingerprint whiz. If I could do it, anyone with the training could, and if that happened, connections would be made that would hurt people I had promised to help.

When I told the director about the positive ID, he asked me what I thought we should do. He was wrestling with calling the cops and telling them we had a match, but I was evasive. I asked him to wait. I had promised Hansen I would cover for him, even if he wasn't going to cover for himself. I'd promised him I'd keep this secret to protect Nestor's family—even if Nestor felt caught in the crosshairs. I was going to do what I had promised to do. Except...now I've got Officer Reines on a mission that could likely take him to Mexico. Who would have thought it would lead to this!

Gary

I left the chief's office feeling even more confused than before. It was pretty hazy how this could-be drug snitch, Paco, was going to tie into anything I cared about, like finding whoever had set Mona up. Was the chief sending me out on a crazy witch hunt? I thought it would be a good idea to let Exeter know what was going on, but he wasn't in, so I left him a message about trying to run down the Paco lead. I changed out of my uniform into jeans and a jean jacket hanging in my locker. I was going to take my service revolver, but I'd leave the Model 10 in the car, locked up, as it was too big to carry around in a pocket and I had no clear idea where I was going to be headed.

Then I took a deep breath. It was obvious that something had snuck up on me. I was feeling it, and it wasn't that buzzing in my head. I went back out to my desk and sat behind it. The blinds were drawn on the chief's window and the place was practically deserted for late Friday afternoon. I didn't even see Chandra around, and I knew anyone on shift would be out in a car or boat. I pulled the phone book out from under the telephone and opened the white pages. Flipped a couple of corners to find the "O"s. There she was: M. Oakheart, Pescadero Drive, Ocean Beach. I dialed her number.

She picked up on the second ring. "Hello?" *OK, what now?*

"Hey, are you OK?" I figured she'd recognize my voice. "I heard what happened. With your car. This morning." I was running out of explanatory phrases.

"Yeah," she said. "I'm OK. I'm bruised from the seat belt, stitches on my forehead, and the car is a mess, I've heard. I haven't seen it yet. I got a ride home from Suze. I was supposed to be in production all day today, but I guess they didn't need me, so I'm home resting. It did kind of shake me up. It's better I'm not at work. How are you doing?"

"Well, it turns out that I got kind of shaken up myself." *OK. Moment of truth.* "When I heard about your accident."

"Really? You're worried?"

"Shit, Mona, I shouldn't have let you go home alone last night. I just didn't know what to think. I *still* don't know what to think."

"So is that a good thing?"

"Mona, I know what I feel, and I want to see you again." Pause. Silence on the line.

"Well, I'm home now," she said.

"There's a little business I have to take care of first. I don't want to worry about what's going to happen to you next. I may be able to come by later, though. We'll see how lucky I am."

"What do you mean, 'what's going to happen to me next'?"

"You didn't get hit because you are a bad driver."

"You talked to Exeter?"

"He confirmed what you told him about your brakes. You were set up. Exeter wants my help with an old report that he thinks has important info, but it's apparently disappeared. A report by Chief Hansen. Did you know him? Ever hear of this report?"

There was a pause. "Never heard of him and no one ever told me about any reports. But you should know, Gary, no one talks to me about anything. I've just been minding my own business. Then this gal Patricia shows up, and the next day she's dead. Nobody talked to me about it."

"I believe you, Mona. Something very weird is going on, and it's on my beat. Even Exeter asked for my help. My chief and my dad both know something about it that I don't know, and it probably has something to do with the secrets you're keeping. But I am not going to sit around and wait for the next shot. I don't get paid to be a target anymore, so I'm going to do a little hunting around."

"What are you thinking?"

"I'm thinking it's a good thing to have friends. I'll call you back later. Take care, lay low, and take it easy, OK?"

"Why are you being so mysterious?" she asked. "I want to know what's going on—and whatever you are doing, if you're doing it for me, then...I don't know what to say. Are you doing something risky?" she asked. Maybe it was my hopeful imagination, but her voice sounded a little different. Maybe a note of concern? Like maybe she cared. Or maybe it was a note of fear.

"I'm just chasing down some leads to try to get the whole story. Maybe we can figure out how you got pulled into it. Believe me, I'll tell you what I find out. Lay low, Mona."

I hung up the phone and went out to the front lot, where my Camaro was parked. I locked my Model 10 into the glove box and turned onto Harbor Drive, right in front of our headquarters, and headed south toward the commercial boat basin and the G Street mole. I wasn't sure why the chief suggested I talk to Matt about the drug deal, but it was all I had and I really had to do something, so here I went. He must have had some purpose, was what I told myself.

The boat basin is a short ten-minute drive from us, and I reasoned that if the *Lady Lynn* was shipping out tomorrow, Matt Coelho would be down there making sure everything was ready to go. I didn't have my walkie-talkie, or I could have radioed to have someone check on the boat, but I knew where his family ranch was if he wasn't there. There was a big city-owned parking lot down by the docks, with only a few cars and trucks parked in it. I locked up the Camaro and walked out on the mole toward the big tuna purse seiners. Smelled like fish and salt water. *Lady Lynn* was one of three tied up on the bay side of the mole. I stood in front of the gangway and called up. A deckhand showed up immediately, and when I asked if Matt was on board he waved me up. I stepped off the solid ground and onto the world of modest motion, a vessel at rest but moving, floating on the bay. A transition I felt very accustomed to.

Compared to the big gray ships the Navy steered in and out of the bay, a purse seiner may not look like much, but they are seagoing ships themselves, and will spend months at a time out working the business of hauling in vast schools of tuna. I got to the deck of the *Lady Lynn* and saw Matt peering through the angled glass window of the bridge and waving me up, so I made straight for the hatch that led to the ladder up to the bridge deck.

"What's up, buddy?" Matt said, after taking my hand and shaking it. Despite the warmth of his greeting, he looked a little wary. "You know we're cleared to take off out of here tomorrow. I'll be out for at least three months."

"I'm trying to help Exeter with his investigation into the floater. Did you talk to him?"

"Sure—everybody talked to him. That's how come we got cleared to split."

A crewman stuck his head through the hatch and smiled at Matt. "Hey, Uncle Matt," he said, "I really appreciate this, I really do. My mama is very happy. Thanks, man." Then he ducked his head out and I heard him head aft.

I looked at Matt, questioningly.

"My newest deckhand," he said. "I don't know what Exeter

heard from Paco, or even if he found him, but that guy disappeared on me right after he pulled the barrel out of the bay, and
I personally haven't seen him since. As we're leaving tomorrow,
he is officially cut from the crew and I've replaced him with a
nephew. I should have done it before, really."

"I take it you haven't heard from Paco all week?" I asked
him. "That's strange. My chief sent me down here to ask you
about him. Apparently, my chief and the DEA know about
some kind of drug thing," I looked at Matt and he nodded, "and
he thought I could learn something about my..." and then I
realized that Matt probably didn't know anything about Mona,
or why I cared, "something," I ended, lamely.

Matt volunteered, "I've been talking to DEA agents for the
last couple of weeks. I'm not supposed to talk about it, but
you're a cop, right? They're convinced that someone—or some
group—is bringing in uncut heroin from the Golden Triangle
—that's what he called it—and everybody has heard the
rumors that they're using the big Arc Light B-52 bombers to do
it. It's not like they talked to me about what they're doing, but I
think they did find some connection to Paco and I sort of
assumed that's why he disappeared. He's probably in Mexico;
he has people in TJ. You want to find him?"

"Yes, I do."

"Ask Tony. They were like buddies. He'd know. He should
be back checking out the net skiff. Can I do anything more for
you?"

"No, Matt, thanks. Good luck fishing—and don't forget your
Saint Chris!"

He laughed and tapped his chest, where the medal hung on a
chain. "Don't worry. See you when I get back—we'll have a party
at the ranch. They're up there making linguiça this weekend."
We slapped each other on the back and I went off to find Tony.

I made it back to the stern and found three guys sitting on
the nets, smoking cigarettes, talking in Portuguese. I grew up

around the Portuguese fishing folk and I knew the sound of the language, but I could only kind of tell what they were saying. It was pretty far off from the Spanish I grew up with.

"Are one of you guys Tony?" I asked. The one with his back to me turned around, and I saw, a little to my surprise, that he looked Chinese. I looked straight at him. "Tony?"

"Who wants to know?" he answered.

"I'm Gary Reines. I'm a Harbor cop. I've known Matt Coelho for a long time—he told me you would know where I can find Paco."

"You're the cop who was there when we pulled up the barrel with the dead gal, right?"

"That's me."

"What do you want with Paco?"

"I just want to talk to him. Why'd he split? Where is he?"

"Paco, he has problems. We're leaving without him. He knows that."

"How do you know what he knows?"

"I talk to him sometimes. He's gone, man."

"If he's gone, how do you talk to him?"

Tony smirked. He looked at the other two guys and they both got up and moved off.

"The telephone, man. We talk on the telephone."

"And when he is on the phone, where is he calling from?" I looked at him directly.

"Somewhere in TJ, man. Why do you want to know?"

"Look, I appreciate your help, Tony." I took my wallet from my back pocket and pulled out a hundred-dollar bill. Cash was not a problem for me. "I just want to know where I can find him."

Tony's eyes widened at the bill. "I can leave a message for him," he said. "He uses the telephone at the Striped Stallion; it's a bar in Zona Río. He calls from there. He's supposed to make a call tonight. I'll tell him you're looking for him."

"No, thanks," I said, "I don't think that's a good idea. But I appreciate the information. No calls, right?"

Tony looked at me like he was insulted I would ask. "Hey," he said, "our secret. I'll be at sea tomorrow and no one hears from me for months."

I climbed back toward the bow and looked for Matt to wave at him, but he was no longer in the window. I turned and went down the gangplank, across the mole, and back to the Camaro and headed south on the Interstate. TJ was only twenty minutes away.

Mama Rose

Sometimes I make plans and they are good, and I feel clever enough to justify all the money the grandfathers pay me. I knew that killing the bar lady would just heat things up even more, so I told the boys to do something that looked serious, but didn't leave her dead. Not yet—we don't know enough. It was risky, but I wanted to buy a little time while it looked like I was still following directions, because in their eyes I am just their arms and legs—they make all the decisions for the Tong. I just do what they tell me to do. Mostly. They are the ones with the money.

Then I got the call from the grandfathers and I was happy. Big mistake, they said. "Don't do anything more!" they said. I knew this was a bad idea, to try to get rid of the bar lady so fast. People know her! I think the banker grandfather talked to somebody he knows, who knows somebody else—who gave us the contract for the lady that we put in a barrel. Now I get the call to say do not, for any reason, cause any problems for the lady who owns the bar. She cannot be a target. Fine. I should get paid twice for this one! Double happiness.

Then the phone rang again. *What now? Busy Friday!* "Embarcadero Souvenirs," I said.

"It's Tony."

Ah. "Yes?"

"I want to let you know, I just had a conversation with a Harbor cop, who came down to the *Lady Lynn*. He says he knows Matt Coelho, and he's hot to run down Paco. I don't think he is with the strike force; I think he's all worked up about the floater. I told him Paco's contact was the Striped Stallion, and that he'd be there tonight. I'm sure this guy is going straight down there, so if you want to take him out he's a sitting duck. Both the cop and Paco, if that's what you want. I'm supposed to ship out tomorrow. What do you want me to do?"

"You aren't shipping out until noon; that's the word on the docks. I want you to go down there and protect our interests. We have many friends in TJ, all the way to Port of Ensenada, if you need more people. But just watch and listen; don't let that cop become big trouble for us—find out what he learns from Paco, but we don't want the heat of a missing Harbor cop right now. I'll call some people for you so you have help if you need it. But don't screw up and don't start trouble with cops—not down there, not up here. Other things are going on that are more important. No trouble! Understand?"

I continued. "Paco should never have gone off. He should have stayed with you. Now he is attracting attention. We don't need attention. If anything goes bad, it goes bad for Paco. The grandfathers won't let it go bad or they end up in hot water. Very hot. You get me?"

He assured me he would go down to TJ—he'd been to the Striped Stallion many times, knew where the bar was and where the cop was headed, so it would be easy to listen and look. He said he'd let me know. That all seemed good to me. Maybe this time, there'd be no fuck-ups. Okay—closing time.

Phil

My wife had given me a handsome brass clock in a walnut case, and it sat across my office on a credenza by the far wall. It read six thirty. My office had some of the few windows in our build-ing, and I could see that the sun had already set. Fridays go by slowly, and things reached me late that should have made it earlier in the day. I knew my staff was out in the reception office working, as they never went home until I did, and I was feeling maybe a little guilty for holding everybody up. I knew that staring at the clock was not going to make its hands roll back to an earlier hour, so I turned back to the paperwork on my desk when the phone rang. My secretary told me the councilman was on the line. She didn't have to say which one.

"Simon Holier," I began, "you catch me trying to get a few last things done so I can go home to my family. Is there some-thing I can do for you?"

"I'm pretty sure there's going to be something I can do for *you*," he said, "and I want you to know that your people have been very good to work with. Better than the police. I got the permit, thanks to you for that, but I thought they were going to start putting the squeeze on that gal who owns the bar and makes the titty movies. And I'm getting a load of nothing from the cops about where they are and what's happening. Have you heard anything? What's going on?"

I involuntarily winced when he said "titty," but it occurred to me that I really didn't know what was going on, and what-ever the cops were planning was a total mystery. Yesterday, I'd heard the plan about Mona getting picked up by the cops and having it orchestrated for the evening news, but today... Gus had told me about her car accident, but only that it happened and that she wasn't seriously injured. I didn't really know what was going on, but I did know that we were running out of time.

Holier told me he got his permit—but what was he going to do with it?

"Are you still planning your big event on the waterfront tomorrow?" I asked.

"Damn straight, I am. This has been planned out to a 'T.' We are going to start a cleanup like this town hasn't seen in decades. They're already talking about it in today's papers, if you haven't seen. And I've got them ready to put this on the front page of the Sunday paper. Couldn't be better! They know the theme is 'The Big Cleanup,' but my spark for the event was going to be police action against that woman, and I've kept it quiet because—well, you know, I need it to happen. Nothing's happening yet. Sounds like you don't know anything, either."

"All I can tell you is that the Harbor Police have your event on the calendar for tomorrow. They'll be there to provide some security. I'm glad we were able to give you a discount on the permit fee, but that's where I get the funding for the Harbor Police team, so your discount is going to chew into my overtime budget. But you know that."

"And I appreciate it. You'll get something out of this. Redevelopment, and the big bucks that go with it. We'll have a project on the waterfront. You'll find the city will work seamlessly with your agency on some projects we both have an interest in. But I need action on that woman! And it's got to happen right away!"

"Don't tell me about it; that's not on my watch. I don't know anything about her," I said into the telephone, looking at the photograph of my wife on my desk.

"Well, for you it's easy, right? Your work is all done. For me it's just starting! We'll talk tomorrow." He hung up.

I put the receiver down softly in its cradle. I watched the sweep of the minute hand on my wife's clock across the office. Holier couldn't be more transparent. He only cared about how all this would look, and how he would build on it for his own career ambitions. Of course, Mona didn't even matter to him. But even though it was a long time ago, I'd be an even worse heel if I didn't try to help her. She did matter, and she'd suffered enough, and by God I wished there was something I could think of to do—but not something, of course, that would give my wife a clue. That life was far behind me, and the evening was wearing on. I had to get through this stack of paper so we could all go home. I hadn't heard from Gus in a few hours. What *was* going on?

Gary

It was a short, straight shot down Interstate 5 to where it dead-ended at the border crossing, but I knew to turn off on the exit before the gated entry to Mexico. I needed to get some pesos, and the banks had all closed hours ago. The commercial blocks of San Ysidro, on the cusp of the border, clustered along the side of the freeway and were jam-packed with shops and storefronts offering Mexican auto insurance and money changers, as well as the ubiquitous churros and chicharrón. I needed the money changers and automatically bought the insurance—but no churros for me.

Standing outside the shop on an early Friday night, I looked up and saw that the sky had already darkened. Bright neon lights in primary colors hung in the windows, flashing messages in Spanish and English: *Money Exchange! Cambio!* A steady stream of customers went in and out of the border stores, and the crowd of cars in front of the gates had thickened with people driving home from their work in the north. I got back in the Camaro and drove into the southerly stream. They say this is the busiest border crossing in the world—and tonight, it looked it.

I edged back out onto the freeway and thought about the crush of people headed south. Because my mother was Mexican, and she spoke Spanish to me at home, and I took classes in Spanish through high school (easy good grades for me), I was pretty bilingual, so I wasn't worried about communicating. But I *was* worried about what I was doing. I was surprised when the chief told me to check up on Matt and gave me a lead to follow on my own. On my own. What was that about? Off duty? Was it some kind of setup? I couldn't believe I was being set up by my own chief; we connect in too many ways. But there is a sense of paranoia you get from serving in country. Just because someone is in charge doesn't mean he is there to help you. I heard stories of officers in Nam whose days had ended more suddenly than was expected. Your own people could turn on you, I knew. But the chief, my dad, Mona—it couldn't all be for nothing. She was being chased, and the chief thought I could help find out what happened from this guy Paco, who apparently pulled the barrel out of the bay. We couldn't chase him to TJ officially. OK. I was on my way. The last thing I'd told Exeter was that I was going to the tuna boat to look for Paco. He was not going to figure I'd decided to cross the border south. I was kind of out on a limb, here.

I moved slowly closer to the gate. To the left, the gates manned by the Border Patrol guys were stacked way deep back into Mexico with drivers headed north. I could see on the other side of the gates the children selling Chiclets, churros, and stuffed dolls of Mickey and Minnie Mouse. Plaster Virgin Marys. The side going north went slowly, Border Patrol agents stopping each car to look inside.

I knew it was totally illegal to bring any firearms into Mexico, but my service revolver was in the glove box. This could land me personally in big-time trouble, and my department as well. I knew that. I drew closer to the gates. Why was I taking these risks? What was pushing me to try to run down some witness in a place that, let's face it, could be all kinds of dicey? I wouldn't be able to call for backup. I wasn't supposed to even *have* a weapon, let alone use it.

I looked to the left again—the border gates were a bottleneck behind which pooled a sea of cars, trucks, and vans headed north. I looked ahead. A stream of cars headed south. It was a little crazy for me to be going south, but somehow, this guy who disappeared after he pulled the barrel out of the bay was linked to the attack on Mona. Chief as much as said it. But it's TJ. Cars going north waited while the patient Border Patrol interviewed and peered at the occupants. Over and over.

"Where are you from? Got anything to declare?" The typical violator was probably a senior citizen bringing back a load of Chivas and Smirnoff at Mexican prices. The crowd going south, workers headed home and people out for a rousing night in TJ, went faster. I had a brief memory of lying next to Mona, naked, running my hand down her back, and then I got to the gate. The Mexican patrolman hardly looked at me as he waved me through.

Tony

I got across *la linea* early. Drove the Toyota pickup with the nets in the back down from the tuna boats in San Diego to the fleet in Ensenada. At least that's what I told them at the border. I go through all the time. No big deal. But I didn't go to Ensenada. I drove down Zona Río to Zona Este so I could pick up Avenida Revolución. The Striped Stallion was down there near Davila. Striped Stallion, my ass. Stupid reference to the painted mules that tourists sat on for photographs. The TJ Zebra. I drove past the bar and parked the pickup around the block. Not that anyone would want it. It was a beater with Baja plates. Held together by rust. No value.

It wasn't late—maybe seven. Night was falling and lights were on. Music was just starting. I slipped into the bar and went to the pay phone at the back. Not too many pesos. She picked up.

"Mama?" I said, as I have called her that since I was a teenager.

"You there now?" she said.

"Yeah, I'm in place. Nobody's here. I don't see Paco and the cop ain't made it down yet."

"Keep your eyes open, but stay out of sight. I want you to look, but nobody can see you, got what I mean?"

"Yeah, Mama, I got it."

"I called some people. They're going to come by for you.

They'll do whatever you say. They'll be there soon to meet up with you, but keep it very quiet. You understand?"

"Yes, Mama, I understand." Jeez, these old people can be slow.

"You look, you watch Paco, and if he is trying to play a game —it is his last game, you understand?"

"Yes, Mama, for cryin' out loud, I understand."

"And don't let the cop get fucked up, you understand? He has to come home or we have bigger problems. You understand?"

"Mama, I'm not Paco. I won't fuck up. I get it. I'm in the back. They'll never see me. I'll wait and let you know what happens, OK?"

"You're not so bad, Tony. Almost Chinese. I'm counting on you."

Gary

Even though it was nighttime, it was still warm. I cranked down the windows on my Camaro and leaned an elbow out as I drove slowly down Zona Río toward downtown. Music was coming from different sources: a blaring radio from a storefront, a live quartet with a trumpet from a bar, people spilling out of lit buildings onto the sidewalks, full of life for the beginning of Friday night. I stopped at a stoplight and asked some people through my window where I could find the Striped Stallion. One of them said I should go south and then east a block more. "*Gracias.*" I nodded, and drove farther once the light changed. The people in TJ were either vivacious and energetic or they were shuffling around wrapped in serapes and looking like they were on their last legs. Both types were out tonight. Some rich kids in Corvettes and plenty of rusty old Volkswagens and pickup trucks. Just crossing was all it took to remind you it was a different world. People might be the same, but the environment was different. Less formal, less orderly, and in less good repair. Things were just generally more broken down.

I found the bar and parked on the street in front, thinking that the more obvious it was, the better off the car would be. Several young men, my age and younger, were sitting stooped on the street corner across from the bar, smoking cigarettes, open cans of beer between them. I felt their gaze on me as I locked my car and headed over to the bar.

The Striped Stallion made Mona's place look like the club she always called it. The Stallion was no club. The front entry was a pair of winged shutters, like cantinas in an old western. I pushed through and tried not to be too obvious about taking in the scene. It looked like I was the only Norte Americano in the joint. Back in high school I must have gone in and out of TJ a hundred times or more—but that was a lifetime ago. Now it felt like the foreign land it was.

The bar was already half full, with guys wearing cowboy hats sitting at round tables, and some guys at the bar dressed in the remains of what looked like old American military uniforms. Cigarette smoke hung in the air. A busty young woman in a white flouncy blouse was delivering an order of beer off a serving platter. She looked up at me as I came through the door. So did a couple of the other patrons, but only for a glance; I didn't make much of a ripple in the murmuring Spanish conversations going on around me. There were a couple of pool tables in a back room with some young toughs in white T-shirts shooting under lowered fluorescent lighting, and they ignored me completely.

I moved slowly over to the bar. It ran the length of the room, and if I sat down at the far end I could swivel the stool around and see who was coming and going. There was a pay telephone at the other end of the bar, near the pool tables, and I could keep an eye on it perfectly. I ordered a Dos Equis and quietly looked over the people in the place. I could see most people and more in the bar mirror, but there were a few way in the back behind the pool tables beyond my vision. I'd only seen Paco once, last Monday, but he and I had talked and I'd gotten a good look at him. He wasn't in the Striped Stallion. Maybe I should have asked that guy, Tony, to call him and tell him to meet me. Maybe it was a little crazy to think that if I just went to his contact spot I'd find him. But Tony seemed to think that was exactly what would happen, and I felt sure that if Paco heard I was looking for him, I wouldn't find him. So I stayed, sat there, sipped my beer and waited. The flouncy barmaid brought me some tortilla chips and *salsa roja*.

Over the next two hours, I watched three guys and a couple of girls (one who was definitely working for a living) use the telephone, but none of them even looked like Paco. I had another beer; nobody tried to talk to me and I just kept my eyes open.

Around ten or ten thirty the swinging doors pushed open, and out of the corner of my eye I saw another guy, kind of shabby, amble over to the telephone and feed it some pesos. He had his back to me, but I could see he was talking. He was an energetic talker—jabbing with his hands to emphasize things he said. Someone on the phone must have told him that he might have picked up a tail, because he stopped talking and looked around the bar, and he and I connected eye to eye. We had only looked at each other face to face for a minute or two Monday morning, but we knew each other. He'd made me. His demeanor changed abruptly when he saw me, and he said a few more things and hung up the phone.

Then he walked over to the bar where I was sitting, very confident in his stride, if slow paced. The stool next to me was empty, and he climbed right up on it and smiled at me. He had a gold incisor. "*¿Qué onda wey? ¿Cómo estás?*" he asked.

"*Hola*. I've been looking for you, Paco."

"Why are you looking for me? And how do you know to look here?"

I had been considering what to tell him as I nursed my beer.

I thought I'd throw him a shocker to put him off balance. "I talked to your buddy Tony. He told me this is where you come to call in to him."

"Bullshit, Tony didn't tell you nothing like that. He wouldn't talk to you, cop. How did you find me?" His tone was distinctly less friendly.

"Hey, you don't want to listen, fine. But let me tell you something—when you flee from a crime scene it leaves you looking guilty. What are you guilty of, Paco? Why did you disappear after you hauled that barrel out of the bay? Now your buddies are getting ready to sail off for tuna and make some good money, leaving you behind in TJ. Why's that?"

Paco stared back at me defiantly. His face shifted as he chewed on my news. "You think you're smart, *omes*, but you ain't. You are in my place now. Why you looking for me? You don't get to push me around here. You ain't no cop here." Then Paco turned around and talked to the guy sitting one stool over, dressed in fatigues with an Army cap that said García on the name tag. "You hear what he says, *ese*?" The guy in the Army hat turned from the conversation he was having with another guy in fatigues next to him and gave me an eye. "No *mames*," he said, "this guy is a cop?"

He slipped one stool closer to sit next to Paco on a stool that had been empty. The guy he was with shifted over to the stool the first guy had just left. Now they were kind of crowding in on me. The three of them were all peering at me, and I was starting to feel that kind of fizzy buzz in my head that I've had since the war. It comes on me when I get tense, or worried that something bad is coming.

"What is it you want to know, cop?" Paco asked me.

"I'm not a cop here, Paco. I'm here to try to help a friend. I'm just trying to find out who is threatening her. I know that's not you—you've been down here in TJ since Monday, right? I just want information."

"What friend are you talking about?"

"Her name is Mona. Mona Oakheart."

He squinted. "Mona who? I don't know nobody named Mona."

"Did you know about the card they found on the body of the woman in the barrel?"

"What card? I don't know anything about a card. The *chica* in the barrel had nothing, man, just a dress."

That made me stop and think. "How do you know? You weren't even there—you split before the barrel got popped open. What's up, Paco? Who are you covering for?"

Paco stared back at me, his dark eyes expressionless, and then he smiled, showing his gold tooth. "I tell you what—I give you the whole story, man, I tell you all about it. But you got to buy us all a beer and," Paco turned to the bartender who was staying away from us at the other end of the bar, "we need a round of tequila reposado, *comprende*?, for my amigo. No, *todos*, we need a round for everybody—give the bill to my friend here." He looked at me. "*Problemo*?"

"*No problemo*." My scalp was tightening. There was an increasing sense of menace falling on me, and I figured if buying a round of drinks lightened up the tone it would be good.

Four bottles of Dos Equis appeared, one in front of each of us, and we all took a swallow. Then the bartender came back with a serving tray that held four shot glasses of amber tequila, and Paco picked them up one by one and carefully placed one in front of each of us. Paco picked up his glass, took it down in a gulp, and nodded to me—"drink it, ese, and I'll tell you the story." I took it in a shot, then turned to look at him.

"I don't know nothing about no *chica* named Mona. Never met her. Don't know why anyone is threatening her. How is that happening *norte*, where everything is so squeaky clean?"

I tried to sort out my thoughts about how I could approach this. "Paco," I said, "why did you run after you pulled the barrel out?"

"I tell you what, *omes*, I didn't stick around for the cops because I knew what was in the barrel."

I didn't expect that. "How'd you know that?"

"Because I helped put that girl in it!" He laughed and slapped his hand on the bar. The two guys sitting next to him didn't smile. I noticed that the bar had somehow emptied out of most of the drinkers sitting at tables. "I heard that they found that card on her. Not good, eh? Bad thing to find card on a dead body. You know she got no fingertips?"

I nodded, and the movement sent trails behind my eyes. "We cut off the fingertips so they can't know who she is. Smart, eh? But then they find a goddamned card on her. *Puta*. You know why she came to San Diego? She told me, because she thought I would feel sorry for her and stop cutting off her fingers." Paco leered at me. "You know what—I enjoyed cutting off her fingers. A little screaming makes me horny. It was all good for me, but not so much for her."

At this point it looked like Paco started swaying—and he was getting bigger. Was he growing? Something weird was going on and I was getting hazy... Paco looked at me, probably assessing how fucked up I was—because now I felt it. Some shit in that shot. He'd slipped me something. I couldn't get my mind focused—I kept thinking about the fingertips. And it occurred to me, slowly through the thickening fog, that Paco was essentially making a full confession to me. That couldn't be good. I realized my limbs weren't responding to my mind—and now what was disquiet became full-fledged dread.

Then I noticed that three of the guys who had been outside, stooped on the sidewalk, were now walking through the wing doors of the bar. Purposefully. They were walking toward us. The last two tables emptied out. One of the street guys was holding a sweatshirt in his hand. In my peripheral vision, I saw the group of young toughs at the pool tables slip out through some back door. The place was empty. I tried to stand up from the stool to put my back against the wall, but my arms didn't want to move. I felt like I was swimming in molasses. The guy with the sweatshirt came up to Paco and held it out to him. There was something under the sweatshirt. Paco reached out and his hand came back with—oh shit—my service revolver! I had replaced the grips with Pachmayr aftermarket grips; I'd know that Model 10 anywhere. And I could see it was loaded. I had left a box of rounds in the glove box.

Paco hefted the pistol in his hand. "This feels good, bro. Nice weight." He sighted along the barrel and pointed it here and there in the bar. I was fighting to get off the stool and turn so I could draw my backup pistol, but my body wasn't responding, not even in slow motion, like in a nightmare where you're trying to run but your legs aren't going anywhere. Except I wouldn't be waking up from this one.

"You have a nice car, *omes*, so I think we take a ride. I tell you the story, like I promised. But it has to stay with you, *sí*? I can't have you telling it, you know? That would be very bad for me. Let's go for a ride in beautiful Mexico." The two guys sitting next to him slid off their stools and came over, hustling me off my stool and onto my feet. My bad leg was frozen solid and wouldn't move. They grabbed my upper arms and essentially took on my weight, lifting me. I felt like it took all of my energy just to move my legs back and forth; I could hardly hold myself up.

Paco nodded at them and they braced up against me. The guys from the sidewalk circled us. Paco laughed again. "Funny thing is, man, that now I think I know who this Mona must be. While I am using garden shears on her fingertips and my fun is just starting the lady is crying at me, says she came back to do a good deed. She wants mercy so she can deliver her message to someone who she hurt. She begs me to spare her life for this— so that she does something good in the eyes of God, she says. But I am no priest. I don't give a shit what she was doing. I just got a job to do and people who pay me to do it. That's me, gringo—I do my job and take care of bad shit. She was bad shit to someone, no matter how she talks. No matter who she gets a message from and who she is supposed to give it to. And now I think that somebody might be this broad you're telling me about, Mona. She loses a couple fingertips, and then told me she knows where the bodies are buried, man, can you believe that? Like I care? That was the whole deal. She knows where the bodies are buried. Shit—I gave her a speedball after we finished with her fingers and having fun with her. I didn't want her to feel the water coming in, man. That would be hard. I would hate that."

Through my fog and stupor I heard what he was saying, and I understood him to be telling me he thought the floater had come to give Mona a message about where the bodies are buried. *Jesus, Mary, and Joseph*. Was he saying the floater knew where Mona's "bodies"—her daughter among them—were buried?

"Wh-wh-where?" I managed to croak out.

"In a church, *ese!* Where else!" Paco laughed again, slapping his hand on the bar. Then he stood up in front of me, but I was gripped by the two in Army fatigues. Between them and the mickey he'd slipped me, I was immobilized. He got up right in my face. "Capilla del Perpetuo Socorro." Then he smiled a wicked smile. "Maybe we'll go leave some more bodies there, you know? It's the place for it."

Then the two goons holding me up jerk-walked me toward the door, and Paco got behind us, with my own damn pistol pointed down at my legs. "Start walking, *wey.*" The bar was empty, no bartender, no girl in a flouncy blouse, and no customers in sight—they'd all disappeared at the signs of trouble that I was too slow to pick up on. The bar was quiet and I was lurched forward because my own legs weren't doing the job—but I was sure if I let my eyes close like they wanted to, I likely wouldn't ever open them again.

It was an interminable passage across the empty floor to the wing doors. Everything seemed deathly quiet. I could hear the men beside me breathing as they lugged me along. They pushed aside the doors and drew me forward. I hoped there might be someone outside on the street that I could somehow signal. But I didn't think I could mouth a word. The outside air seemed as still and dense as the air inside the cantina. The street was empty—not at all what I remembered from downtown TJ on a Friday night. No innocent bystanders. My orange Camaro was across the street where I'd left it, but I could see that the driver's-side wind wing was busted out. Damn it—they'd busted into my car! They *were* going to kill me! I figured I had nothing to lose; I had to try to get the gun out of Paco's hand. My legs were working—I just couldn't control them. My arms ought to work, but I couldn't chance flexing them while being held.

Tiring of carrying me, the goons were now relying on me holding some of my own weight. Still no one out on the street so I could somehow make a scene—maybe they'd call for help, I don't know. I didn't have a better plan. They pulled me out onto the street toward my car, and I could see Paco was looking up and down the street; he wasn't looking at me. The pistol was pointed into my thigh.

Shit, I thought, *I've been shot in the leg before and lived through it. Maybe if I can grab the gun it'll go off, or if I don't he'll shoot me somewhere I can live with—and someone will hear it.* I knew it was not much, but it was all I had. Once they got me in the Camaro, I was toast.

As soon as I saw Paco swivel his head to check the other direction down the street I slowly drew a deep breath, and while the goons were content I was under control, I put everything I had into twisting around. They were surprised, their grip slipped, and I did get around. Paco looked immediately up at me and started to raise the hefty revolver, no doubt to hit me in a deadlier spot than my legs, but I had just enough control to swing my hand around and slap his, knocking it to the side and causing the pistol to discharge. I followed through on my twist as I slipped out of their grip and fell onto Paco with my full weight. The pistol discharged a second time—but harmlessly out to the side. The unexpected noise and mess must have slowed the reaction time of the goons and their car-wrecking helpers, but I knew to expect a boot in the back any moment, and tensed myself for the impact. I curled on top of Paco, who started to push me off of him.

There wasn't much I could do to resist, and then a pair of arms pulled me up. I was still slow with the drugs in me, but I tried to turn to protect myself, assume a defensive stance, when I saw that Paco's buddies and two of the three guys who came from the street were all lying on the ground. At least five or six of the tough young guys from the pool tables were standing over them, holding pool cues, spinning them in their hands as though they were more than just pool cues. They looked at each other, and then at the guy who pulled me up—obviously some kind of leader, a young guy; he looked Chinese. Not odd; there are a lot of Chinese living in northern Mexico, at least since the last century. He turned to me and asked in Spanish if I was all right. Paco still stayed on the ground, sitting with his hands behind him, looking at the scene.

"Ugh," I managed to grunt. "No, *malo*." I took a breath; my lungs were working again. "But thanks. I think you saved my ass. Who are you?"

"Hmmm, no matter. We were just playing pool; we saw you were in trouble and had to help, you know? So—we help. Can you drive home?"

"I don't think so." The pins-and-needles feeling in my legs was receding. "But I'm getting better. Ten minutes ago I couldn't even talk. Now I think I might be able to stand up."

"I tell you what, man. You sit in your car for a while until you can drive. I'll get them to bring you a *cafecito*."

My mouth was dry but beginning to work again. "Make sure they don't put anything in it!"

He couldn't have been older than his early twenties, black

hair combed straight back, white T-shirt like his friends—all local guys, apparently. Then I spotted a figure standing to the side in a connecting alleyway. He was standing there, watching, but I couldn't make out who it was, even though he seemed somehow familiar. Had I seen him before? I was still foggy.

The young guy turned back to me and smiled. "Don't worry," he said. "I don't think you are dying tonight." Then he nodded at the figure in the shadows by the side of the bar and turned to talk to the others. They had already pulled the fallen men out of the street and frisked them for weapons. A couple of them were recovering and were apparently allowed to skip. Paco scuttled backwards on the ground and then flipped over and stood up. He looked ready to run when I heard the figure in the alley call to him, and he froze in his tracks.

"Paco. Come with me," said the voice.

There was a familiar quality to the voice, I thought I knew it, but it was not loud enough for me to hear well, and my head was still thick with the effects of whatever it was they'd slipped me. Thankfully, it was fading, and one of the pool players came out with a mug of coffee, helped me into my car, and left me there, nursing the hot mug. Just then I heard what I thought was a muffled gunshot, and when I looked back up at the alley, Paco and the guy in the shadows were nowhere to be seen.

Within seconds, the street was empty. No toughs, no pool players, no partygoers stumbling into another bar. While I drank my coffee, though, a couple did walk into the bar. Minutes later, the jukebox started up again. I patted my pockets and found my keys. I looked across at the dashboard. The glove box had been opened with a pry bar. It was never going to be pretty again. My service Smith & Wesson was on the front seat, although I hadn't seen anyone put it there. I finished the coffee and realized it was after midnight. Friday was over and I'd better get back.

6

SATURDAY

Gary

Thankfully, the Camaro started right up. The street was still showing signs of people, even though it was in the earliest hours of the morning. It was a deep black night—not so many streetlights in TJ. I cautiously motored out into the street and headed left to hook up with the big boulevard, Avenida Revolución, so I could get back to the crossing. The air was hot and dry. I rolled down the windows and let it wash in, glancing down at the empty triangle that used to be the wind wing. *Assholes.*

Crossing the border north at this hour was easy. No huge crowds, although the kids hawking Chiclets were still around. They were an older group; the youngsters must all be asleep. It took less than five minutes of idling up to the gate, where the bored border guy gave me a glance.

"Someone break into your car?" he asked me.

"Yeah, good thing I had insurance. I have nothing to declare." The guard waved me through and like that, I was back in the USA. As I drove out onto the five-lane freeway that leads straight north, the air in my face helped me wake up, and my brain shook itself off and started working again. If I believed Paco, he'd tortured and then killed the talent agent because he was paid to do it. So—who paid him? And why? And if he was the guy who killed her, how the hell was he also the guy who pulled the barrel out of the bay, right by the *Lady Lynn*—sort of pointing directly right back at him?

Going back over the night, I was gripped by uncertainty about the message Paco had "intercepted." The dead agent was supposed to tell Mona (she was carrying Mona's card, wasn't she?) something about "where the bodies are buried"? Paco did not think that was a metaphor. If there were buried bodies, could they be...from the kidnapping? How would the agent know about that?

I felt like I was filling in blanks, but that there were big holes in what I knew. What, for example, did my dad have to do with any of this? And why didn't the chief just share the whole story? I knew he was holding something back, and he had to know that he was sending me on a chase that would lead me into Mexico. Being on the strike force, he had to know Paco had skipped south. Why'd he let me—hell, why'd he *lead* me—to track him down? So many different questions were bouncing around, it was almost as dizzying as the mickey.

I was anxious to talk to Mona, but I needed to get a little rest. Thank God it was Saturday and I was off work, though I was sure the chief was going to want to hear from me. I was less sure what I should tell him.

It was almost three in the morning, so I turned off the freeway and headed up toward Kensington and my casita.

Gus

Christ, I hadn't heard anything from Gary. If I sent him into something bigger than what he could handle, I'd never forgive myself. And probably a few other people wouldn't forgive me, either. I still felt, though, that it was the right thing to do, because I was keeping my promise to a dead man—but one who I owed. Still, I let Gary put himself at risk. This was all spinning out of hand, maybe out of control. I wanted to know who was doing what, and once I'd heard that Mona was threatened, I couldn't leave it alone. The boss never had to tell me what to do—I knew what had to be done, now and before. I'd man up and cover for everyone.

Gary was my best shot at getting me some inside information. I hoped. Meanwhile, I had another angle on trying to undo this mess that, let's face it, I guess I created. Hansen had been dead for years, and here I was taking all kinds of risks to keep a promise to a dead man and protect his buddy the boss. Was it the code of honor we learned in the streets growing up? Was it the morality I learned from the priests who taught at St. Augustine? It's basically hell to be a good Catholic.

I glanced at my watch. It was about three thirty in the morning. Dark outside, but not cold. Sunrise in about three hours. I was sitting in the shadows on a bench across from the parking lot for the County Administration Building. I watched the big wooden *Star of India*, tied up at the bulkhead along Harbor Drive, floating in the bay, its old painted masts moving gently in the swell. I waited for my old friend, Sticks.

Alonzo and I had been street punks together in National City in the forties. The Navy was king then—they were selling old equipment, dumping what they didn't need any more right into the bay, often enough. Or burying it over. Alonzo was raised first in Hong Kong, so he could speak Mandarin and Cantonese when he was just a kid. Selling old Navy equipment (however he got it) led him into a Toyota car dealership, which led to a new Volkswagen dealership. He was very good with money, very connected. With everybody.

Once I'd matched those prints for the director, we both knew that Mona's talent agent was really Freddie. Back, just as Hansen knew he would come someday. The director had wanted to think about what to do. He was obviously wrestling with calling the cops so they could grab Freddie, despite what it would do to him and his family. But I knew that he would end up taking heat he shouldn't have to face. I did what I thought I had to do. I took it on myself to call Alonzo. Privately. One ex-street punk buddy to another. "I'll be straight with you," I told him. "This can't come back. I just want this evil shitbird to disappear—forever. He may look like a woman, but he's got the fingerprints of a kidnapper with ice in his veins. Send him to Antarctica, I don't care. What do you need from me to make that happen?"

Sticks didn't play games with me. He was already too rich and we went back too far. "Can you come up with twenty G's?" he said. "I think that's what it's going to take."

I knew where I'd get the money. "Not a problem. Put it up, get it started. I've got a source and I'll cover you in a day or two. I don't want to know anything about it—just get rid of this person. I owe you."

"We owe each other," he'd said.

That's how I ended up sitting on the bench in the early morning hour and considering how things had gotten to this point. It struck me that there had to have been interventions for it all to have come out like this. Like, divine interventions, you know? Now it was my turn. Alonzo was supposed to meet me here and he was a little late, but not much, because there he was.

"Hey, *hombre*," Alonzo said in his best Clint Eastwood voice, sitting next to me on the bench in the shadows, "things got pretty fucked up here."

"You think you can fix this?" I asked him.

"Yeah. I got the guys waiting, just like we talked. But you don't meet them and they don't meet you. You got what we need?"

I had explained to Alonzo that, as chief of the Harbor Police, my duties included fire protection on the bay, and of the public structures alongside the bay. As one of the authorized law enforcement responders, I had the master key that would get entry into public buildings in times of emergency. That key worked for the County Administration Building, and the morgue that was in the basement. I handed the key to him. "This isn't a copy; this is my official key. I need it back asap." Alonzo told me that the people he, *we*, hired, the Tong— whoever they were—were "good" for it. They didn't want more money. They knew they had to fix this problem.

"The team will be done before daybreak. I'll have them drop the key at your house. Do you still have a mailbox slot in the front door?" Alonzo had been to my little house in "Portuguese town" a couple of blocks north of Rosecrans, near Shelter Island.

"That'll be perfect," I said. As he rose to leave, I said, "So why did Oakheart get targeted? What the hell was going on?"

Alonzo paused. "I don't really know," he said. "The thing is, Stones, that everybody sees only their own little slice of the big picture. I got mine, you got yours. Nobody knows the whole of what's really going on. Nobody *can* know everything."

Enough damned philosophy, I thought. "It's good for her now, right? She's off the radar of whoever this was? No more threats?" I asked, even though he had assured me on a phone call hours ago that it was covered. He nodded and patted my knee. I stood up and walked away toward my car. Even though there were a few hours left to the early morning, I didn't think I'd get much sleep.

Exeter

Seven thirty in the morning! I definitely didn't need this phone call at my home on Saturday morning. My chief, who'd already talked on the phone with Councilman Holier, had to listen to the good councilman being pissed off because we'd never organized a perp walk with Oakheart for him yesterday. Holier thought I should do something, but this was never anything more than a staged press event, so I wasn't too excited. Holier's big "clean up the city" event wanted a photo of an arrest of a sex queen (give me a break) as its backdrop—but he never got his queen.

I explained to the chief, sitting in my boxers drinking coffee while my wife stared at me in her pink hair curlers, that we didn't pull the broad in because the picture was changing. She looked to have become the next target. I was going to go talk to her again today—but she was not looking as good for this as she did earlier in the week. "No," I told him, "she doesn't have any infractions at the bar we can pull her in for. No," I told him, "she doesn't have any community complaints from her movie biz. She was in the hospital yesterday—I don't think this is going to play out for the councilman just the way he wants. Yes," I told him. "I'll let you know."

My wife and I looked at each other for a second. "I got to go," I told her. "I won't be out all day—and I promise to be back in time for a date night, like we planned." We missed *The Godfather* when it opened last year, but it had come back to the Fox and I promised her dinner and a movie. She smiled at me wanly and told me she looked forward to it, then she picked up the coffee mugs with a clink and took them to the sink. The sooner I got going, the sooner I'd be done.

Showered and dressed, I climbed into my city ride and looked at my watch. Nine a.m. Not too early to surprise Miss Oakheart for some frank talk. She may not have done the deed, but I was sure she knew more than she was spilling. It occurred to me I might need something tangible to break through to her. I radioed in to the department and asked the desk sergeant to call detectives and have whoever was on call get down to the morgue and get me the written report. "The coroner told me his findings and said he had a report coming," I told him. "I think I am going to need it now. Have someone pick it up and meet me down in OB."

"Ten-four," he said.

We'd see what Oakheart had to say about her Patricia now that we knew she used to be a he.

I went to a little coffee shop on Newport Avenue to wait for a black-and-white to bring me the report. The couriers were supposed to bring it asap for my interview. All the while, I was considering what I wanted to get out of Oakheart and how the pieces would tie together. They were late, and I was drinking way too much coffee. I was getting a little anxious when my pager buzzed. I automatically dropped my hand to touch it on my belt, to reassure myself that it was buzzing. I was having trouble getting used to the thing, but it worked, and it had a message to radio in. I went back to my car.

"Exeter."

"Call your dispatch officer on the telephone, Lieutenant—there's something they have to tell you and it's an emergency which shouldn't go out over the air."

OK. So now I had to go back into the coffee shop and use the pay phone. I fed it a dime and then I remembered they need two. New thing. I called in. "What's up?"

"It's crazy, sir. We have two units down at the Administration Building. Morgue staff opened up and it appears they were robbed last night."

"Right. What did they want, a dead body?"

"Uh, yessir."

It clicked. "You're telling me someone pulled a corpse out of the morgue?"

"Yessir."

"The gal found floating in a barrel." It was a question, but it came out of my mouth like a statement of fact.

"Yessir."

"What about the report? The lab workups?"

"There's nothing there, sir. They're going through the place now. And no signs of a break-in. She's just gone, and all the files connected with her are missing. And that seems to be all that's missing."

"When did this happen?"

"We don't know, sir. Sometime last night."

"Get forensics down there and don't let the uniforms mess up the crime scene. Get some prints. Get whatever they can get. I need a copy of the report immediately. Got it?"

"Yessir."

I hung up and looked around the small coffee shop. No one was paying me any particular attention. This changed things. They probably wouldn't be able to hang this on the Oakheart dame. How would a bar owner spirit a body out of the morgue? I headed down to the morgue to see what I could see.

Mona

Horizontal. Floating back to consciousness. I lay in my bed under just a sheet, as it had been a warm night. The morning breeze, coolest breeze of the day, drifted in off the Pacific, swirling up gently over the cliff and across the little beachside community of OB. Over and through my little cottage, which snugged up right to the edge of the cliff. I was feeling pretty good; I didn't have a headache and I couldn't feel the stitches in my forehead. I looked at my belly, and I could see the bruises from my seat belt had started to turn from an ugly purple to a dark brown.

I lay back and felt the breeze, wondering what the day would bring. Anybody's call.

When the phone broke my train of thought, I looked at the clock and saw it was already eight in the morning. The cops, the studio, Gary...?

"Hi, Mona," said Gary. I felt a huge wash of relief, which almost embarrassed me. *Jesus*, I thought. *I've only known this guy a couple of days and he's already starting to fill my mind.*

"Hey, Gary." I paused, almost afraid to ask. "How'd it go for you last night?"

"We have stuff to talk about. Can I come over?"

"Yeah, I'd like to see you. I want to know what happened."

"Give me twenty minutes," he said, and hung up. As I showered, I thought about what I should wear, rejecting my short silk French robe, or tap shorts and a halter top—shit, I might as well have put on a bikini. In the end, I put on a casual blouse and my bell-bottomed jeans. We probably still had some ground to cover.

He knocked on the door right after I got the percolator going. The smell of coffee filled the cottage. I opened the door. It was a surprisingly awkward moment. I wanted to hug him, but I wasn't sure that was the best way to say hello.

"Hi," he said. And he reached out and took my hand in his as though he was going to shake it, but instead he brought his other hand up and held my hand in both of his. My breath caught. "Let's go sit down—we need to talk," he said, and dropped my hand to walk into my living room and sit on the couch. I didn't know what to think.

I closed the front door. "Coffee?"

He patted the couch next to him. "Later," he said. "I was out late. Got back just a few hours ago. I've been tossing and turning since then. No sleep for a couple of hours, because we have to talk. I want to share what I know with you, and," he looked at me, "I want you to share what you know with me."

"OK," I answered, and sat down on the couch, but at the other end, leaving a little space between us.

He looked at my face, and my bandaged forehead. "How are you feeling?"

I tore the bandage off to show him my stitched-up cut. Four stitches. I lifted the hem of my blouse, which I wore outside my jeans, and he could see a little of the bruises from where the seat belt had dug in. "I'm fine," I said. "How are you?"

He sighed and told me, "It's been a night. And today might end up being one hell of a day, from what they're telling me."

"What are they telling you?"

"I've heard that Holier, the councilman—you know him, right?"

I nodded. I listen to the radio, even if I don't read the papers.

"There is some kind of big deal he's going to make to clean up San Diego. Sex, drugs, crime, whatever. He is starting a campaign to make everyone happier with downtown."

"I didn't know anyone was unhappy with downtown," I said.

"*He* is. Maybe he figures it's his pathway to become the mayor. The governor. The whatever."

"What's this have to do with me?"

"He had some kind of deal set up so that the cops were going to arrest you, or at least herd you into a black-and-white, and the whole thing was supposed to be staged for the press."

I looked at him quizzically. "Wow. Whoa. What do *I* have to do with anything?"

"His plan ties you into the murder of that talent agent I found floating in the bay, as a result of your evil involvement with the sex business—through your front, the movies, no doubt—and your ownership of a downtown bar where nefarious things happen. You get picked up, and, let's face it, you're a pretty attractive person to be on anyone's front page. You, the cops, a story full of sex and murder. Sounds like a total winner. They'll probably try to close down all your businesses to preserve morality."

I thought about the years I'd spent trying to get the club in shape, and the money I'd poured into making the movies to make something. "Whoa," I said again, softly. "I'm screwed. How'd you learn about this? Who all is into this plan?"

"I got it yesterday. Jim Exeter told me about most of it. I made some of it up—but I can see it happening."

"Exeter! He's a snake. I saw him yesterday at the hospital, but he never told me about any of this crap."

"I'm not too sure Exeter is all snake. He told me. And he has kind of figured out that telling me means telling you. And the big arrest of the beautiful star criminal didn't happen yesterday, did it?"

"Where does that leave me? What do *I* do?" I asked him, starting to feel a little fearful. The walls of my little cottage living room seemed to shrink in around me. I sat still next to him on the couch.

"Hold on. There's more." He stopped talking and closed his eyes for a moment, as though he was rearranging his thoughts. "There are big holes in what I know, but I know who killed the lady agent, and I know why."

I was immobilized with shock and dread. "What do you know?"

"She was killed by a deckhand on the *Lady Lynn*. This part is crazy—but she was killed by the same guy that pulled her out of the water where she was found floating in the barrel."

"What? How do you know this?"

"He told me. Right before he tried to kill me. And he told me why."

I closed my eyes, not knowing what I would hear. My thoughts about someone trying to kill Gary, and the story he was telling me, got jumbled. "What?"

"He was paid to do it. It was a contract hit. The thing I don't know is who paid him."

I took a minute to take this all in and think about it. "He tried to kill you?"

"It's a long story and kind of crazy. I got a lead to him through another deckhand, a guy named Tony." He stopped abruptly. "OK, I have to ask you something. Straight up. You didn't pay this guy to kill the agent, did you?"

"Wha-a-t?" I looked at him, bug eyed. "Do you think I *paid* someone to kill a person...?"

His face was serious. "I am just asking you direct. Did you

pay money—or do you know someone who did? Someone did."

Jesus. If Gary was willing to believe I made a deadly call about Patricia, then I guessed it was not so far out that Exeter was sniffing around. "No, Gary. I didn't pay to have anyone killed. I didn't *ask* to have anyone killed. I don't *know* anyone who would have someone killed. *No one.* Why are you asking me this?"

"Because there is a connection. There is a connection between this talent agent and the kidnapping of your daughter. The deckhand who admitted killing her told me so."

"He admitted?"

"He didn't think it was going to matter—and I figure he wanted to distract me so I wouldn't notice what he was doing, which was setting me up for a hard fall. But he admitted he was paid to kill the gal who told you she was an agent. And he told me more." Gary took a breath, then went on. "He said that the talent agent had come to see you with a message. A message about the kidnapping, I think. She didn't say anything to you? Nothing that made you suspicious she had some connection?"

We came to a hard stop in the conversation. I thought about what he'd asked me, looking straight into his candid brown eyes. How'd I get so tangled up? Here's this guy who seems to care about me. I think I care about him. Now he's taking risks and even though he's kind of a cop, I think he's doing things he isn't supposed to. I'm moved. What can I tell him?

"I'm going to tell you all I can tell you, Gary." I turned away and looked at the wall in front of me. "When Patricia Peteaut called for an appointment, I didn't think anything about it. But when we met, it was a strange meeting. She had all these shiny new photographs of her talent—but they looked like stock photos, head shots that she could have just bought someplace —brand-new prints. No bodies. Shiny finish like they just came out of the studio, just printed. It's just not what I'm used to seeing. Her letterhead said that she had an office in the Philippines. I get the same feeling Exeter does about the Filipino connection. My housekeeper and her dead husband were Filipino, and I heard talk of a Filipino connection with the kidnapping, but no one ever told me why or how. There you have it. It struck me as odd." I thought back and remembered sitting with her at my table in the studio office.

"She was dainty, petite, and spoke and acted like a female, but her hands, when she shook mine, and when she fanned out the photos on my table, looked strong and muscular. It was at odds with her appearance. I didn't think much about that, either, but she was unsettling. We agreed she would come in on Monday and bring some of her actors. When she stood to leave she walked to the door, opened it, and then turned and looked at me appraisingly, as though it had all been some kind of test. She said she was going back to her room at the Holiday Inn—you know, the big round tower by the freeway—but that she would see me on Monday. Then there was this look, and she paused, and made it sound really important."

I turned back and faced Gary. "She told me that she was bringing me a message from someone from a long time ago, a message that would *matter*, and she was going to be happy to share it with me. But before I could ask her about it she closed the door and left. That was that. It weirded me out. I had no idea what she was talking about—but it all seemed either like cornpone or just plain wrong."

I looked at him, listening intently. It felt good to tell the truth. "I've been in this business for a long time—and she left me feeling like she wasn't really here to get me new actors, but for something else. The Philippine connection felt creepy, after the Lazaragas. There was absolutely no one I felt I could turn to. I had to unload or I would burst. So I made a call. This I will tell you. The only call I have made to him in over ten years. And never since. Angela's father. I promised I would never say who he was, but I know he can get things done, things, and..." I paused, rethinking. "Never mind about him. I made a call." I looked him in the eye. "I made a call, told him what happened, and I was told to take a walk, leave the photographs on the table, and be out for an hour. That's all I did. That's all I *ever* did."

Gary

"You're not going to tell me who you called?"

"No, I can't. I promised. But Gary..." Her hazel-green eyes looked almost tearful. "I can tell you it was *not* your father. He's only been a gentleman and a help to me, the one time we met. Long ago. I've already said too much. Gary, forgive me."

It felt like a big hand around my chest just let go, and I realized that I had been holding my breath. "You made a phone call." She nodded, and looked at me from under lowered eyelashes.

"Whoever you called may have made another phone call. That could make you an accessory in the eyes of the DA."

"I have no idea what he did, other than that he was arranging to check the photographs, I suppose for fingerprints. I never thought anything would happen except maybe he would make a call to the cops if he figured out that there was a connection. I can't believe anyone ordered a hit."

"The hit man was real, and I believe what he told me. Somebody paid him. And he told me the message that the agent lady had for you."

"You mean there really was a message?" She seemed to go blank, as though she didn't know whether to be glad or frightened. "About what?"

"According to the hit man, the agent was going to tell you she knows where the bodies are buried."

She just looked at me. "What bodies...?" she asked, almost in a whisper.

"I'm guessing they are bodies that would mean something to you." I couldn't bring myself to be more direct. I watched her closely, to see how she was taking all of this. She was hard to read. I think she had kept things bottled up for a long time.

"And Paco told me where they are," I finished.

"Oh my God," she said. Her eyes widened and I heard her breath quicken.

I went on. "To tell you the truth, I'm not even sure Paco is still there, or even still alive. I haven't been able to sleep. I have to go back down there and check. He gave me the name of a church, and if it's real I can find it. I'm going to go back there now, and I'll call you if I find anything."

"There is no way you are leaving me here in this room while you go looking for my daughter by yourself. I'm going with you."

I thought about telling her that she should stay home and recuperate, then I thought of telling her the cops would be pissed if she went to TJ, then I thought of telling her how frustrating this would all be if it turned out to be a story, like I half expected. But instead I told her to get some good shoes, as I didn't know where we would be walking.

As we walked out to my car I told her, "Oh, and there's another thing you should know."

"Jeez, Gary, what else is there?"

"Exeter confirmed he's going to investigate your accident. I haven't been able to reach him to find out what he knows, but somebody may be trying to kill you. I'm going to leave a message for him and my boss to let them know I'll call when we get back."

Exeter

From Ocean Beach I turned around and went straight back downtown to the County Administration Building by the waterfront so I could take a look at the morgue. I parked on the lot right by the southern doors, now flanked by a pair of uniforms and four black-and-white units with lights flashing.

I badged them at the door, then went inside and downstairs to the basement. Two uniforms at the door; the coroner was standing there in blue jeans and a white shirt, looking very pissed.

"Tell them to let me in there," he said. "Right now!"

"Hold on, sir." I was extremely polite. I turned to the officer at the door. I didn't know him, but his badge said "Harrison." "How many people have been in there, Officer Harrison? Give me a rundown."

"I met with one of the—uh—doctors here at eight thirty to get the report that you called for. I was going to run it up for you. Doc was friendly, not too pissed about being asked to come down and get it out for us, and he opened the door with a key—there was no sign of a break-in. We two walked over to the trays on the reception counter that had the mail that was supposed to go out on Monday. The report was supposed to be in there, but he looked three times and couldn't find it. He and I both went to his office to see if it was somehow put back on his desk, but there he realized that the file with all the lab reports about the floater, which had been on his desk, was gone. Then we went in to check on the floater, and she was gone. Then I called it in, and they told me you wanted the scene closed until you got here. Sir."

I turned toward the coroner, who had been listening, and said, "Sir, could I please ask you to wait here while I do a quick reconnaissance, as I'm sure we are going to need our team of forensic specialists to go over this place with a fine-toothed comb. Literally."

"I just want to make sure nothing else is missing," he said.

"We're going to need you to do that, but please, your office is a crime scene now. Let's not lose any evidence, OK?"

I took only a few steps into the reception area, and I left the door open so that the coroner could look in as well. Everything looked very tidy. Nothing out of place. No dirt on the floor, which was still shiny from an end-of-the-week waxing. I backed out. "The forensic team is on route—they should be here soon. I called for them while driving over. Let's close it up for now." I turned to the coroner. "Can we go find an office that isn't part of this crime scene, where we can call my boss and let him know what's going on?"

We marched up the big, stained mahogany staircase to the first floor, where the tax collector had his offices. The coroner told me that there were always people working in here on the weekends, and when he knocked, the frosted glass door opened quickly. He talked quietly, and the clerk backed up and waved us to a room that was empty of people, but had a desk and a telephone.

"Come on with me," I said to the coroner, "in case there are questions you can handle better than I can."

I called in to Nancy, the administrative assistant to the chief of police. I knew he was taking heat about this case becoming the star attraction for the city's big anti-smut event this evening, and I thought he ought to know these developments right away. I wasn't surprised to find her in the office. I told her to call our boss and read off the number he should call me at. "Don't worry about pestering him; he's going to want to talk to me."

The phone rang within minutes. I picked it up.

"Exeter," I said.

"What?" He put a lot into that one word. It was clearly telling me I had better have something worth having him called at home on Saturday morning. Not to worry.

"We've had an incident at the morgue," I told him. I was met with silence.

"Somebody got in here and stole a body, along with an autopsy report."

"Somebody broke into the morgue and stole a body?"

"There's a first time for everything," I said. "But this one gets worse." I took a breath. "It's the floater. Which I know was going to be a big deal for Councilman Holier and his plans for today." I didn't have to say more. I had his full attention. "There's more you haven't heard yet. Last night, I got a verbal report from the coroner," I glanced up across the desk to where he sat, ramrod straight in an oak chair, "and it was surprising. Apparently the floater was not a woman. Or at least, was not born a woman. The coroner told me she'd had some kind of sex change operations. But now she's gone. Or he is. There was a complete report with details, but it's gone, too." I looked up at the coroner, who was watching me. I asked him, so the chief could hear, if there was anything he wanted to add, but he shook his head no.

"This is all we have right now, Chief. But I think we got to keep this buttoned up while we figure out what is going on. I don't want the press all over the fact that the floater wasn't born a woman, or that the body is gone. I don't think that's good for anybody. You got to talk to Holier and get him off of this. This is no time to be going to the press with what we have—and what we don't have. I know this is above my pay grade, sir, but I wanted you to hear from me as soon as I got the lay of the land. I have a tech crew coming down to go over the scene, but I'm telling you—it looked clean. It didn't look like there was much there."

"I think you're right, Lieutenant. This can't be turned into a media circus now. I'll call Holier. Keep me informed if you learn anything. Let me know if you need more resources." There was a pause at his end. "Are you alone?" he asked. I looked up and asked the coroner if he could step out and let me have a word in private with the chief. He readily left and I let the chief know.

"There's a Joint Strike Force operating in the bay for the last few months. Drugs coming in on B-52s, they think. Feds. NCIS. Us. Others. Top secret. Need-to-know *only*. They were very unhappy to hear that Councilman Holier was going to have a big press event about this floater to kick off his smut stuff. Very. They're trying to conduct an undercover operation and the good councilman is trying to put it on TV to score points. I don't know how the floater is connected to their investigation, but they were looking for a way to close down Holier's plans. They'll be happy to hear about this. Except, of course, that they won't be. Who the hell took the body? Get back to me, Exeter. As soon as you can."

I hung up and looked at my watch. *Damn!* It was practically noon already. I figured I'd head back to OB even without the reports, and see what *Mizz* Oakheart had to say for herself.

Mona

It's funny, but I think I've been to Tijuana only once or twice in all the years I've lived in San Diego. It just wasn't a place I traveled to regularly, even though plenty of girls from Tijuana were in my movies. I was busy with work; they came to me, I didn't go to them. I really didn't get far past my little circle of the downtown club, the Kearny Mesa studio, and my OB home. It's like a triangle that surrounds me, but I don't even notice it's there; I just go from one station to the other.

Now here I was, sitting in Gary's high school ride, a flashy orange Camaro, driving through OB and headed for the freeway. I asked Gary what happened to his car—the wind wing was busted out completely, and the glove box was closed with duct tape. He told me not to worry about it. Right. This he shares with me right after he tells me that somebody is trying to kill me. I wasn't even going to try to figure it out. It didn't make sense, but in this world, little does.

Within minutes we were on the freeway headed south, the wind whistling noisily past the gap where his little triangular window used to be. I had to speak up. "You said 'hard fall'?" I asked him. "What happened?"

"I went to a bar in TJ to try to find out why you were being targeted. My boss suggested I talk to a deckhand at the *Lady Lynn,* and that's where it led me. The lead was to the guy who pulled the barrel out of the bay, a guy named Paco. I went down to brace him, but he distracted me with his story while he put something in my drink. I guess. Some kind of drug. I was paralyzed, practically, and he was going to have me killed and dumped somewhere."

He glanced over at me, my eyes wide open and staring at him. Maybe he could see that this story had petrified me. He kept talking. "At least, that's what I thought was going on. I made a desperate move that never could have worked, but all of a sudden these guys showed up and whupped the crap out of my goon squad. They said they saw me in the bar and just wanted to help, but I don't know. Really? I am alive now only because they helped me." At this remark I felt another sharp pang of fear. Gary went on, "I don't know what happened to Paco—somebody walked him off somewhere after he tried to croak me. I think I heard a gunshot; I don't know if Paco got away or what. I thought I might have known the guy who called Paco over to him, but...hell, my head was still fuzzy from the mickey. Once I tell Exeter what Paco told me, law enforcement will reach out for him in Mexico and they'll get him. I'm calling Exeter as soon as we get back."

I took a deep breath. "Gary," I said, "why did you do that? It sounds like you took a crazy risk."

He answered, looking ahead at the freeway flying by under our wheels, "I was motivated."

"You think it would be good for your career to bring this guy in?" I asked him.

He laughed out loud. "My career?! Are you kidding? I was in Mexico armed—strictly against the laws of both countries— way out of any jurisdiction a Harbor cop could have, which didn't matter because I was there on my own time. Putting mostly me at risk. Chief Gus told me he would disown sending me anywhere. My neck couldn't have got much more stuck out." He turned away from watching the road and smiled at me. "I didn't want to leave you high and dry, Mona. I wasn't going to do that."

I swiveled from looking at him to staring out the windshield. I didn't mean to do it, but as I understood what he said I just started crying. I don't know why. The craziness of yesterday, exhaustion, or...whatever. I can't ever remember anybody telling me they were willing to risk it all because they were trying to help me. I was embarrassed—and I don't embarrass easily—but even as I tried to stop crying, I was sniffling. Gary pulled a little packet of folded Kleenex out of the car's door and handed it to me. It took me a minute to get control of myself, and then I sat quietly as we approached the border gates for the crossing.

Traffic was flowing easily. We came up to the Mexican guard and he hardly looked at us, just kept waving his hand for us to come on in, and there we were, in Mexico.

"What are we going to do, Gary?"

"Paco told me that the woman was going to give you her message about knowing where the bodies are buried, and he said she told him they were buried in Capilla del Perpetuo Socorro. Chapel of perpetual, um, help. I speak Spanish because of my mom. If that's a real church, we should be able to find it. I figured we would go ask the boss—the padre at the Metropolitan Cathedral, Our Lady of Guadalupe. I've been there. Long time ago, with my mom. It's a classic cathedral, really, beautiful stained-glass windows. Close to the border in Zona Norte. Benito Juárez Avenue, I think."

"What if this guy, Paco, what if he's there waiting for you at this place?"

"Capilla del Perpetuo Socorro? I don't think he's camped out there."

"If he told you things he shouldn't have, he's going to be looking for you so you aren't a threat to him."

"I think he missed his shot at that. I don't think he's lying in wait for me there. And this time," he said, looking at me as we pulled into a parking spot by the cathedral, "I'm not armed. Less chance for trouble."

I wasn't sure what he meant by that, but I got out of the car and followed him toward the doors of the big church. I use Spanish all the time at work, but I wouldn't say I was fluent. Gary was lovely to listen to. He knew how to ask very respectfully for information about the chapel, and it turned out he didn't have to find the boss. The first cassocked guy we met right after entering the cool, dark space with its vaulted ceilings knew exactly where the chapel was. I heard them talking in low tones. Colonia Libertad. Nearby. Gary thanked him graciously and we went back out to the car.

Gary grinned at me. "The chapel is apparently the oldest church in TJ. Everybody knows about it."

It was only a short distance from the Metropolitan Cathedral, really. In the north part of town, near the border. Colonia Libertad was maybe the oldest part of Tijuana, Gary told me. We drove there in less than fifteen minutes, and it only took that long because the streets were small and full of people. When we got there, its front looked like a miniature version of the Alamo. A mottled adobe wall with an arch leading in. Gary looked at me.

"Are you ready for this?" he asked.

"Kind of depends on what we find, don't you think?" I answered. "I don't know what I feel. Now that we're here, I guess I am sort of scared. Mostly that we won't learn anything."

Gary reached out and took my hand in his. "It's high noon, Mona. Let's go out and confront the bad guys."

I sincerely hoped there were no bad guys to confront, but I figured he meant it in a metaphorical way, so we got out of the car and walked to the chapel.

Exeter

I got back to Oakheart's place in OB around noon. There hadn't been much for me to learn at the morgue—the scene was too clean. I hoped the techs would come up with something, but I had a growing sense that they wouldn't. I pulled over and parked in the alleyway that seemed to be the only way to get in or out of the cottages at the cliff top where she lived. Once I got out of the car, it struck me how it smelled like the beach. Salt water, sand, breeze. Out here by the water, the hot Santa Ana wind was more bearable.

It was the middle of the day, but the alley was empty. Nobody dumping trash or walking a dog. I got out and crossed over to the little courtyard that her house shared with two other little houses. They were all grouped in a rough U shape, and had views out over the ocean, but Oakheart's was in the center, and had the most windows. Looked nice. X-rated movies must pay good. I walked over to the front door and knocked. She ought to be home; she'd just gotten out of the hospital yesterday, right? No answer. I stepped back and glanced around to see if there were any worried neighborhood faces peering out at me.

I knocked again, louder, and stated in a voice loud enough to get through the door that it was me, Detective Exeter, and I'd like to talk with her. No shit I'd like to talk. For one thing, what did she know about the floater being a guy? Still no answer from inside. There were some low bushes in front of the houses, but they didn't prevent me from being able to walk up and look into Oakheart's front window. Nothing. The place looked empty and quiet. Lights out. This did not make me feel better. I hadn't been able to do any follow-up at all on Oakheart's little car sitting in impound, but I was worried she had become a target. Now she was missing, even though she should have been at home, recovering. Maybe a second try would work better than the first. Christ! Why did this have to happen on date night?!

I thought about radioing in a BOLO on Oakheart, but I really didn't have that much to go on yet. How worried should I be? I needed to know more. Like always. I drove over to a pay phone hanging on the wall of a local bank and tried calling Reines again—did the kid ever get through to a lead? No answer. I noted the number on the phone: 224-2478. I got back in my city ride and switched to the radio frequency that included all our emergency responders, including the Harbor Police and Fire. I knew that it was monitored all the time by everybody, just like it was at the PD.

I sent out a call: "This is Detective Exeter, SDPD badge 2803, calling Harbor Police. Harbor Police, do you copy? Over."

Brief pause. "Harbor Police, we copy. Over."

"Advise Chief Mendoza 10-21 at 224-2478 ASAP. Over."

Briefest of pauses. "Harbor Police. 10-4."

A guy ambled up to use the phone, but I badged him off. "Police business." The phone rang five minutes later. I picked it up and turned with my back to the wall and my eyes out toward the parking lot.

"Gus Mendoza," he said.

"This is Detective Exeter," I started. "I'm the guy assigned to the floater your people fished up on Monday—"

"I know who you are."

"You do?" I didn't think I'd ever met the chief of the Harbor Police.

"Of course. Gary Reines keeps me fully advised. What's up?"

"Yeah, well, I asked Gary to get me your copy of the report about the old Oakheart kidnapping perp, but I haven't heard back from him. Have you seen him?"

"I saw him yesterday, when he came and asked me for the report. Sorry to say we couldn't find our copy, but we're still looking for it. Why is it useful to you?"

"We're convinced there is a connection between the floater and the kidnapping, but we can't untangle it yet. Do you know where Reines is?"

"I know he's not on duty today, and I'm not either. He left a message for me that he'd have a report later in the day. I thought he was going to tell you the same thing?"

I felt like snorting into the phone—why was this guy being

so difficult? He was the chief of the harbor cops, so I tried to be polite. "I can't just wait around until he's ready to call me—I have questions I want answered by Oakheart. Turns out the floater only recently became a girl. She started out life as a he."

"Really?" the Harbor Police chief said. Neutral and calm, not sounding too surprised. "I didn't know you could do that."

This was not helping me. "Did you know that someone took a shot at Oakheart yesterday?"

"You mean shot at her?"

"No—I mean someone sliced her brake line and tried to take her out of the game."

There was a pause. "What are you going to do about it?"

"Right now, I'm just trying to find her. I have reason to believe she might be with Reines."

"I'm sure I have no idea how my officers spend their off-duty time. Not my business," he said.

"I suppose she's better off if she has Reines with her. Especially if she's a target. If you hear from him, tell him to call me, OK?"

"Thank you for keeping me informed, Detective. When I hear from Reines I'll pass your message on." We hung up.

I don't know what it was, but something seemed off about Mendoza's reaction and his response to my questions. He didn't seem like he was trying to help at all.

Mama Rose

I checked the would-be Buddha's belly and saw it was one o'clock. The grandfathers told me they'd send a helper to keep the store open while I had the meeting they'd set up. Every meeting was dangerous, and we did our best to avoid them, but our partners had let us know they had something to tell us. It was my job to listen.

A young man came in and bowed respectfully. "Nothing missing when I come back!" I told him. He nodded. No one was going to cheat the grandfathers. I went out of the shop and onto the walkway by the water and headed toward the Broadway pier, where the ferry to Coronado docks.

Funny thing! As I walked to the pier I saw that the *Lady Lynn* had left her moorings and was making slow passage up the bay. What a coincidence I should see her leave! I looked hard to see if I could spot Tony on the deck, but I knew he'd had a long night, very hard, lots of work all night long, and he was probably sleeping below. I said a little silent prayer as the big tuna boat glided by and turned to head out into the ocean. Tuna is a very good business. Every business is the same. Risk and rewards. I should have insisted Tony do the job in the first place, instead of that stupid Paco. But Paco was not a problem anymore. I told Tony what to do and there he goes, shipping out today and taking our problems with him.

The white ferry pulled up to the pier and emptied out its passengers. Foot traffic and some bicyclists. It was much easier to get on the ferry now, a few years after they built the big bridge. Not so crowded. I got in line and boarded with about a dozen others. Light day, for a warm Saturday afternoon. Not too many people. That was good.

I went up to the open-air deck and took a seat on one of the long benches that were bolted to the deck. With the radio mast on the top of the pilot's house, it almost looked like a Christian cross, and all the benches resembled pews at a church. But I had not come to pray, and the man who sat down next to me was not a holy man. He was middle aged, no spring chicken, balding with a very short haircut. I knew him to be Italian, and too much spaghetti made him pudgy. He wore the dull khakis of a Navy uniform and looked just like a great number of people in Coronado. As far as I knew, he was the head of the Navy team that arranged for the chandoo to fly out of Andersen on Guam. We sat in the back row of the ferry, where we could see everyone on deck. The city skyline started to fade away as we pulled out into the bay. Not too many tall buildings anyway.

"So, Mama." He said the name like he didn't want to use it. "Things got pretty screwed up this week, didn't they?"

"What's the problem? The load came in, we got it, it's shipped out already."

"The problem," he says, "is that one of your boys tried to pick up a little extra on the side." He looked at me closely, but there wasn't much to see on my face. "We figured you didn't know, because you wouldn't have risked what we have going for some stupid side scheme."

"What are you talking about?"

"Look, *Mama*, nothing goes on in this bay that we don't know about. We have eyes and ears everywhere. We have to, if we want to survive. Remember that! We saw your boy—what's his name, Paco?—out in a Boston Whaler last Sunday night. We have equipment, you know? Night vision? We can see him plain as day, even though he's running slow and quiet, with no lights. How about advertising, huh? No lights. That's asking for trouble. He's got a big oil barrel in the boat and he's trying to avoid lights and head out to the channel. We see the whole thing. We know your boy—he's been on your pickup team for months, when he's not out to sea. What was he doing out there?"

I said nothing. I thought I could see where this was going.

"You know that the DEA has been climbing all over us at the base. They got some special kind of joint task force now. There is more heat on us than ever. If we get another good year out of the Arc Light flights it'll be a miracle—but if we do, we are all going to be set for a very long time. No one is going to take a risk on that. Especially for some low-life punk who is obviously trying to make some change on the side, doing something that can only get more cops all over us. No way. You hear me? No. Way."

He had worked himself up a little bit, and he caught himself, lowering his voice. "We figure whatever he's doing, it's got to be some kind of maverick deal. No matter what he's got in that barrel, it's got to be a bad idea. Right?"

I still said nothing. I was working on my inscrutable look.

"You can see everything from the Air Station. We followed the whaler as it went out of the bay, but he didn't go far. He turns right at the range light on the shoals and tips the barrel out of the boat. The idiot doesn't even turn around to watch—he just heads back into the bay, but this time he turns his running lights on. So guess what? The barrel isn't sinking. It's floating. And dummy didn't even see it. We're not going to sit around and add more problems to our operation. You wouldn't want us to do that, would you? It's not happening. We watch your punk head back to the commercial docks, while we send a couple of our boys out in an inflatable to recover the barrel. Paco—that is his name, right?—tries to leave some kind of shit on our doorstep, which favor we then returned to him. The boys in the inflatable tow the barrel back to the purse seiner that Paco is crewing with. Tide was coming in. We left. Now we hear that Paco has split and is in Mexico, because the goddamned barrel had a dead body in it. And now it's in the newspapers. Does any of this sound familiar to you, Mama?"

I listened quietly, and now I knew how two and two became four, and why the barrel ended up knocking on Paco's boat. I nodded my head but didn't say anything at first, while I organized my thoughts.

"Paco did a bad job," I said.

"And now he's in the wind in Mexico!"

"Thank you for this knowledge, which I will tell to the grandfathers. We will make sure nothing threatens our operations again." The ferry had chugged up almost to the Coronado landing and was starting to maneuver to its dock. "I am sure the grandfathers will prevent Paco from being a problem anymore."

"I don't want to see him again. And definitely nowhere near any of our operations."

"I will tell them what you say, and I'm sure you will not see Paco again."

The ferry docked so lightly you couldn't even feel it. The deckhand jumped onto the dock with the heavy hawser in hand to slip it around a bollard. The man in the uniform next to me stood up. You could tell from the grease under his fingernails that he was a mechanic. But you had to know him to know that he worked on the big B-52s that flew in from Asia every week. He didn't look back as he walked to the stairs that led to the lower deck and the path out. I didn't leave my seat. I would enjoy the sunny ride back to downtown and tell the grandfathers what I learned. It was a good thing that our partners didn't know we hired Paco to do that job. But there would be no more jobs for Paco.

Frank

"You're telling me this is really over," I said, into the telephone receiver. "You're not going to need any more money? The risk to us is over? The risk to me?"

"The job is done," said Gus, on the telephone. He had called to tell me about Mona's car wreck, and how the bodies and the evidence were all gone, and how my role was now totally hidden, and things really ought to be over at this point. Of course, he had told me that before, when he needed the twenty G's to deal with this killer. I understood that he didn't want to put the director in the middle. The less you know, the better, it sometimes seemed. But for cryin' out loud, coming up with that kind of money for Gus, even though it went to help Phil, stuck me way out there and I admit I was nervous about it. "This time it is final," he said.

"Thank God, because I was losing sleep over this. And my son—not telling him anything, it's been bad. Gary was here this morning," I told him, "but he left pretty early. He didn't say anything to me."

"I got a message from him," Gus told me, "but I don't expect to talk to him until later today. And I just got a call from Exeter, following up on a few things, but primarily he wanted to know where Mona was. She wasn't at home, where he thought she was going to stay put. I'm trying to track them both down."

"He thinks they are together?"

"He didn't say as much, but that's the impression I got."

"And what kind of impression do you think you gave?" I asked Gus.

"If I'd been Exeter, I'd have been pissed at how useless I was." That provoked a laugh from both of us.

I paused, taking it in. "You're telling me that the killer is gone, and you believe Mona is now out of trouble from whoever was threatening her. What about all the flack she was looking at from the city and its smut campaign? That's still out there. And she and Gary are both AWOL. Have I got it right?"

"I wouldn't call him AWOL—it's his day off."

Pause on the line. I thought about things and took a breath. "Thanks, Gus. Now that I don't feel so exposed, I think Hansen would have been proud of you for pulling all this off. The killer returned as he always said he would, we found justice for Angela and Mona, and Phil is not on anyone's radar screen. That's what Erick wanted."

"Thanks, Frank. We were both at risk trying to protect Phil. Now it's over, I did what I promised Chief Hansen, and the fact that you're satisfied means a lot to me. Now let's track down your boy. Wherever he went, he didn't take his walkie-talkie and he isn't responding to our call-in request."

"I'll call you when I hear from him," I said, and we hung up on each other. I was at our house in Kensington, and I briefly recalled that the whole subdivision had been developed by Buster Keaton decades back. Movie money. I hoped movie money has been worth it for Mona. I wasn't sure how I felt about her, now that it seemed she had struck up a thing with Gary. I mean, her club was really a seedy bar, and her movies were all sex films. I was sure she didn't go to church, but then Gary hadn't for a long time, either, and I still loved him. She had certainly been at the receiving end for trouble in life. How far was this thing going to go with the two of them?

I sat in my large house. It was empty, but for me. The house-keeper was the only other person usually around, except for the gardeners, and she only came in the mornings on Satur-days. The house seemed cavernous. It had always seemed so full when Maria was here. Maria played some piano, Gary ran around, life was full. I was not going to lie on my bed and mouth "Rosebud" because things didn't work out like we wanted them to. I still had my son, and by God, what was good for him would be good for me. But where were they now?

Mona

We stepped out of the dusty, hot Tijuana street into the dark doorway built into the adobe façade of the chapel. From hot to cool, in an instant. At first, our sight still dazzled by the bright afternoon sun, all I could make out was two points of light in the near distance. As my eyes acclimated, the lights became candles. Gradually, I could see that the two candles flanked an altar: an oil painting of some angel, or saint, or maybe it was Jesus Christ, his hands clasped in prayer. I didn't know what all the symbols were for, what things meant, and I felt like we had crossed another border and were in yet another foreign land. It was just a little room, and it was empty but for the altar and the candles, the painting and some benches that were set facing it.

Then a thick cloth curtain rustled at our side, and we were joined by someone who wore robes that looked like a monk's—without the collar priests wore. He looked from me to Gary, and he smiled and asked why we were there. I was able to follow, and Gary's Spanish sounded like he was speaking poetry. He asked the monk if there was a place we could sit down and talk, and the monk motioned to the bench at the front. "We don't have much space here," he said, "but you are welcome to sit in the house of God and tell me why you have come."

"Father," said Gary, "there is a very sad story I have to tell you, from some years ago." The monk just nodded. Gary looked at me, and then he took my hand in his and held it, as I caught my breath and he turned to tell the old man, "This woman had a little girl. The love of her life. When her little girl was only three, she was taken from her mother by a very evil man, never to return. Mona," he said, squeezing my hand, "has suffered as no mother should have to suffer."

The monk looked at me kindly but piteously, and he made the sign of the cross in front of me.

"The child had been home with an *abuela*, and when Mona came home, she was gone as well. And lying dead on the floor was the *abuela*'s *marido*. It was a terrible day."

The old man muttered something to himself. It sounded more like Latin than Spanish but I couldn't really make it out, as I could hardly hear anything over the pounding in my ears. It was starting to come home to me where we were. What we could find.

"The man who did these evil things," Gary went on, "is now dead. But before he died he told someone that the bodies from that terrible day ended up here, in your chapel's graveyard." The monk looked at him thoughtfully. He asked when this happened, and Gary told him: April 1967. I mouthed the words "the fourteenth," but could hardly get them out.

My eyes had now adjusted to the dark and the gloom, so I could see the monk's face clearly, and he had tears in his eyes. I thought I knew what that meant, and I choked up immediately. I couldn't breathe. He put his hand on my knee and said, "Come with me, my child." I was right. He stood, and Gary and I, still holding hands, followed him to the dry and desolate graveyard that was stuffed into a small bit of land behind the chapel. It was as far the opposite of something like Forest Lawn in LA that you could imagine. Simple stones and markers, not in symmetrical order, or any order other than certain names found grouped together with dates going back more than a hundred years. I stumbled on the uneven ground and followed the monk to the back of the graveyard, to a far corner under a spindly jacaranda tree. There I followed his pointing finger to two wooden markers, still legible: "Tia, April 1967" and "Nina, April 1967." That's all they said, but it was all they needed to say. I fell to my knees sobbing, and Gary gently knelt down next to me and put his arm around me as I shook and cried. The monk stepped back, then told Gary he would wait inside.

"Oh my God, Gary, oh my God. This is really her." Gary didn't say anything; he was choked up himself. All the years of horrible nightmares—things that could be happening to Angela that would be worse than death. This, the evidence of her death, was in a strange way a relief. Even as I stopped crying, I thought about all the sleepless nights, wondering if my baby was alive and missing me, needing me. "Oh my God."

"Look," said Gary. "I know this might not mean a lot to you —but as a Catholic, she is buried on sacred ground. That means that she had holy rites and, in my book, she's in heaven now, Mona. From a Catholic's point of view, she's in heaven."

I had been kneeling on the ground almost as if in prayer, but when Gary said that I sat back up on my knees and hugged him as he knelt next to me. "That's the sweetest thing you could say," I said, speaking into his ear with my head on his shoulder. "Even if it is bullshit." I took a couple of breaths. "I'm not leaving her here. She's coming home with me."

He looked at me seriously. "I'll help. We'll make it happen."

We sat on the loose scrabble dusty dirt, while the monk watched us from a shaded doorway at the back of the chapel. I wondered how much of all this was my fault. Was it something I did that left my little girl dead in a Tijuana grave? Maybe if I had lived a different life? Would it have mattered if I wasn't away at work all day long and needed to hire Lola? Was it Lola's fault? She'd paid for it dearly. Would it have mattered if he, *him*, had left his family and come to take care of his daughter? If he had owned up to being the father he was?

The long years I'd borne the secret of his fatherhood now seemed wrong. I needed something more. Angela was due something more. Setting us up in the beginning was appreciated—but looking back on it, I could have used a little acknowledgment. A little support during the years no one knew anything. At least that's something Angela would never know she missed. That thought made me angry. I hadn't noticed, but my breathing was deeper and faster, and Gary did notice.

"Hey," he said, "what are you thinking about? It's obvious this has stirred you up. What can I do to help?"

"I'm not going to lie to you, Gary. I am feeling very mixed up here. On the one hand, my baby's life ended too soon, and this kind of puts that right in my face. That hurts. But other things I used to worry about, like a life of drawn-out torture, I can push out of my mind, and that's good. I couldn't rule it out before. Not only that, but I'm feeling kind of pissed off, now more than ever. This has been weighing on me for seven years, and I've gotten no support from anybody." I looked up at him, feeling it in my heart. "Until you. I'm thinking that it's time the father owned up to her life."

"What can I do?" said Gary. "You want me to go shake him up?"

"You don't have to do that, I'm sure." I looked at him. "I guess it's all going to come out. I promised to keep the secret, but now, I don't know..."

"So you're going to tell me what my dad did?" Gary asked me. I think we always think of our own families first. The ties that bind.

"Yeah. I am." I took a breath. The sun seemed high in the sky for October, beating down on us as we sat in front of Angela's grave. "There's more to every story, you know. Nothing is ever simple. But the simplest facts are these: Angela's father is Philip Nestor. The director. Your boss." I didn't look at Gary—I knew Phil was someone Gary had known all his life. What was this going to mean? "We had a thing—it was more than a decade ago, hon'. There's certainly nothing left of that now. Your dad, his buddy, helped by setting me up in a house in National City. I sold it to buy the cottages in Ocean Beach later, and he also set me up with Tell No Tales. Your dad did all the paperwork, I guess. He was a gentleman with me the two times I saw him, and he did all the paperwork for Phil. And that was that. You happy now?"

I watched Gary as I told him, and his tense foreboding melted as he listened. "I'm not sure that 'happy' is the way to describe it, but I feel better that you're sharing the truth with me. Much better, actually. Philip Nestor? I guess I can't blame him, but who would have thought? What do you want from him?"

"Good question," I said. "I'm not sure. There has to be a funeral, though. He has to come. Don't you think?"

"If that's what you think, that's what I think. We'll make it happen."

"No, Gary, this is not for you to do. Your dad might not like that much. This is for me. I'm going to call him."

"We can't change the past," he said. "But we can work on whatever happens next."

We both stood to walk back to the cool of the chapel, where the monk waited, watching us. Gary asked him what he knew of this—how had this happened? The monk explained that almost everyone buried there was from this neighborhood, Colonia Libertad. "Families that have been here for generations. So it was highly unusual when a young woman came here seven years ago. I never heard of any man. I wasn't at this chapel, then, but the story was passed on to me. The young woman was very respectful, very humble, and she was clearly a devout Christian. She told the monks then that her auntie had died of a terrible illness while they were trying to make it from Mexico to the US, and that her daughter had died from it as well, but that they were devout Catholics, and needed a burial on sacred ground, and she was able to contribute"—at this, the monk looked a little embarrassed—"a significant amount of money to the chapel for the cost and inconvenience. It must have been a great amount of money, as the graveyard was already quite full. Apparently, when she said she was going to retrieve some papers, she instead left very quickly, surprising everyone with her stealth. She had given the chapel her money and the dead, and they never knew her name, or theirs." He motioned to the outside. "Then there was nothing to do but bury them, so they did. It is a story that has been passed down. Now that you know this, what will you do?"

"I will bring my daughter home, Padre, I will bring her back home. She was such a sweet and happy little girl. She had her whole life in front of her. Even though this is a horrible ending, it is an ending. I thought it would never end. For that I'm very grateful. Thank you."

We walked back across the street to Gary's Camaro, the vinyl seats hot to the touch from sitting in the sun. We got in the car without talking, and Gary started it up and headed back north.

Gary

The ride back was uneventful and quiet, each of us lost in our own thoughts. I pulled off the freeway and retraced the path back to Ocean Beach and Mona's cottage. My car seemed almost as big as her driveway when I pulled into it. It was approaching evening, and the streets seemed calm. As we walked toward Mona's front door, she reached out and took my hand.

"I've got to make a couple of phone calls and check in, let people know what's up," I told her.

"Fine," she said. "What are you going to say?"

"I'm going to tell my boss what we found, but I don't think I have to tell him about Nestor. It isn't his business, is it? And whatever I tell him is going to go straight to Philip Nestor anyway, you know."

"Are you going to tell your dad what you know?"

"I want to. But I'll tell him not to say anything to Philip yet, until you've thought about how you want to handle this. OK? He'll respect that, I'm sure. I'll make sure he appreciates that this is your call and I'm behind you one hundred percent."

"OK." It looked like she visibly let herself relax. "I've got some beer in the fridge," she said. "Want an Anchor Steam?"

"Sounds great." I went over to the corner of the living room, where Mona had a chair and a telephone on an end table next to it. I fell into the chair. Took a deep breath and made my first call.

"Dad?"

"I'm so glad to hear from you! I've been on pins and needles since I got your message this morning. What happened? People have been calling."

"I'll bet. Don't worry about it—I'll call my chief, and I'll call Exeter, after we talk."

"Did you get in any trouble down there?" he asked.

"A little, but it all worked out. But that was yesterday. Yesterday was a little sticky for me, but I learned something—I learned Mona's daughter was buried in Tijuana, and today, Mona and I went down there and we found her." That hadn't come out right. "We found the grave where her daughter is buried. Or at least, that's what we believe."

There was a pause while my dad took this in. Then he asked me, "How's Mona?" and it just made me feel so good, that he was concerned enough to ask about her. Now I was really torn. I'd been fearing the worst there, half-expecting he was going to be dismissive of her because of her sex movies. The bar wasn't too bad, but I hadn't thought that either the bar or the movies would be a selling point with my dad, and now I had to talk to him about the old secrets, revealed.

"It's all still new, but I think this has been a very good thing for her. She had all kinds of terrible thoughts about what could have happened to Angela. I guess you knew that's her daughter's name."

"Yes, I know."

"Sitting in front of the grave was hard on her. She shared how hard it was to have been all alone for the past seven years. And that led to her telling me something else." I took a breath. "She told me who Angela's father was, and the role you played in all of it." Another pause.

My dad finally spoke. "She has kept that promise of secrecy for a long time. I can see how discovering her daughter's grave would jar her. What do you think she is going to do now?"

"She needs Philip Nestor to acknowledge the death of their child. I don't know how."

"Does she intend this to be a big public thing?"

"I don't know. This is all new territory. They should probably talk about it."

"And you are in the middle of this?"

"Yeah, I am. I'm sorry if that is a problem for you."

"No, that's OK, I saw this coming over the past couple of days. I kind of knew it was happening, I guess."

"I don't know what to tell you, Dad. Who knew things were going to go like this? It certainly makes me feel differently about Philip, even though he's your buddy. I'm sticking with Mona."

"Gary, I know that it's hard enough in this world to get by on your own, and having someone to share it with makes all the difference. This I know."

I wasn't sure if he was talking about Mona's relationship with her daughter, or her lack of a relationship with the father, or his own relationship with Mom, or what. And then it flashed on me—he was talking about my relationship with Mona. He was giving me his blessing. It stopped me. But only for a moment.

"Dad," I said, "we'll work out something for the funeral. Let Mona deal with it. This means something to her; it's important, OK? I'm sure it can be a very private affair. No one has to hang, just provide a little support. And, I guess, a little living up to the consequences of life. Let Mona work it out, I'm asking you. And while I'm on that—do you know anything more about this city plan to put Mona on the front page and run her out of town on a rail? Is she still going to get slammed?"

"I don't know, Gary. I haven't heard anything about it for a couple of days now. Check with your people; they ought to know. I think I ought to call Philip and let him know the lay of the land."

That stopped me. Mona had told me her secret in confidence. She should be the one to tell Nestor she'd shared it with me. That was between the two of them. "Whatever you want to share with him, don't tell him that Mona told me he was Angela's father, OK? She's trying to work out what she wants to do. Hold back on that just a bit, until after Mona and I have talked some more." I thought about everything he'd done to protect Philip Nestor so far, and added, "You'll be able to tell him more once he and Mona talk. Look, I have a few more calls to make," I told him. "We'll talk soon."

My next call was to my chief. I heard Mona get into the shower in the small cottage and turn on the water.

"I'm glad to hear from you," Chief Gus told me. "I've been sharing nothing but ignorance with anybody since I got your message this morning. I was glad to get it, by the way, glad to know you didn't run into too much trouble wherever you were…I have to admit I was getting a little worried."

"Well, Chief, your lead to the *Lady Lynn* got me connected with the deckhand who pulled the barrel out of the bay. His name is Paco, but like you said, he had flown to TJ, and that was where I had to go to find him." I paused, waiting to hear if I was going to get reamed out for such a breach of jurisdictional protocol. Silence. So far, so good.

"Turns out, I did find him. And for reasons I think we should not go into, he confessed to being hired for the killing of the talent agent. He didn't know why she was a target, or who hired him; he was just paid to kill her and dump the body. So he said. I can't imagine how the damned barrel ended up banging against the hull of the *Lady Lynn*. Seems crazy, but that's why he split as soon as it came out of the water and he saw what it was. He figured he was a sitting duck, so he fled to TJ. I followed a lead from another deckhand on the *Lady Lynn* and found him at a bar there."

"What happened?"

"It wasn't good. I was stupid and got in a fix; he was all over me. But some guys intervened and pulled him off me—they said they were just locals, but they knew what they were doing and they acted like a team. When it was over, Paco was going to split, but some guy called him over and they left together. That's the last I saw of him. And, I think I may have heard a gunshot. I didn't get a good look at the guy who called him over, but he showed up right when I needed him and he had some kind of relationship with those guys who helped me out. I don't get it, Chief. It could have been bad, but it turned out OK. And Chief, while Paco was trying to distract me, he told me where Mona's daughter was buried. Apparently the lady, that agent he killed, had come with a message for Mona, who never got it, but Paco learned what it was. Don't ask how." I forged on. "I came back here to get Mona, and after I sent you and a couple of other people messages that I'd report later, we went to TJ—totally on our own, very legit—and we used the information Paco gave me to find a grave site that looks like it's for Mona's kidnapped daughter. And the housekeeper, too, I think." I stopped to take a breath.

Chief Gus sounded like he was all business. "Call Exeter and tell him about Paco. He'll want to get cranking on having our friends in TJ pull him in, assuming we still can. They are going to want to know who started this."

"Will do, Chief." I took a deep breath. This was not the time or the place to go into Mona's new feelings about the director letting her down all these years, and for all I knew, Chief Gus had no idea about the director's old relationship with Mona. Besides, the chief had been pretty exercised about me even being seen with Mona. She was a suspect in the eyes of the PD, and she was a woman with a history. But it is what it is. "Chief, what can you tell me about the big circus the city was going to put on to play Mona as the Wicked Witch of the West and run her out of town?"

"All I can tell you is that the event is starting in about thirty minutes. They got the permits, they put up the bleachers and the stage, but the PD hasn't made any arrests or public statements. I think we'll find out together. Call Exeter; he might know."

I had the feeling that Chief Gus wasn't being entirely straight with me—but I wasn't being entirely straight with him, either. Was I supposed to keep pulling the truth out of him? "And what about the threat to Mona?"

"I haven't heard anything from the PD about it. Check with Exeter and see what he knows." Although this was not helpful, the tone of the chief's response suggested he was not troubled. I didn't know what to think.

"Hey, Mona," I called to her, hearing the shower had stopped. "Nobody seems to know anything about the big political rally that Holier planned. I'll check with Exeter."

I made the call to Exeter's office, not expecting to find him there. He was apparently out of touch for the night, so I left a detailed message at the desk about finding Paco and his confession, and letting Exeter know that he needed to get the paperwork going so we could pull Paco out of Mexico, if he was still breathing, and learn who paid him for the hit. Then I hung up and took a long pull from the bottle of cold beer that Mona had put on the end table by the phone. Mona came out from the kitchen and sat down on the couch, looking at the ocean and horizon. Her house was close enough to the ocean that a fall over her backyard fence would topple you down a cliff and into the water. The sun had set and the light was getting dimmer.

After a moment's silence, she turned to me. "Let's take a walk, OK? I need to get out and breathe."

I had reached the bottom of that bottle and felt better for it. I stood. "Where to?"

"There's some old steps the city put in a long time ago that lead to a path down by the ocean. Let's go down and watch the waves crash."

We went down the ancient steps, using the old galvanized pipe handrail, and into the briny mist that hovered in the air as we stood on the rocks watching the waves roll in and crash around us, over and over.

Gus

I picked up the phone and called Philip Nestor at home, even though it was getting late. He'd want to know. His wife answered, and she recognized my voice. I was over at their house often enough, and we saw each other frequently at events. "I'll go get him," she said.

"Yes?" he said, a minute later.

"Sir, there's some things I think you need to know. I heard back from Gary Reines, and he said that he lost Paco, but in the process he learned, uh, he and Mona found the grave of...the child. And the housekeeper. In Tijuana."

Pause. I couldn't tell what he was thinking. "Everything else good?" he asked.

"I think so. I can give you a fuller briefing later, but for now I think it's all wrapped up. No more threats to Mona, and one less killer in the world." I heard no comment from him.

"There's something else you should know, Gus." Pause. "I heard from Frank, who talked to Gary, and Mona had apparently shared my history with him. She's going to make some 'requests' of me, but I don't know what they are yet. I'm not sure where things are going to end up."

I was concerned about Nestor and his troubles, but in truth, I cared more for Mona. "Sir, what's going on with that big show for the 'Cleaner San Diego' program Holier is ready to hype up? Mona still faces some threats there, I guess."

No pause this time. "I wouldn't worry about that one. A little bird told me that it was looking dicey for any arrests, especially now, with the morgue having been burgled—and without their star witness being frog-marched to the police headquarters they've lost their front-page sizzle. They're doing something different now."

"Sounds good, sir. I think."

"Good night, Gus. Looks like you did a good job of cleanup. Hansen would be proud."

That made me feel good. Everything I'd done was to honor my promises to Chief Hansen, who'd pulled me out of the barrio and given me a career. Phil Nestor was just the lucky one who'd gotten the benefit of that promise. At least so far. "Thank you, sir," I said.

7

SUNDAY

Gary

I woke up before the sun was out. I slid out of bed and pulled on my boxers and jeans, then walked softly out to the living room and sat on the couch and looked out the big window over the brooding Pacific. It was quiet and still. I went outside, barefoot and shirtless, and turned to walk down the lane to where it dead-ended at the cliff's edge. There was a fresh breeze coming in from over the sea. I took a breath. Clean salt air. Looked like the Santa Anas were done blowing for now and the wind was coming in from the ocean. After a minute I walked back to the cottage and found Mona up and in her short red French robe, putting coffee on the stovetop to percolate.

"Sleep well?" she asked.

"Yeah. It felt good. You?"

She smiled. "I fell asleep thinking of Angela. I dreamed about her, and it wasn't a nightmare. Yeah. It felt good."

"Have you thought about what you want to do? Did you hear me tell my dad not to tell Philip what you've told me? It's up to you. Now you just have to figure out what you want."

"I don't know," she said. "I don't want a pound of flesh. I just want him to acknowledge that his child died."

"We're going to bring her back and have a funeral here?"

"Yeah. But it doesn't have to be in the papers. It's for me. And for her. I think he should be there."

"Do you want me to tell him?" I asked her. "I can set things up for you."

She shook her head. "No," she said. "This is for me to handle. I'll think about what I want and what I want to say."

"You're the boss. What about bringing Angie home? Are you going to call some place and make arrangements?"

"Well, it's not like I go to the red brick church by the high school, Gary. I don't know how this stuff goes... I don't even know what or where the graveyards are here."

"How about," I said, "if I find out whether she can be buried near my mom?" And as soon as I said that, she threw her arms around my neck and started crying again. It only took a minute for her to quiet down, and I held her, feeling her breathing slow. We sat on her couch and looked at the ocean. We weren't out of the woods yet. I didn't want to get into it, but there was no dodging it, either.

"I didn't see a newspaper out front...?" I asked her. She sat up and took a Kleenex to her eyes.

"I don't get one. Never had time to read it."

"You want me to go get one?"

"Let's not. If I'm getting screwed, let's put off thinking about it as long as we can. Right now, I feel like just having some coffee. This morning feels better than a whole lot of mornings I've lived through. We'll deal with trouble later—it's always there, you know."

She poured the coffee into a couple of mugs and we went back to sit on the couch and look out the window at the brightening ocean. I thought of all we had gone through this week, and my phone call with my dad last night.

"I have sort of a crazy idea," I said to Mona.

"Shock me," she answered.

"In about two hours there's a family Mass at our parish church, Saint Didacus."

"Okay," she said. "You win. I'm shocked."

"I haven't been there in years. Since before I left for the war, in fact. The last time I was there it was for my mother's funeral. Maybe," she looked at me, "I remembered something when we walked into the cathedral in TJ. It felt like...something. My dad goes every Sunday. He'll most likely be there with Nestor and his family. There used to be a threesome for church. Erick Hansen was an original in the gang, but he died and it's not the same with Chief Gus. Hansen started the Harbor Police when Nestor became the director. They were a trio; they were all in the war together. Gus never really filled those shoes the same way. Nestor is a deacon, you know."

I didn't know what Mona knew, and what she didn't know. She said nothing, and just looked at me with a very solemn gaze.

"With everything that's happened this week, I feel like it would be a good thing to do. And I'd introduce you to my dad."

She just looked at me.

"I know you've met him. But this is a do-over. I want to introduce you and tell him we're a pair."

Now she smiled. "A pair?"

"You're my girl."

"Ya think?" she said, sounding just like a girl from Arkansas.

"And we'll make sure Philip Nestor knows it, too. He'll probably be there. Maybe it's the right time to let him know what you're thinking?" Now I smiled. "Go get dressed. Look nice. Then we'll go to my place so I can get dressed. It's church, right?"

"Well, I don't know, really. I've never been in one. Not a Catholic one, anyway."

"It's probably not all that different. Just watch me and do what I do."

Half an hour later, showered and dressed, she came out. A dark blue pleated skirt that was demure but sexy at the same time, a white blouse buttoned up the front, and a white jacket. Nylons in black loafers. Pearls. Bandage over the stitches on her forehead. "You look great," I said. "Let's go to my place."

I wasn't sure my dad was going to be at the Kensington house, and I wondered what I would say to him if he was, but his car was not in sight when I pulled into the driveway. I knew he went to Mass every Sunday, and from living in the casita I knew that he often went out to a coffee shop on Adams Avenue before heading to St. Didacus. It put him halfway there. I turned the key in the Camaro's dashboard and I was out of the car before its shuddering parts settled, calling over my shoulder for Mona to follow while I hurried it up.

I dove into my own shower and dried off in minutes. Pants and a white shirt weren't too hard to find, but I had to look through everything I had before I found the one sports coat I had left. They were going to have to accept me without a tie, but I didn't think that mattered. Hey—Vatican II was years ago; we're all kind of casual now. When I emerged, I saw Mona standing on the balcony and looking out over the garden. I had no newspaper, so there was nothing to tempt her curiosity. She saw I was ready and smiled. "You clean up pretty good," she said.

Funny. Here we stood, getting ready to go to church, looking like Mr. and Mrs. Cleaver, when what we really were is two new lovers: a gimpy and wayward boat jockey cop and a bar owner who makes sex movies. I guess things aren't always what they seem. Time for church.

St. Didacus is a square Romanesque structure on a quiet residential street that seems bigger than it is, once you're inside. I grew up in the parish, which includes Kensington. It's the open wood-beamed ceiling that makes it feel as high as heaven. Especially to a five-year-old boy, going to Mass and attending

the church school, which was housed in a couple of long buildings next door.

I stashed the Camaro in the church lot and crossed the
street with Mona. A knot of people clustered about the steps
leading inside. Jackets and ties. Dresses. Families in their
Sunday finest. Mona and I stood in front, and I pointed out the
rooms that had provided me with my elementary education. I
caught sight of the top of my dad's head, at least I thought I did,
but he was at the front and headed through the doors. The
church bells were sounding, it was time to begin, and even
though the double doors were opened wide it was a slow surge
to the oaken pews. We were in the back, and I could see my dad
had gone up to the front. He knelt and made the sign of the
cross before sliding into a seat that had obviously been saved
for him. It was next to Philip, no surprise. Who had his wife
and daughters with him. From where I sat it looked like he
patted the pew and my dad sat next to him, but as they were
engaged in talking, he didn't look back and see that Mona and I
had slipped into the rearmost pew.

Music had begun floating out over the congregation from
the choir balcony upstairs and in the back. From where we
were sitting you couldn't see anything—it was as though the
music just drifted down from the sky. A piano and a couple of
voices. *"Gather at the water..."* Even though the lay officiants
were bustling about and trying to get things started, old friends
had stopped to talk to each other in several knots scattered
about the big church. Men and women with arms around each
other, engaged in some topic or other. I kept waiting for my dad
to look back and see us, but he was talking to Philip, and never
did. Mona just sat and took it all in. The stained-glass depic-
tions of Calvary in the windows weren't as large or impressive
as those at Metropolitan Cathedral in Tijuana, but they were
beautiful. An elderly woman walked up to a lectern and began
making announcements. "The Divine Mercy Group," she said,

"will be making tamales again to raise funds for the school. Make sure you place your orders in advance..."

I turned and looked at Mona. She looked back at me, a sardonic smile on her face. "What?" I asked her.

"You're so cute," she said to me. "You brought me here to show me where your life started, didn't you?" Her smile grew larger.

The priest had started:

"Have mercy on us, O Lord.
For we have sinned against you.
Show us, O Lord, your mercy.
And grant us your salvation."

I leaned over and whispered in Mona's ear. "It always starts by accepting that you are imperfect, you have sinned, and asking forgiveness. You don't actually have to do all the things I do—you can just sit and listen." She just smiled at me.

I kept whispering. "I felt this at the cathedral when we walked in. A cool place on a hot day. The church reminds me of that." I sat back as the familiar service rolled slowly on.

We must have soon gone through the Apostles' Creed, because I could see the ushers start to walk down the aisle with their baskets, working the collection. Ultimately, we got to the Liturgy, and the priest recounted the parable of the prodigal son. Having gone out and wasted his inheritance, the son comes home willing to be a servant to his father in abject apology for the error of his ways, but he is instead welcomed back into the household by a father with open arms. Love conquers all.

At the end of this, Mona leaned into me and whispered in my ear, "And here I thought that prodigal meant he had a really big dick."

"Sounds like you've greatly recovered," I whispered back.

"Who, me? I'm just a sweet little Sunday school gal."

All of this whispering, accompanied by some squirming around on the pew, brought a couple of glances our way, but people tended to look more amused than annoyed. I sat back, and my thoughts might have slipped from the sacred to the somewhat more profane. I felt really good. I was comfortable, connecting with a past self and a state of mind that accepted the world as beyond my control, sitting next to this lady who was smart, sassy, and sexy. Even if she did look like June Cleaver today.

Mona

Even in Arkansas my mom didn't do much about going to church, and I just didn't remember the last time I was in one. I'd never been in a Catholic one before. Lots of stuff was going on, but it must all have had to do with history, because it wasn't like anybody was explaining anything in a way I could get it. As I looked around and the Mass went on, my mind drifted. Naturally, I started to get ideas about scenes and settings and how I could riff off of a religious thing in a whole new series of short movies. Probably sell like hot tamales.

I was sort of absentmindedly considering this idea when I looked up and froze. I'd made eye-to-eye contact with Philip. Probably for the first time in eleven years. A lot had happened since we sat on that pier in San Clemente and said goodbye to each other. He had turned around and looked toward the back from his pew, seen me, then quickly turned back to face the altar. But it only takes a flash to know, and he now knew I was there. *OK*, I thought, *this is going to get a little weird*. He was up there sitting next to Frank, and I was back here with Gary.

Gary leaned over and told me that now was the time when people were offered Communion; he'd explain it later, but we could just sit it out. Fine. The priest called out:

"*Behold the Lamb of God,*
behold him who takes away the sins of the world.
Blessed are those called to the supper of the Lamb."
The congregation replied:

"Lord, I am not worthy
that you should enter under my roof,
but only say the word
and my soul shall be healed."

We sat it out as most everyone in the room rose and filed slowly toward the altar at the front, where I was told the priest and the Eucharist ministers were turning wafers and wine into flesh and blood. Gary said the Mass was almost over, and that we should just sit tight so his dad could see we were here and we could connect. I said nothing, but I kept looking at the back of Philip's head. He leaned over and talked to the woman sitting next to him. I had never met her. She was obviously the wife. You could tell by the way they leaned in together. Teenagers next to them—two girls. Got it. I was no family wrecker. I just wanted acknowledgment. Philip and his family and Frank all did the Communion thing. I told Gary he should go up there, but he shook his head. "Not for me," he said, "at least not yet."

Ultimately, people did start flowing out the big front doors and pooling about in front of the church, talking and touching each other. We kept our place as the worshippers went down the side aisles between the pews and the glowing stained-glass windowed walls, and down the wide center aisle. Because Philip and his family sat close to the front, I could watch them wait patiently for others to leave before they headed our way. Gary's dad, Frank, noticed his son quickly, even though the place was still crowded. I could see his face light up with a smile. He was obviously surprised to see Gary here, and when his recognition took in the two of us his smile didn't go sour. It got bigger.

Frank's warmth, and the happiness he radiated at seeing his son in church, was a contrast to the face of the man I had once loved freely—which was stolid and blank. His wife held him by the arm and their daughters trailed them as they advanced down the wide aisle toward the door and the rearmost pew, where we sat. We shuffled ourselves along the oak floor and slid along the pew from its outer end to the middle, where we would be closest to them. The big flush of people had become a trickle, and only a few were still in the big room with the pews. Others had mostly gone outside. Frank reached us first, and Gary stood up from his seat and they embraced with a hug. It sure looked like the real thing.

Gary backed up just half a step, and said, "Dad, I know you and Mona have met, but that was then, and this is now. Now I'd like to introduce you to Mona Oakheart. I think you will find her a very engaging woman and you will likely see a lot more of her."

Jesus, I thought, *where did* that *come from?* But before I could make a comment, Frank leaned over, reached out, and put his hand on my arm. He squeezed it and said, "Mona, I couldn't have imagined a better surprise than meeting you here today in this house. It's a real pleasure." And then he turned to the side and looked at Philip, so my gaze turned as well. And we looked each other eye to eye. Now that I was up close I could see that he did look older, and, yeah, fatter. But I could see the old line of the smile he had for me under his flesh, and I could remember how we'd had so much fun together. And our daughter, now dead in Tijuana.

"Mona," Frank was saying, playing his role, "let me introduce you to my very good friend, Philip Nestor, the director of the Waterfront Agency, and his wife, Cynthia, and their daughters, Linda and Marie."

I turned to face him, and he slowly lifted his hand, reaching out to give me a neighborly handshake. I took his hand in mine, and he squeezed it.

"Mona," he said, "let me just say that Chief Gus, of the Harbor Police, has given me a report, and I know you've found the place where your daughter was buried. Angela. I don't know what to say," he added, not noticing that his wife was clearly aware of how long he was holding my hand. Then, as though he suddenly got the message, he let go of me and stepped back.

"Frank told me that you are bringing Angela back to the States to be buried here, near you. Can I join you for the ceremony?"

Frank told him?! I thought Frank had agreed to leave this to me. At this point, his wife seemed thoroughly perplexed. She clearly felt undercurrents of something, but...? It was so strange being here, with Gary, his arm around me, his dad, and his dad's best friend Philip staring at me, and the wife, who didn't know he'd fathered my little girl. Thank goodness I looked like Beaver Cleaver's mom, assuming she had a head wound. Gary was looking at his dad and his face was clouded. I was riveted on Philip, who turned to his wife and said, as we all listened together, "Cynthia, I asked Father Joseph if we could visit with him after Mass."

"But he'll be in confession," she said.

"I asked him to be available to us. There are things that he knows about that you should know. Things I have only shared with him in confession. Frank, can you take the girls, maybe go out for lunch, and we'll pick them up from your house?"

Frank said, "Of course." Gary had pulled away from his father, his arm still around me.

Cynthia looked at Philip, and at Frank, and at me. They turned and walked back toward the altar to find Father Joseph. Gary turned to his father. "You told me you'd stay out of this. This isn't your world to orchestrate anymore." He was visibly upset.

"Gary," his dad said, looking at the two teenaged girls, who seemed far more attentive to the retreating backs of their parents than the quiet anger between Gary and his dad. "This has been a long time coming. I owed it to him to try to smooth things out."

I watched him carefully, and while I was annoyed with Frank for butting in, Gary looked as angry as I'd ever seen him.

His jaw was clenched. "Good to know how you feel, Dad," he said through his teeth, then turned, taking my elbow to walk us away.

I let myself be steered by Gary down the big steps that spilled out onto the street. I looked up and who was parked at the curb, leaning against his Ford Vic with the moon hubcaps, but my "friend" Jim Exeter. He smiled and waved as we exited the church, indicating we should come on over. *Perfect*, I thought. *If he plans on pushing me into his car it'll happen with everybody watching. Not that it ever helped in the past.* Frank and the girls were right behind us. Gary turned to them and said we would check in with them later, and he held my arm as we broke away to join Exeter.

Exeter was smiling a big, shit-eating grin. He had a folded newspaper in his hand and he kept slapping it into his palm. "Hey, kids," he said, looking at Gary. "Your chief told me I could probably find you here, and I was hoping to find you both."

"Cut the crap," said Gary, ready to get bristly with him. "Did the chief give you my whole message? If Paco is still standing, we have to start things going to reel him back. He gave me a confession because he thinks he's safe down south, so we need an international warrant. Don't we? Unless somebody else got to him first."

Exeter eyeballed him. "I heard a gunshot," Gary told him.

"Slow down, hotshot. First, I heard about what you found in Mexico." He turned his gaze and looked at me. "I hope it came as a comfort to you." Then he turned back to Gary. "We do need a warrant, and we're on it. It's not as easy to get lost in Mexico as the movies make you think, and our extradition partners work with us pretty good. We'll find Paco, and the feds want him too. We'll get him, and we'll squeeze him, and maybe we'll find out who paid him. OK?"

By this time, Gary was smiling. It was like the cavalry had shown up.

"And maybe you two haven't heard, but there's news about the floater."

We looked at each other. "You know who she is?" Gary asked him.

"She was a he. Sex change operation. So we haven't really pinned down who he or she is, because something really hinky is going on with the fingerprinting, and I don't just mean that her fingers were cut off, either. A lot of people in my world believe there's a connection with your kidnapping case, but belief is one thing and evidence is another. Funny thing about evidence," he said, then slapped the paper in his hand one more time.

What a jerk, I thought. *Why is he smiling?!*

"Did you see this?" he asked, and handed it over. OK. I unfolded it and there was a big picture, in color, on the front page, of some kind of event—a rally downtown by the tuna boats. Looked like bleachers and a crowd of people, a stage with some guys on it, a microphone, and a banner in the back with "Clean Up San Diego" emblazoned across it. My eyes drifted from the picture to the headline: "City Councilman Vows to Clean the Bay."

"Apparently," Exeter went on, "the city has decided to team up with the Waterfront Agency and fund a big program to clean up the environmental hot spots around the bay. New program." I quickly scanned the page. Nothing about the tattoo parlors and locker clubs, small bars and sex shops. Nothing about a downtown bar owner who makes sex movies. Looked like they took a new direction, and left me out of it.

Gary had been reading over my shoulder as I held the paper. I looked up at him, and he was smiling. "I'm all for a clean bay, Mona. Aren't you?"

"Well," said Exeter. "It's stranger than that." It looked to me like our good friend Jim was really enjoying feeding us new facts, one at a time. "While you were in Tijuana yesterday," he turned and looked at me, "lucky thing for you, I guess—the body in the morgue disappeared. It was stolen, along with the autopsy reports."

"What?!"

"Lucky for you, because you can't be blamed for it. This whole mess is getting bigger, and I think it's going to end up being a federal mess. Emphasis on the mess. All I can tell you is the body is gone. We have no fingerprints, we have no positive ID, and the self-confessed killer escaped to Mexico."

"What about me?" I asked, pointing to the bandage on my head. "What about somebody trying to kill me by sabotaging my car?"

"We opened an investigation, forensics has been over your car, but so far I've got absolutely nothing. Frankly, I'm hoping that Paco may have some answers for us on that one, because it sure looks like somebody tried to set you up. As far as my department can tell, we're going to have to catch up with this Paco character, assuming he's breathin', in Mexico, but don't hold your breath. The wheels of justice turn slower than a Benz." He smiled at his own joke. "Anyway, try to stay out of trouble, OK?"

I started to give him a smart-aleck answer, but before I could even say it he cut me off. "I don't mean you, Mona—I mean the boat jockey." He got into his car, cranked the window down, and started it up with a rumble. "I'll be seeing you around. Maybe," and he drove off. Jim seemed like kind of a hard guy to read.

I turned and saw that Frank and the girls were looking at us from across the street, perhaps wondering how things were going and what the police were telling us. But no one had been arrested, voices weren't raised, and the only thing disturbing the tranquility of the sunny Sunday morning was Gary, angry that his father had given Phil a heads-up. I could see this was really gnawing at him.

Frank asked as we got closer, "What was that all about?" and Gary told him, sounding a bit cold and distant. "That's the detective working on the murder I reported. The body in the barrel—last Monday. He was telling us that he thinks he's going to be off the case soon. It's going to go federal."

Gary stood there awkwardly. I could see that he wanted to let his father know he was really pissed, but with the girls standing there he controlled himself. Everybody seemed acutely conscious of the girls listening. I wondered what I would talk about if I had to make conversation with the girls. My daughter? My movies? My recent car wreck? Maybe I'd stick to the weather.

The youngest daughter leaned over to her sister and cupped her hand over her ear, whispering something. The sister answered in a totally bored tone, "I don't know, why don't you ask her?"

"Is it polite?" the girl asked. Her sister shrugged.

The younger girl, maybe she was thirteen—it's hard to tell —turned to me, not Gary, and shyly asked whether I was Gary's girlfriend. All eyes were on me. You could have heard a pin drop. But before I could say anything, Gary put his arm around my waist and said, very seriously, "Just because I have a girl-friend doesn't mean we can't still play Monopoly once in a while, Marie. There's nobody I would rather play Monopoly with than you, but things change all the time. They're still changing, and the next time you and I play you're going to have to watch out for Mona—something tells me she's going to be killer at Monopoly."

Well, I thought to myself as we all started to move toward our cars, *this is going to be new and different*. I wondered when, or whether, I might see the girls or their mother again.

Frank

The sun had set a short time ago. I held a short glass of Chivas in my hand. No ice, just a splash of water. I sat in my favorite overstuffed armchair and looked out the big windows to the garden beyond. Gary had come home and in half an hour had packed up and moved out. He was angry, and he hadn't come in and said anything to me. Not hello or goodbye. Here my heart was filling with happiness as he was finding a girl, a woman, but now I guess I truly screwed up. He figures I don't respect him, I guess, and all because I felt like I had to call Philip. God help us get past this. I wished again I had Maria to lean on...

I took a sip of the whisky, and the telephone rang. There was a phone right on the end table next to me, so I reached over and answered. "Yes?"

It was Phil. "How are you doing, Frank?"

"Not so good. Gary is angry that I called and told you what Mona was thinking. He had told me she wanted to tell you herself. He seems to think I betrayed him. What about you?"

"I guess betrayal is the word of the day. That's what Cynthia thinks. Cynthia has been crying. Not just because of the affair. She says it's because I kept the big secret. She's angry I kept it, and Angela, hidden all these years. She's very upset about Angela. The girls' half-sister. I figured this would be hard, and now it's time to reap what I've sown. She said she's taking the girls—and I'm not invited. I don't know for how long. I never imagined this happening, not in my wildest dreams. It's not good, Frank."

This was sad. It was what we had hoped to avoid. Still, I had to ask. "You're sure that no one is going to pop up and start to point fingers at who, what, and when? That's all we need: lose our families and go to jail, too."

"Believe me, Frank," he replied, "it's over. Gus has assured me, although he is also vague about what exactly happened, and how. I think we should leave it all alone.

"Look," he added, "you've been a rock for me through this whole thing. And funding everything. Getting Mona set up with the house and bar all that time ago, then putting up the bucks for MASTCO to pay for an international investigation after the kidnap—none of that would have happened without you. I doubt that Mona knows what you've really done for her, and for me."

I thought it was best not to mention the last twenty grand I'd put up recently for Gus to get the job done. No reason for Phil to even know about it. "What about Mona?" I asked. "Shouldn't we tell her that we positively ID'd that agent, so she knows the guilty were punished?"

"Think about it, Frank," he said, "I'm sure she gets the picture. She gave us an alert, and that was that. She can guess that the prints we got off the photos were a match for the creep, or why would anything have happened? How am I going to tell her—or Gary, which is probably the same thing now—about how we positively ID'd the killer without going into explanations about who did what, when I don't even know what happened next? And that would risk the careers of more than just me. If not much worse."

"So we say nothing." Even though Philip couldn't see me over the phone line, I shook my head. I get it. We were really vigilantes, outside the law, skirting on the edge even when we funded Mona's house, even when Hansen had first run down the prints in Manila, and even when Gus then confirmed them. "It should be a good thing, but it's not."

"We did the best we could with the hand we were dealt, that's all I can say. I think it *is* a good thing. However it happened, a bad person came to a bad end, and now we have to live with the consequences."

"I suppose somebody is going to get away with murder," I said, "but it was the murder of a murderer."

"I think that the less said about it, the better. Let's try to pick up the pieces."

"Give my best to Gus. I'll see you later this week."

I hung up the telephone and walked out onto the porch that looked over the garden. Not far from where Gary had been so upset with me earlier in the week. I guessed he'd moved in with Mona; he sure hadn't told me where he was going. Nighttime, and Maria's garden was full of scent. I could smell the heady aroma of flowers, but I wasn't sure which ones I could smell, and for some funny reason, that thought made me smile. I took a deep breath and turned to go inside.

Freddie

What a nightmare! First he chops off my fingers, then I'm in a barrel, the morgue, a backyard, and now I'm here. And so is Paco, but Paco isn't talking. I think he's very pissed. And he's got my medallion! We're both of us all cut up and crammed in here in these slimy bags and it's cold and dark. Jesus, I'm in pieces. How am I still talking? Maybe I can never die. Reminds me of juvie in Manila, the Old Bilibid Prison right in the middle of the city. The *Carcel y Presidio Correccional* was an old building, falling part, full of rats, long before I was thrown in with the rest of the lost souls. If you didn't have money to buy food you would starve and die. During the war, the Japs put the Americans in there and they did mostly starve and die. Then they built New Bilibid, after the war, and moved everybody there, but still Old Bilibid was the jail, and it was where they kept the kids. Lots of kids; I was only one of many. Nobody had any money. You don't get pesos for nothing—but you could get something for something. We traded what we had—our young bodies.

I was sent there because I killed the dog of the fat old fart who was supposed to set me straight, but instead I was keeping him straight—you know where. He was a very dirty man, and I was disgusted, and the dog barked at me as I started home from his house. Easy to choke the dog—it was scrawny and tied up outside. I just didn't know I was being watched. Next thing you know I'm in court and I'm in jail, and Auntie Lola is glad to be rid of me. She was never happy to have me to care for, and Uncle Pedro could give a shit. They never even came to visit after the first month. Of course, Old Bilibid stank and

felt like a cave, so who would want to come for some skinny
little dog-killing boy? They left me to die. And then they left
the country! I was her sister's baby, and they left me in Old
Bilibid and they went to America! You can't be more alone
than I was. I dream of the day I would meet up with her and
make her cry. I lay on my cot with its wire mesh bed that hurt,
in my room of stone, and I held the one thing I had from my
mother—a small Virgin Mary medallion that I wore on a
chain around my neck—and I planned on how to make my
auntie feel as bad as I did.

I stayed awake thinking on how I could do that. Old Bilibid
was not like New Bilibid. Not so much security. Plenty of jailers
(but they didn't do anything) and lots of cops, too. But people
came in and out all the time. Our cells were not usually locked
(the locks didn't work right), but the hallways were always
locked. So we could get around some. I'd seen boys get out, but
they were always brought back. Then it was worse for them. I
had to think how to get out and not come back. When I finally
figured it out, it was not so hard. I just needed to die there. At
any rate, somebody had to die there, and everybody had to
think it was me. But I wouldn't die. I couldn't. I was very sad,
very sad, not about choking some *pipi tao* but because I thought
the only way to make people think it was me was to leave my
mother's medallion behind. The one thing I had left from her. I
was not so *tanga*, though; I could do this.

I spent some of my valuable pesos on cigarettes, and for two
weeks I was smoking in my room. I knew how to collect some
of the ragged cloth they gave us to sleep on, and I got some
stinky paint thinner from the maintenance closet. This was all
not so hard, really. I'd been in this place for a long time now—I
knew the tricks. Picking which boy to be me was also not hard.
Nobody was my friend. I didn't care. I just needed someone my
weight and kind of like me. Enough like me. The really hard
part was getting that boy to sneak into my cell at night. That
could have been bad for both of us, if we were caught. Very bad.

But I lured him with the promise of sucking his dick and sharing some beer. They made beer in the basement.

It's only fair, so I made him happy before I choke him dead. I switched clothes with him and put the medallion around his neck. That made me cry. From my mama, you know? The extra sheets I bundled up around him and doused with my stinky paint thinner. I made sure to pour some on his face. I left some cigarettes on the floor, and I checked out in the hallway, which at this hour was empty, and the jailer at the end of the hallway was asleep. I started the fire and let it burn so much that smoke was filling the room; it stank when the body was burning. I waited for it to be a big fire, then I ran out in the hall and yelled that there was a fire, before ducking around the corner to be as invisible as I could be. The fire was pretty stinky now, not like grilling a pig; people were coming out of rooms and the guard was up, churning through everyone, and it was starting to look like a big mess. Nobody noticed me. I slinked around the corner and I ran out as others were running in.

Let me tell you, making money on the streets of Manila is not so easy. Everybody is selling everything. All the time. I could sleep under a piece of cardboard, sure, no problem, but that wasn't going to get me to the US. I had a score to settle, and I needed money. I knew how to make a guy scream with pleasure, but I was not the only one who could do that, and there were others younger than me and even better-looking now. I'd never make enough selling my sexy stuff. But—there's lots of gang people in Manila. Not just one or two. You don't have to find them—they find you. All the boys in Old Bilibid knew about the gangs—most of them were in one. They got money and they wanted people like me, who could get close in and choke a dope. I could do that. This way, I could make some money.

I joined the Makabansa; they are very tough. I had to kill two people just to prove I could do it, but I was good at being friendly, getting close, and using my little chain to choke. I

started making money right away. I used sexy to get close, but
not everybody likes the boy thing, so I grew my hair out and I
got some falsies. That really worked! I could cut a mark out of a
crowd and have him down in ten minutes if I was in a good
place for it. I looked very sweet and young, so men all thought I
was *marahuyo*—a little enchantress. Made me happy to have
people *like* me. This way I would find *hiraya* and reach my
dreams, yes? Being a choke lady, it took me less than a year to
make almost fifteen thousand dollars! I mean dollars, not
pesos. After a time, I went back to Auntie's old house in my
dress, and asked the neighbors about her. They didn't recognize
me; they didn't see Freddie in a dress. They told me that Auntie
had left the islands and gone to National City—near San Diego.
She and Uncle Pedro lived there—ooha, I thought they must be
rich Americans now. I planned a visit.

I had money to buy a passport and get a visa, no problem.
Plenty of passports in Manila. I went to Consul for America and
gave them a photo, and they took fingerprints and my name. A
little money. Not Freddie Lazaraga anymore. He's dead in Old
Bilibid. Now I was Princess. Princess Aquino. And she bought a
ticket and flew to Los Angeles. I had a pistol and my money
packed in my suitcase, but no one knew and no one suspected
the sweet girl of being so nasty. Motels near the airport were
very expensive! But I got a newspaper and checked the classi-
fied ads so I could get a van. My plan wasn't all the way thought
out—but I wanted to put Auntie in the back of my van and lock
it up so she felt scared. Scared as I was when the doors closed
behind me.

They were very easy to find. I knew Uncle Pedro worked for
MASTCO and they were living in National City. When a sweet
little girl asks for information about her uncle, the answer
usually bubbles up. I watched their house for a day, and saw
them both leave in the morning, Pedro to work and Auntie Lola
to another house down the block, where she spent the day
before coming home to meet Pedro in the evening. I was

thinking that Auntie was working at the other house, cooking or cleaning or something, and that I could show up and grab her while she was alone, wrap her hands and mouth with duct tape, and get her into my backed-up van pretty fast. Then I'm gone. Seemed easy-peasy.

I watched their house the next morning. Big house; they shared it with other people. Uncle Pedro went to MASTCO early in the morning, and shortly after, Auntie Lola walked up the street to the house she spent the day in yesterday. I waited and watched. A white woman came out of the house and got in a little car and drove off. Lola was now alone. I thought of my plan as mostly just needing duct tape, but I might also need a tarpaulin, so I drove my van back into town to buy some things. After that I had lunch. American hamburger! Then I slowly drove back to the house I saw Lola in. I ripped off some pieces of duct tape and stuck them inside my jacket so I could grab them. I had a little clutch purse, and it had my pistol in it. I looked like who I was—Princess Aquino—but when Pedro opened the door he saw the real me instantly. Pedro!! What was he doing there? And he was about to call out to Auntie, I could see he knew who I was, and he was about to say "Freddie"—I just knew it—so I quickly pulled out the pistol and pressed it against his chest, right in front of his heart, and pulled the trigger. You see, if you hold the gun right against the person you are shooting it makes very little noise.

He fell and I got my second surprise: a little girl started crying and screaming, clutching her mouth and staring at the fallen Pedro, who was already starting to leak blood on the carpet. *Shit!* Where did she come from? As I was staring at her, Auntie Lola came in from the kitchen and stopped in the hallway, taking in the fallen Pedro, the screaming kid, and me, with a pistol. Auntie Lola was wearing my Virgin Mary medallion around her neck! I was so angry, I reacted fast—in two quick steps I was by the kid, gun at her sobbing head, and I told Lola, "You lie down on the floor now, or I shoot this girl." Once she was lying down, sobbing about her Pedro, it was easy to wrap her hands with tape, and then use some for her mouth. I thought it wasn't going to stick because of all her tears and snot, but I wrapped it all the way around her head. That worked. Then I wrapped some tape on the screaming girl's mouth to shut her up, and taped her hands. I looked out the door. The van was backed up in the driveway. No one was looking, so I marched Lola into it and pushed her onto the floor of the van, and then I wrapped her feet in tape, too. I went back for the girl, because she'd seen everything, and even though she was very young, I don't know, she could talk, probably. As I was carrying her out to the van, I noticed that someone walked out to the sidewalk, a couple of houses down, staring toward the van with mouth open.

I ran back to the house and closed the door, trying to lock it, then to the van, slammed the rear doors shut, and jumped in the driver's seat. The keys were still in the ignition. It started right away, and I got out of there as fast as I could without running into anything. I could hear them in the back, rolling around. Now what?

Then I went to a remote spot I found, down by the bay. I drove on all the little streets. Along the edge of the bay at its southern end was a huge building, made of wood, some kind of factory with chutes and rails and cranes and piles of—I wasn't sure. It looked like a mountain of...snow? I had never seen snow, but I knew about it and it was too warm here for that. Salt? Had to be. A mountain of salt. I drove past the big building to an empty lot, a little place where there were the wrecks of abandoned cars and trailers. Even the hulk of an old wooden boat, falling apart. I pulled the van up and just sat there for a bit in the quiet car. I had waited for this for a long time. I could hear them moving around in the back, but they really couldn't go anywhere. There was nowhere for them to go.

I got up out of my seat and crept back into the open rear of the van. The little girl was petrified, and so was Auntie Lola. I gently moved the little girl to lie down and turned her so she was looking at the van's side. I sat between her and Auntie Lola, who couldn't really move and looked like she was having trouble breathing. I scooted up so I could place her head on my lap, and I stroked her hair. I don't know what she thought.

"Dear Auntie," I told her. "Remember me? I didn't think you did remember me." Still lightly stroking her hair. Her breathing was labored, as it all came through her little nose. "You want to know how I felt?" I asked her. While my right hand stroked her hair, my left hand reached over and pinched her nose shut. She right away started bucking and thrashing. She was strong! But I just threw my leg over her and rode her while she bumped around, which didn't last long. She was gone in a minute. Maybe two. I stayed on her, though—I didn't want to have to do that again. When I finally rolled off her and turned around, I saw the little girl shaking and crying. I was pretty full of emotions and maybe I was not thinking good. Later I was angry at myself, because I felt like I wasn't thinking good. Later I regretted it. But right then, I reached over and pinched her nose shut. She was not so strong as Auntie. She quivered like the little dog did in Manila. Then she was still.

It was a little hard to wrap up the bodies in my tarps. Lucky they came in a pack of three, as I didn't know I'd need more than one. The Virgin Mary medallion was mine again. Now that they were cooling, I pulled the tape off both of them and started thinking about what I was going to say. I could clean them up just a little bit, wrap them up like a lumpia and toss the spare tarp over both of them. Then I headed south. The van reached the border in less than ten minutes. I was carrying my painting supplies, I planned to tell the border guard, but he didn't stop to ask me anything, he just waved me through, and there I was in Mexico with the two of them wrapped up in the back. I had to think of something before they started to smell.

I could just dump them someplace and get out of town, but I was already starting to feel bad for the little girl. I looked for the church that was closest, and I found an old adobe building not so far from the border, and—better yet—near the airport, Rodriguez International Airport. This was so easy. I parked the Econoline in the front and went in to talk to the priest. From the bright outside, into the dark chapel where it was cool. I found a friar, on his knees before a simple altar with two candles. Very nice, except I couldn't wait.

"Excuse me," I said, "I have a terrible problem and I need help..." and then I whimpered a little, wondering if it was better for me to just cry loudly, but the monk made the sign of the cross—forehead, lips, and heart—and looked up slowly at me.

"It's my auntie," I said, "and my little cousin. We have come to Mexico from the Philippines, and it cost us all the money we had in the world. We are trying to go to America, where we have family, but they wouldn't let us get visas, so we came through Mexico City. We have been traveling for days. My cousin got sick, and she made Auntie sick, and there were no doctors, and now both," I paused for effect, "have died." I knelt down on the floor and held my hands in front of me as if in prayer. "So close to making it to the United States and our family, and they die!"

I looked at the monk with pleading eyes. I can make tears come and the monk saw that. "She was a devout woman. I cannot leave her without burial on consecrated ground, it cannot be, but I cannot take her into America with me, and I cannot just leave her to a pauper's grave." Another pause, and I looked at the monk like I was studying him. Which I was. "She has some money we planned to use when we got to America. But now, she will not need it there. I cannot take her money, but I must go on." I drew a pre-counted stack of hundred-dollar bills out of my purse. Fifty of them. Five thousand dollars. The monk was looking at the stack of money. "Please," I said, "you must help. You must agree to bury them on your sacred ground so they can rest with God and I can go on. When I am rich in America I will come back for them and move them. Please."

The monk had come over to where I was, and sat on the edge of the bench nearest me, which I had placed the stack of money on. He reached out and picked up the money and weighed the bills in his hand. "Please," I repeated, sniffling, "please bury them and give them the right words."

A caretaker, the monk, and I carried the bodies from the van out to the back of the chapel, at the edge of the small graveyard. The monk asked me to come in and fill out some paperwork—names, dates, the things they need to know. I told him I would come right in, thanked him so much for being a compassionate man of God, and went around to the front, where I hopped in the van and took off quickly. Not my problem, now.

I drove to the airport and left the van in the parking lot. It didn't cost me so much, anyway. Inside the airport hall I saw the next international flight was to Thailand. So, that takes care of that. Princess Aquino is off to Thailand. I needed to get far away from America, and connections could be made from me to the Philippines, so why not choose Thailand? I had only my one suitcase, even if it did still have a pistol and my money wrapped up under some underwear. Nobody ever looks.

Once on the plane, I settled down and accepted a cup of tea from the stewardess. I expected to feel happy, elated even. I had dreamt of this moment for years, Auntie dying under my hands, but it really didn't make me feel good. I thought some more about the little girl and that didn't make me feel good, either. So sad. I fell asleep and woke up in a foreign land.

In Thailand, I got connected with the right people *very* quickly. I was making good money in no time, stashing it away each time I did a choke. I branched out—I learned how to use a hairpin. In the ear, in the eye, very quick. All the time, I kept thinking of the little girl. I thought now that she was so young —she wouldn't have been able to describe me to police, she wouldn't be able to talk about who I am. I probably didn't have to put her down. This made me sad, but what can you do? What's done is done.

Now I found I was girl all the time. It was better for me. And I thought, if I go back home I should go so changed that no one will know me. I don't want to just do nothing but kill people. I should go home to Manila and maybe I can just live quiet. Whatever I want, I should be a new person. I feel much better as a girl. It feels more like who I am. There are men who are very upset when they find out I am not a girl, but I usually kill them, so it hasn't mattered. Still, I think girl is better, and the place for that is Bangkok.

Hey! What's that! I feel someone come over and pull on the top of the bag I'm in. It's that shit-hole friend of yours, Paco, it's Tony. Tony is wrestling me up and dragging me over the cold floor and pulling me onto a cart. I'm talking to *you*, Paco. Can't you get through to this idiot who killed you? Paco doesn't say anything. My bag with all of my pieces is pushed up to the front of the cart. Within minutes I can feel Tony drop the bag Paco is in next to me. I know what's what. I better get through the story fast, because I think this time I'm not going to be put in a barrel and there's nowhere to float to. There's some links of heavy chain at the bottom of my bag, and I'm sure they did the same to Paco.

Where was I? Oh yeah, in Thailand I became a new person. Whole new. I bought a French passport. Now I was classy. I was Patrice Peteaut. I would call myself Patricia, because I don't speak French. I got the goods, just like all the other girls. But even while everything should be so nice, it wasn't. I still felt bad about the little girl. I didn't feel bad about any of the guys I'd killed, but there was only one little girl. I felt bad. Now I was a girl, and I knew how her momma must feel. I would feel that way myself. It bothered me so much that I started not sleeping. Some things I learned very fast, like how to stay alive, but some things I didn't learn so fast, like how to *be* alive.

I was in Thailand for a couple of years before I decided to come back to the Philippines. I was sure no one knew me anymore, or even knew of me. I had plenty of money; I was not going to go back to Manila where so many bad things happened. I was going to go where the country is clean and beautiful. I took the bus ride up the winding mountain roads to Baguio City. From crowded city streets to clean-smelling pine trees. As soon as I got there I thought it would make me feel better. The town was high in the mountains, up north on the island of Luzon. The weather was colder than Manila, and everywhere there were tall trees. It smelled fresh and pure, a chill wind blowing through the forest. I rented a little house just a short walk from the village center, and I thought that here I would find myself. Find peace. But I couldn't stop thinking about the girl.

Some men in town noticed me, but I let them know I wanted to be alone, and they left me alone. I took long walks in the forest. I thought about the girl. I started to think I needed to do something more to find peace. I couldn't bring her back, but I could at least tell her mother where she was. A holy graveyard —that's not too bad. It was the best I could do. It's crazy, isn't it? *Ulol.* I could live happy up here in the mountains of Baguio City, I had plenty enough money, I didn't need to do any more killings that I didn't want to do, and instead of enjoying my life I thought I should go back to America and talk to the mom. Check her out. I did the research; I knew who she was and what she did. I knew just how to approach her. She would not know me, but still, I was taking a big risk! This I knew full well! To myself, I said I wanted to look her in the eyes and say I'm sorry, and tell her where to find her daughter. But I'm not sure if I was lying to myself. I do that, sometimes.

Dammit, I feel them start to push the cart with Paco and me in it. Paco's bag tossed next to me. Garbage on top. Great. I don't even want to know. The cart is moving, I can tell that, and I can tell we are on that stupid boat I banged into when they had me in the barrel. I don't know how I can tell—I just can. I never should have let go of that Virgin Mary medallion. That was the first step in my bad path. I sent a lot of souls to hell, but I had earned a peaceful life, why not? Then I took a huge risk, for what I don't know anymore, and I lost big time. Paco—you never even told me if you told the woman about where her daughter is. You are just a piece of garbage. The whole reason for risking my good life, leaving my Baguio City hideaway, was to make amends, but the only one I got to tell was you— because you cut off my fucking fingers and it really hurt! And then you killed me. Did you tell her?

I waited to hear if he would answer. Nothing. I could be talking to myself. I think I am.

The garbage cart gets pulled to the back of the boat, and I feel it tipping over. Maybe some whale will eat me and I'll come back as Moby Dick. Whoa, whoa, we're tipping and sliding and splashing into the sea.

THE *LADY LYNN* kept churning away, headed westward into the setting sun, while the jettisoned garbage slowly bubbled, settled and sank.

The End

ACKNOWLEDGMENTS

I didn't realize what a community effort writing a novel can be, and until I did, I didn't get very far with it. David Madsen, who I met while converting a by-the-hour motel in Santa Monica into a cheesy apartment building, a friend for half a century, was the first to offer both encouragement and the advice of experience. He helped me unwrap what I was trying to get at without trying to pack it into a traditional three-act format. Pat Dobie, of Lucid Edit, had both a big-picture outlook of the story and an attention to detail—not to mention the time and patience to walk through different approaches with me as she shared her editorial wisdom. To my publisher, Cornelia Feye of Konstellation Press, I owe a great debt, because she helped me see things through yet another set of eyes and pushed me to make the story tighter, clearer, and more readable. I have been fortunate in my friends and advisors.

To my most important partner, Ann Poppe, who I met in 1973 and have loved and lived with ever since, my oh my, where do the years go? It's what they say about having fun, right? Here's listening to you, babe.

I also owe a debt of gratitude to a few friends who all pitched in and helped me along the way. Chris Dworin, who cast an editorial eye over the earliest draft and gave me pages of notes to help redirect my worst impulses, and Ron Little, who helped with my nautical bearings to save me from several embarrassments. Thanks to Linda Beresford and Steve South, who told me about St. Didacus, as well as Andy Schell, who kindly pointed out a particularly sticky wicket I needed to avoid, and Jonathan Louie, who leaned on his friends to make sure I knew about an obscure little church in Tijuana, and others who provided support or encouragement when things seemed bleak – thank you, Marie Tatar, Wes and Nico Opper, and Philipp Scholz-Rittermann, who introduced me to Cornelia.

ABOUT THE AUTHOR

Former professional photographer and TV-show host, lawyer Richard G. Opper went on to serve as Attorney General for the Territory of Guam, where he was awarded membership in the Ancient Order of the Chamorri upon leaving office. He left the islands to settle in San Diego, where he established a career in environmental law and was regularly identified by "Super-Lawyer" magazine as one of the top environmental lawyers in southern California. Opper was also a founding director of Progresso Fronterizo (Foundation for Border Progress), an organization focusing on environmental and health conditions along the US-Mexico border. An avid photographer and cyclist, Opper has published articles in the San Diego Union Tribune and professional journals. *The Body in the Barrel* is his first novel.

www.Richard.Opper.com

Made in the USA
Las Vegas, NV
04 December 2022